Praise for *Insomnia*

Book 1 of The Night Walkers

"Cleverly written and dangerously dark, *Insomnia* will take you to the brink of insanity. A must-read for thriller and romance fans alike."

—Elana Johnson, author of *Possession*

"*Insomnia* is suspenseful, fascinating, and completely unputdownable. I've decided to nickname Jenn Johansson 'Scary McScarypants,' because she spooked me in all the best ways."

—Carrie Harris, author of *Bad Taste in Boys*

"A riveting story of terror and despair that will keep you up long past your bedtime."

—Jennifer Bosworth, author of *Struck*

PARANOIA

Book 2 of
The Night Walkers

PARANOIA

J.R.
Johansson

flux
Woodbury, Minnesota

First Edition
First Printing, 2014

Book design by Bob Gaul
Cover design by Lisa Novak
Cover image © Shutterstock/84980068/Suzanne Tucker

Flux, an imprint of Llewellyn Worldwide Ltd.

This is a work of fiction. Names, characters, places, and incidents are either the product of the author's imagination or are used fictitiously, and any resemblance to actual persons living or dead, business establishments, events, or locales is entirely coincidental. Cover model used for illustrative purposes only and may not endorse or represent the book's subject.

Library of Congress Cataloging-in-Publication Data
Johansson, J. R.
  Paranoia/J.R. Johansson.—First edition.
    pages cm.—(The Night Walkers; Book 2)
  Summary: In the aftermath of the events that nearly killed him, Parker Chipp is trying to learn to cope better with life as a Watcher of dreams and struggles to rescue his father and his town from another breed of Night Walkers: the Takers.
  ISBN 978-0-7387-4018-8
  [1. Dreams—Fiction. 2. Rescues—Fiction. 3. Sleepwalking—Fiction.] I. Title.
  PZ7.J62142Par 2014
  [Fic]—dc23

                                                                        2014002443

Flux
Llewellyn Worldwide Ltd.
2143 Wooddale Drive
Woodbury, MN 55125-2989
www.fluxnow.com

Printed in the United States of America

For Wendy—
Thank you for always reading
(even before it was any good),
always supporting (even when I seemed crazy),
and always making me believe I could be
or do *anything* I wanted. Love you, Mom!

ONE

Weird stuff was going down in Oakville, and this time I was definitely—well, fairly—sure that I had nothing to do with it. The Sunday morning news headline on the muted television above the kitchen counter read:

Another Mysterious Withdrawal

Finn sat beside me at the counter, still in the sweats he'd slept in after our kung-fu marathon last night. He tossed a Cheerio through the air. It ricocheted off the cupboard and then the TV screen before bouncing into the right side of the sink.

"Score." Finn grinned.

I let one fly, but mine hit the angle wrong and landed behind the toaster. Hand-eye coordination had never been my strong suit ... foot-eye coordination, if such a thing existed, was a completely different story. Being pelted by breakfast cereal made the extremely stern expression on the male news anchor's face even more ridiculous.

Mom cleared her throat from the doorway. "I hope you're keeping track of where all those are landing, Parker."

Finn coughed and sat up a little straighter, smiling over his shoulder and trying to look innocent. A feat that probably would have been easier if his shirt didn't read *If We Get Chased by Zombies, I'm Tripping You.*

I nodded without glancing in her direction. "Easy. A few of mine are behind the toaster. All of Finn's are in the sink. And yes, I'll clean them up."

She kissed the top of my head as she walked past and grabbed the remote. "That's all I wanted to hear." Her red-painted nail pressed the volume button and Bradley Kent's voice rose until it echoed softly through the previously silent room. Then she grabbed an apple and began slicing.

"-sibly more puzzling, is that in spite of the fact that he's plainly shown on the security tapes, Mr. Jameson claims to have no recollection of draining his savings account or where the money is now. The police are investigating to determine if there is any evidence of impersonation or identity theft involved in either case."

The channel went to commercial and Mom pressed the mute button again. This wasn't the first time we'd heard bizarre stories on the news lately. A couple of people had woken up in different parts of the city with pockets full of money, and others had attacked people while asleep. Last week, an entire family just disappeared overnight. Although the authorities were considering the possibility that they'd left due to a family emergency or something, it struck me as very odd. They'd left literally everything behind, including shoes, pets, and cars, and someone had seen them walking down the street in the middle of the night in their pajamas.

These things went beyond regular sleepwalking, and they were starting to freak me out.

Mom shook her head, then smiled up at us. "Isn't your flight today, Finn?"

Finn swallowed a massive spoonful of cereal before answering. "Yeah."

"Have you been to Disney World before?"

"Nope."

"Why didn't your family wait until school lets out for summer? That's coming up fast." She picked up a stack of mail in front of her and started riffling through it.

"They got a deal because it's before the summer season really hits. It would've cost twice as much if we'd waited. At least that's what Dad said." Finn dropped his spoon back into his cereal. He glanced at me before his eyes fell to the dark green countertop before him. One hand snuck up and tugged on his right ear the way it always did when his brain threatened to start a fire from working too hard. I knew what he was thinking. It was the same thing he, his sister Addie, and our friend Mia Green had been worrying about for almost a month straight. How was I going to handle seven days without them?

More specifically, would I be able to handle seven straight days without being able to sleep in Mia's dreams?

I'd barely survived years of watching other people's dreams, and subsequently going without real sleep, before I met Mia. Being a Watcher, as I called it, was a living nightmare at times. The self-hypnosis that Mia used to get to sleep made her dreams especially calm and peaceful, at least when it worked and kept her horrific nightmares at bay. One week without her amazing dreams would definitely not be fun, but it shouldn't be that bad.

And if I kept repeating that—it might be true.

"Your dad needs to find deals for me next time we go on vacation." Mom stared at the top of my head until I looked up, then tilted her head toward where Finn sat still staring at the counter. She raised her eyebrows. When I shrugged, she tossed one apple slice into her mouth and put the rest in a sandwich bag, then grabbed her purse off the counter.

"Well, I'm off to work." Mom patted Finn on the back as she passed him and gave my shoulder a quick squeeze on the way to the garage. "You'll have fun, Finn, don't worry. And Parker will survive without you. I'll make sure of it."

The door to the garage closed behind her. Finn pushed his empty cereal bowl to one side and rubbed his palms over his face. His grumbled words barely escaped from behind his hands. "You sure you haven't told her that you almost died of sleep deprivation a few months ago? Because that was a seriously bad choice of words."

"I haven't told her and you need to chill." I really didn't want to go over this again. They had to leave. It really wasn't optional. I tried to keep my voice light. "You're going on vacation to Florida—land of sunshine and bikinis. Shouldn't you be more excited?"

"Oh, right." Finn dropped his hands and his grin almost reached his eyes. "Screw you, then. We may never come back."

I laughed. "That's more like it."

Finn tried to laugh, but it sounded more like a groan.

Chasing a few stray Cheerios around my bowl with my spoon, I spoke fast and tried not to let my own concern show through. "Seriously... don't you think Addie and Mia do enough worrying for the both of us?"

"Whatever. If Mia wasn't still—if I hadn't choked—" Finn's voice locked up and neither of us spoke. I sat in stunned silence. In the two weeks since we'd lost the soccer championship game, he'd never mentioned it once. And unlike his parents and Addie, I never tried to make him talk about it. Can't really blame a guy for not wanting to relive the last half of a crucial game in which he failed to block a *single* goal—not one. We were slaughtered.

Not that anyone really blamed him. Even at school, no one gave him any crap. Our soccer season had been messed up from the get-go, since it started only a couple of months after the football season ended as a joke. Not the funny kind of joke, but the sick kind that was whispered about in hallways across the state. Some of our offensive line hadn't even shown up for the last game. Almost no one was in the stands, and the cheerleaders spent more time crying than cheering. I guess that's what you get when you play a game only one week after your quarterback/senior class president/ star soccer player/psychopath extraordinaire Jeff Sparks tries to set a couple of students and the school on fire.

Finn, Mia, and I had all survived—more than we could say for Jeff. I'd finally proven to Mia, and myself, that Jeff was the stalker sending her creepy messages, not me. We'd even healed, at least on the outside.

So we'd thought soccer season couldn't possibly end worse, right? Right, but it could still be pretty bad. We tried to pull it together at the end, got the wins we needed for the playoffs, but we weren't the same team we'd been before.

I would never be the same again. Turned out, neither would Finn.

Standing, Finn walked over to the sink, rinsed his bowl, and put it in the dishwasher before turning to face me. "We wouldn't even be going to Florida if my mom didn't think everything could be fixed by throwing Mickey Mouse at it."

"Maybe it can be." I swirled my Cheerios around in my bowl without looking up.

"Only when you're five."

"Don't knock it 'til you try it."

The doorbell rang. Finn sat up straighter and ran his fingers through his hair, trying to smooth it a bit. That meant Mia was the one picking him up. Finn had never said a word about liking her, but it was pretty hard to miss.

The whole thing seemed a little awkward to me. Mia's parents had been killed in a fire, and she'd been in foster care ever since. When Jeff, who was Mia's foster brother, attacked us at the school over fall break, the foster system needed a new home for her. Addie and Finn's parents had jumped at the chance. It had seemed ideal. The Patricks were great and Mia was very happy there. About a month later, Finn started acting different around her.

I figured having the girl you liked living in the same house with you could either be really great or really uncomfortable. Given how much time Finn had spent at my house the last couple of months, I guessed he leaned more toward the uncomfortable side of the scale.

When I opened the front door, Addie and Mia's hushed voices stopped immediately.

"I can leave the door shut, if you like." I leaned against the doorjamb and smiled. "For future reference, though, don't ring the bell if you aren't ready for someone to answer it."

"Good morning to you too." Mia gave me a quick hug, her brunette ponytail swinging in my face and making me sputter, before walking past me toward the kitchen and leaving Addie and me alone in the entryway. I watched Mia's retreating back for an instant. It was still hard to get used to her not freaking out every time she saw me. And even though she didn't act like it, I knew from watching her dreams that it hadn't been easy for her to adjust to the idea that I wasn't the enemy.

Addie's auburn hair blew loose around her shoulders in the passing breeze. It looked carefree...like she used to be. Her hazel eyes studied the ground between us. I wanted to see the swirling browns and golds in them even though I knew they only showed me what she was feeling when she wanted me to see. She'd always been the hardest for me to read.

The only time she'd looked truly happy over the last few months had been when Finn learned to play the ukulele

7

so he could sing her Happy Birthday. He was hilarious, and she couldn't stop laughing. Even though she'd turned sixteen a week before Valentine's Day, we hadn't been able to celebrate either event the way we wanted to—together.

I reached out and brushed the back of her hand, hoping for a smile, but when she looked up I saw only worry.

"Don't." I kept my voice soft. "It's going to be fine."

"No repeats, Parker. You need to keep control." She curled her fingers around mine and pretended not to notice when I glanced back toward the kitchen to make sure Finn wasn't looking our direction. I still hadn't managed to tell him how Addie and I felt about each other, and with his recent struggles in the soccer championship game, I didn't know when I was going to.

Addie continued making a list of all the things I wasn't ever to do again, staring hard at my hand while she did so. "No hallucinations. No car accidents. No coming back from vacation to find you in the hospital."

"I know, I kno—"

"Most importantly," she interrupted, squeezing my hand and lifting her eyes to mine. This time she let me see it: the pain she still felt every time we talked about the day Jeff had attacked us. "No disappearing. No running away and leaving me nothing but a stupid note."

Her words fell like anchors on my shoulders, tying me to her in ways a rope never could. But we both knew—now and every time she'd asked me before—that I couldn't, I wouldn't promise her that. If it came to keeping my friends safe, I'd run again. What could I say? Any response from me would either have been a lie or the exact opposite of what she wanted to hear.

So I said nothing. I just led her out onto the porch, out of view of the kitchen, and wrapped my arms tight around her. We stood in the warm air of late spring and I breathed in the light citrus scent of her hair. Waited one—two—three full breaths before she finally relaxed against me and I felt the warmth of her hands on my back.

"Why does this have to be so hard?" Her voice was muffled against me, her breath warm on my neck.

"I'll figure it out. Give me time." The words sounded empty even to me. I'd been telling Addie this same thing for months now, but I hadn't made any progress. I didn't want to sneak around like this any more than she did, but Finn had made it clear, many times, how bad of an idea he thought it was for anyone to date his sister—especially his friends. And with everything else that had gone on in the last year, a solution wasn't coming quickly enough for either of us.

"Come on." She sighed and pulled back, stuffing her hands into her jeans pockets. The space between us made me feel colder than I should have when standing in the sunlight. "We need to talk to the others."

Without a word, I followed her into the kitchen. There really wasn't anything else I could say. Our relationship, if you could call it that, was more than complicated. If you took complicated, mixed in fifteen pounds of confusion and messed-up crap, then you were getting close. Keeping it a secret had definitely caused problems, and having my life depend on me spending most of my nights in another girl's head didn't help much either. But I felt even stronger about Addie than ever. I had no idea how to sort it all out.

As soon as we were back in the kitchen, she spun on her toes to face me. "So what's your plan?"

I scratched my elbow as Finn turned off the TV and slid around on his barstool. They all watched me, waiting, but if they wanted an answer, they needed to be more specific.

"What do you mean, 'plan'?"

Mia leaned back against the counter and folded her arms. "Well, can we just make eye contact now … and then you not look at anyone until I come back?"

I sighed and shook my head. "No. That would be the simplest option, but it won't work after the first night. Ever since the hospital, my mom has been very … attentive. She stares me straight in the eye every time we talk, and if I won't look back at her she asks what's wrong, over and over. I'd have to avoid her completely all week and that doesn't go over well either, especially since she's just beginning to relax a bit lately. I'll just have to deal with it until you get back. It's not like I haven't done this before."

Mia frowned but didn't argue, and since it looked like Finn and Addie were about to, I kept my attention on Mia as she asked, "Who is your backup if we're all gone? Your replacement-me? Have you been thinking about it?"

"I was thinking last night that we should try using video chat right before you go to bed," I said with a shrug. Finn and Addie visibly relaxed at just the idea. "I mean, if you're willing?"

"Of course." Mia's response was immediate. She didn't even need to consider it.

"Thank you." The words weren't enough, but I knew she understood how much her help meant to me. It was literally life or death. She saved my life every day. How could two words ever be enough for that?

Addie looked thoughtful. "Do you think that will work? Maybe we should've tried it before now ... "

"I have no idea, but it's worth a try." I shrugged. "I thought about testing it last night, but if it didn't work, then it would just have been one extra night of no sleep. Besides, you guys *have* to go; it's not like you can just decide not to. If it fails, it fails. I'll be fine. My mom won't be able to help with the sleep issue like Mia can, but at least her dreams are usually safe and boring. She's definitely Plan B."

Finn nodded. "I think that's the best choice. With your top three options gone."

Mia rolled her eyes, but the corner of her mouth jerked up. "You make us sound like contestants on some kind of game show."

Finn grinned wide and then said, "Sweet! What kind of game show, exactly?"

Mia opened her mouth, but I decided to cut her off before Finn could derail the conversation even further.

"Anyway, yeah. It will be fine." I tried not to think about the fact that Mom had been on three dates with my physics teacher, Mr. Nelson, in the last month. Or that from the way she'd giggled when he called her on the phone last night, I got the impression she was enjoying herself. That was great;

I was happy for her. I just really hoped he didn't show up in her dreams tomorrow night—or the next five nights after.

I'd learned a long time ago that there are some images that just stick with you, no matter how hard you try to forget.

Mia cleared her throat and her wide eyes didn't leave mine in the awkward silence that followed. I knew they were all going to keep worrying about me no matter what kind of plan we had, but Mia was in a unique position to understand just how bad it could be for me to be stuck in the wrong dreams. Her nightmares had been a literal hell for both of us for a long while.

Even now, though her bad nights were definitely fewer and farther between, when they did show up ... between me not sleeping and her reliving the death of her parents, it made for a rough night all around. On top of that, she'd added a new recurring nightmare featuring the night Jeff attacked us. I didn't think she'd told Addie or Finn about this one, and it wasn't my place to share it if she wasn't ready.

In the seven months since we'd met, Mia and I had survived more than a few nightmares, both in reality and in her head. In some ways, our friendship was brand new and tenuous. In other ways, we'd already survived more together than most friendships ever could. Add in the fact that we both knew she was keeping me alive, and our friendship was unique if nothing else.

"So, uh ... should we watch some TV?" Mia asked, changing the subject as she shot me a sympathetic look.

I glanced at the clock on the microwave. "What time

do you guys have to head home? Need to pack before the flight to the magic planet or whatever?"

This time all three of them glared at me. Mia because we both knew I'd called it the wrong name on purpose, Finn because we both knew he didn't want to go, and Addie...I really wasn't sure. I could probably make a list of reasons why she should be glaring at me and none of them would be the reason she actually was.

I was relieved when Finn's phone rang and he picked it up with a groan.

"Yeah?" He closed his eyes and grimaced. "I'm sorry, Mom. I meant to say 'hello.'"

After another moment of silence he said, "Okay, we're on our way. See you in a few."

"I guess that answers my question," I said as Finn got to his feet.

Addie let Mia and Finn walk to the front door in front of us and grabbed my hand, giving it a tight squeeze. It wasn't much, but these stolen moments were all we had right now and as little as it was, it really did help. I rubbed the back of her hand with my thumb, releasing it only as Finn opened the front door.

Once on the porch, they all turned to face me.

"Have fun, guys." I plastered a smile on my face and did my best to ignore their worried gazes. "Do me a favor and bring me back some of those mouse ears...I'm planning a Halloween costume."

Mia rolled her eyes but smiled, making sure to meet my

eyes for a second before heading for the car. "Take care of yourself. Text me what time you want to try a video chat."

"I will."

She put her right hand on Addie's back and her left on Finn's and propelled them down the stairs. Finn muttered under his breath the whole way to the car, but then beat his chest with his fist and gave me one of his weird salutes before Mia started her purple pick-up and drove them away. She seemed to be the only one really looking forward to the trip. Addie stared at the back of Mia's seat as they left.

Everything I'd seen in her eyes and her expression lately pained me. I hoped when she got back, she'd be more like the old Addie. Her spark was missing, and I couldn't help but feel that I'd been the one to put it out.

Florida might not be as "magical" as Mrs. Patrick wanted it to be, but after everything we'd gone through this year, my best friends definitely deserved a long vacation away from me.

TWO

Sunday night I slept in Mia's dreams. Monday we tried the video chat, but it was no good. I was stuck with my mom's dreams instead of Mia's, so we scrapped that idea. Finn kept sending me bizarre Mickey Mouse jokes via text, followed by a panicked phone call if I didn't respond with "haha" fast enough. Addie called the home phone to make sure I hadn't run away, and Mia sent me pictures of them on rides to prove they were having fun.

Five days left until they would come home, and I was having considerably less fun. School had been much harder for me since the fire. And although I didn't think it possible, without my friends it was so much worse. The district had decided to wait until summer to repair the damaged portion of the building, which meant that the halls were overcrowded and the parking lot was filled with trailers to replace the classrooms that had been destroyed. The locker room and the gym were gone, so P.E. consisted mostly of people running on the outside track and then trying to get dressed in an extra trailer. No one could shower, the halls smelled worse than ever, and everyone blamed me.

People stared as I passed, as they had ever since the fire. Some with curiosity, others disdain. Half the people at school thought I was a hero for saving Mia and Finn, so they forgave me for the inconveniences they held me responsible for. Some even treated me with a weird kind of reverence. The other half thought I was a monster who'd gotten away with killing Jeff and setting the school on fire while somehow managing to pin the blame on my innocent victim. They either glared at me in anger or cowered in fear... and some even picked fights or tried to corner me on my way out to my car. No matter their opinions, though, nothing I did could change their minds about what they believed happened that day.

The whole thing struck me as ironic. They didn't know about Darkness, the frightening piece of my personality that at times had taken me over in the past, but the absolute polarity in the way they treated me reminded me of my other side every single day. Besides taking over my body, Darkness had appeared to me as a nightmarish version of myself. I could see him and hear him as if he were right beside me. I shuddered at the memory. Even though he'd been quiet for a while now, my world wouldn't let me forget him.

Rather than see their stares as I sat alone in the cafeteria, I took my lunch to the hall that had once ended at the gym. One wall was blackened with smoke and soot and the other wall was completely gone, exposing the interior of the building to the outside air. They'd used a row of desks to block this hall off. We weren't supposed to be here, which was part of why I came. Most of the time it was a great place to be alone. But that wasn't the main reason I spent my lunches here.

I came here sometimes to remind myself of the destruction that could happen when I lost touch with the truth. I hadn't started the fire, but if I hadn't been so busy suspecting myself, I might have seen how dangerous Jeff was getting sooner. This was the kind of destruction that could happen again if I ever let Darkness regain enough control to fool me, to make me believe the hallucinations he forced on me or his lies.

To make me lose sight of the person I am.

The old shop room lay twenty feet in front of me. The metal beams that formed the walls were like bones, now bent and blackened as they reached for the cloudless sky. The plaster and sheetrock, the skin that had covered them, was gone. It had been scorched to ashes and buried in snow and later dirt. The bones were all that remained and they were scarred, just like Mia, Finn, and me—every living person who'd been in that shop room when it burned. We were all damaged now.

And I *would never* let it happen again.

———————

The first two nights of Mom's dreams were random bits of memories combined with her brain trying to sort through this week's to-do list. Boring to the extreme, but not bad.

Wednesday night, Mom had a nightmare that featured me being set on fire at the high school.

Man, I missed Mia.

Thursday night, the dream started with Mom's date with Mr. Nelson. It was detailed and absolutely clear. With vividness like this one had, it was obviously a memory. They went out to dinner and a movie. The flirting made me a little ill but besides that it wasn't so bad, and it was nice to see how well he treated Mom. When they got back to our house and Mom invited him in, everything got fuzzy around the edges and I knew we'd crossed over into dream territory.

They sat on the couch and he held her hand. When he leaned over to kiss her, I closed my eyes and sat down against the wall but I could still hear them making out. I didn't want to hear that. I stuck my fingers in my ears and tried to drown out the sound of their smacking lips with my own humming.

A massive crash brought me out of it and I jumped to my feet, struggling to figure out what I'd missed. The living room door was hanging off its hinges and Mom was tugging the strap of her dress back up on her shoulder as she got to her feet. Mr. Nelson stepped in front of her, and they both looked confused. Then a shadow stood in the doorway, and I recognized him even before he walked forward into the light.

Dad wore the same clothes he'd had on the last time I'd seen him—faded black jeans, red polo shirt, and a leather jacket. His hair, his face... everything about him was the same. Not that I thought Mom had seen him over the more than four years since he'd left us, but this dream confirmed it for me. She remembered him the exact same way I did.

He came in and sat in the recliner facing the couch and said only one word: "Continue."

I felt Mom's emotions more powerfully at that moment than throughout the rest of the dream. Her attraction to Mr. Nelson was still forming—she enjoyed his company and he made her laugh—but her pain at seeing Dad, even in a dream, was heartbreaking. She got to her feet and tears streamed down her face. Dad stood up when she approached, and she curled up in his arms and cried.

Then I felt the anger. It wasn't as fresh as other times she'd dreamed about him, but it was still pretty potent. She beat against his chest with her fists.

The rest of the dream faded away—Mr. Nelson, the couch, the room—until there was nothing left but my parents. Dad smoothed his fingers through Mom's hair and whispered "Shhh..." until she calmed down and relaxed against him.

"I hate you for leaving me," she whispered in between sobs.

"I hate me too," he said softly, and even though he was just an aspect of her dream, the pain written on his face made me feel a little better.

"You never came back." Mom looked up at him. "I always thought you would."

"I couldn't." He leaned down and placed a kiss on her lips and then took one step away. As we watched, Dad began to age suddenly, rapidly. The skin on his face and hands wrinkled and then his cheeks hollowed out. His hair grew long and gray and then fell out onto his shoulders. Mom screamed again and again as his body decayed and his ice blue eyes, identical to mine, disappeared back into his skull. All that remained was a skeleton wearing Dad's clothes. Then even that collapsed into a heap on the floor, and we were both thrust out of Mom's nightmare.

———————

I woke dripping with sweat and could hear Mom screaming all the way across the house. Jumping to my feet, I bolted through the kitchen, narrowly missing a collision with one of the dining chairs. When I reached her room, I threw open the door. She was sitting straight up in bed, shouting words I couldn't understand.

My heart pounded in my ears as I sat beside her and grabbed her hand. I kept my voice hushed and level. "Mom? It's okay. It was just a nightmare."

She blinked a few times at my face and began to calm down. Taking deep, shaking breaths, she wrapped her arms around me and cried into my shoulder. "It—it felt so real."

"I know, but it's not. Everything is okay." I was still shaken by her dream, and I'd known it wasn't real the whole time. The mind is a cruel trickster, the way nightmares can make a person believe their worst fears have come to get them. I have enough other problems, so I'm not sad that being a Watcher means I mostly miss out on having nightmares of my own.

The irony of the thought struck me and I suppressed a cold laugh. No, my mind played its tricks on me in the daylight ... when I was wide awake.

I'd seen plenty of nightmares but never been around to witness the aftermath. It ripped me apart to see Mom so upset. She was so strong—always had been.

Her sobbing subsided and she cleared her throat. I could see the embarrassment on her face when she pulled back. "Sorry, I—I don't know what happened."

"Please." I smiled. "I had my breakdown a few months ago and you wanted one too. It's okay to just admit it."

"That must be it." She grinned and shoved my shoulder lightly, but I could see the gratitude in her eyes. "Now go to bed or you're grounded."

"Fine, fine. I'm going." I stood and walked out the door. As I shut it, I spoke five words of absolute truth. "Hope you sleep well, Mom."

———————

I woke up early the next morning. The exhaustion I'd been evading for months was back—and it wasn't pulling any punches. Even rolling out of bed sounded like too much work so I stayed there, listening to Mom hum as she walked around the house. Thinking and floating in and out of the white nothingness that held me whenever my Dreamer was awake. As much as I fought it, my thoughts, just like Mom's, kept drifting back to Dad. I'd been hoping she might be starting to forget him with Mr. Nelson, to move on.

Just like I wished I could.

I'd been doing pretty well for a while there. My anger had always helped me push aside the sadness that saturated me from the inside out whenever I remembered the good times before Dad left. The times he'd taken me into his lab on the weekends, shown me how he could mix two liquids together and somehow make them burn. The way oil and water would never truly blend. He'd taken us camping and taught me to recognize some of the constellations. Every one of these memories was like reopening an old wound, so holding on to the anger instead made his loss more bearable. Besides, when you were slowly dying of sleep deprivation like I'd been, you didn't exactly have time to dwell on things from the past you couldn't change. Better to focus on finding answers to ensure yourself a future.

Turns out, those kinds of quests can be awfully time-consuming.

Then I'd met Jack. Or Blind Skull, as I'd dubbed him because of the emblem on his leather jacket that featured a skull with a patch over each eye. After the school fire, when Jack had showed up at the hospital, he'd introduced himself, told me my dad had sent him, and said he'd be in touch.

That was the last time I'd seen him. It was over five months ago, and just thinking about it pissed me off.

Reaching behind my head, I rolled my pillow into a little ball and fluffed it by punching it a few times as hard as I could. After thirty seconds, some of the seams looked about one hit away from turning my bed into a crime scene from a stuffed animal's worst nightmare. So I tossed it aside and buried my face in the sheets.

Why? Why couldn't Dad just leave me alone? Or have his stupid messenger actually do what he'd promised and come back? Or better yet, why the hell did Dad have to leave us in the first place?

I groaned. Sitting up in bed, I gave up on trying to rest anymore. It wasn't going to happen, and it didn't do me much good anyway. Stiff pains shot up my neck as I rolled my shoulders, trying to relieve some of the tension I always held there. Only two more days until my friends would be back...only two more days.

Changing into sweats, I pulled on my running shoes. Since the end of soccer season, I'd spent more time running. Physical activity always helped wake me up and burn off frustration. After witnessing Mom's latest dream, I needed exercise more than I had in a long time. If I hurried, I could get a good run in and still be home in time for school.

While Jack never coming back was one more disappointment in the long list of letdowns courtesy of my dad, I reminded myself that life was good right now. For the first time in almost five years I had a future, thanks to my friends. I had a present, and I liked it. Whether Jack ever showed up with answers or not, I was done letting my dad and my past mess me up.

Even as I thought this, something was still bothering me deep down. Jack had been around every corner last fall, when everything was crazy. In fact, other than myself—or Darkness, I guess—he'd been my lead suspect as Mia's stalker.

I shuddered at the memory. I tried not to think about that terrifying time very much—doubting myself like that had been horrible. Losing control of myself, of my body, hours of my time...it wasn't something I could ever let happen again. The iron grip I'd held Darkness in ever since had definitely pissed him off, but he never seemed to fade away like I'd hoped. He was always there, watching. Waiting for the next time I'd slip and get too tired. But thanks to Mia, that hadn't happened again.

And I knew this for sure, because every night I'd been watching the Watcher.

Walking over to my desk, I grabbed the camcorder I'd bought the weekend after the school fire. I stopped the current recording and then pushed rewind, examining every movement I made last night in reverse. When I got to the beginning of the recording, which showed me setting the camcorder up and climbing into bed, I released a tightly held breath. Except for running to Mom's room after her nightmare, I'd stayed in bed all night.

This was just one more safeguard to keep Darkness from taking over again while I slept. If he regained his freedom this time, I would know about it right away.

Rubbing my palms against my eyes, I powered down the camcorder and yawned. I just had to hold on until my friends came back. I'd spent every night for months in one of their dreams, mostly Mia's, and so far it was working. The old nightmare images had begun to fade, even those from Dr. Freeburg.

I still didn't know if I'd killed Mia's hypnotherapist; I didn't think I'd ever know. The thought drove me crazy. I'd been both relieved and devastated when I found out they weren't doing an autopsy on him. Still, what could they discover that would be of any use to me? There wasn't exactly a known physical result for what happened when someone like me went inside your mind and murdered you in your dream. I just had to hope it had been a heart attack, a coincidence.

At the same time I had to believe, deep down, that I'd done it. I had to believe it enough to make sure I would *never* do it again.

———

After school, I spent most of the evening at the movies and the mall. I texted Mom to say I'd be late. Every time I closed my eyes, I saw images of my decaying dad. I really wasn't in the mood to watch that again tonight, so I thought I'd take a risk and make eye contact with one of the people from school. Most of them weren't too bad, and I was bound to run into someone at the mall on a Friday night.

When I saw one of the cheerleaders sitting with a younger girl at the food court, I decided she was probably my best bet. She'd had a bizarre dream or two in junior high, but weird was a very good thing when compared to the nightmarish alternatives. Plus, I was pretty sure she was one of the people who considered me a hero, which was much less risky than watching the dreams of someone who saw me as a monster. I stopped by her table.

"Hey, Anna." I smiled when she looked up, straight into my eyes. After more than four years of being a Watcher, it was like I heard a little click inside my head when I made eye contact. Like a mental chain that bound my mind to theirs had snapped into place. "Is this your little sister?"

The girl was probably twelve or thirteen. She looked up at me but I was careful not to meet her eyes.

"Yeah." She gave me a little smile and then grinned back at her sister. "We're having a girls' night out."

"Sweet."

"What are you doing? You here with Finn?" She looked past me, then back to my face. I saw that glimmer of pity I always saw from the people who thought I was a hero ... but also suspected I needed years of therapy after the ordeal.

"Nah, his family went on vacation." I shrugged and started to back away, my mission accomplished. "I'm just picking up some stuff for my mom. I need to run, but wanted to say hi."

"Ah, okay!" She smiled and, with a quick wave, went back to eating. "See you later!"

"Bye." I turned and walked away. I smiled ruefully to myself as I walked through the mall toward the theater, thinking I was getting pretty good at the whole casual-eye-contact thing. If only I'd figured out how to approach Mia that way when I met her, I might've saved both of us a lot of trouble.

I bought tickets to the next movie playing and went directly into the theater. By the time it got out, Mom would be asleep, the mall would be empty, and I could go home. When the movie started and I saw it was some kind of sci-fi/old-west combo, I started feeling lucky. As long as Anna's dreams weren't too crazy, it should be a good day all around.

Everything worked as planned when the movie got out. The stores were all closed as I passed them on my way to the parking lot. I scrolled through my phone and was surprised to find that no texts or messages from Disney World had come in during the show. Maybe my friends had finally relaxed a little. That would be a very good thing.

I was feeling so optimistic I didn't even hear Thor coming, but he hit me from behind so hard it knocked the wind out of me, and my cheek got sliced up when I hit the pavement. I rolled onto my back, dazed, trying to catch my breath. When I looked up, I met his small dark eyes.

"That was for Jeff." I'd known Thor, aka Joey Thornton, for years, and this was the first time I'd ever heard him speak. His words were almost pure snarl, so it took me a minute to make out what he'd said.

"And I'm not done yet," he added.

He pulled back his leg, but I scrambled out of the way just in time. I tried to get to my feet, but I was dizzy and the blood dripping from my cheek and chin distracted me. I fell back onto the hand I'd broken in the fire. My wrist was healed, but I landed wrong and painful tingles shot up my arm.

"Joey, stop it." Some guy ran out of the shadows near the mall and grabbed Thor's shoulder, pulling him back. The guy was a little older, maybe eighteen, and a little smaller. Something about his face looked ragged, like he'd lived a hard life; his eyes looked older than the rest of him. I met those eyes on instinct. I'd literally rather watch anyone dreams—seriously, *anyone's*—than Thor's. He'd been Jeff's best friend, and after Jeff died in the fire, Thor blamed me completely. He'd been furious ever since.

Never mind the fact that Jeff had *started* the fire and was a psychopathic killer—no, it was clearly my fault.

"Get off me, Cooper." Thor shook his shoulder and the other guy dropped his arm. They both backed toward the other side of the parking lot.

Cooper looked at me over his shoulder. "Sorry, man."

I got to my feet without a word, pressed the end of my sleeve against my bleeding cheek, and stumbled back to my car. Maybe today hadn't been so great after all.

Leaning against the car door, I watched Thor and his friend climb into the backseat of an already-running sedan. A girl sat in the driver's seat. Her short blond hair shimmered almost white in the moonlight streaming through her window. Even from across the parking lot, she seemed afraid...or maybe upset. Her motions were jerky as she turned the wheel, and I could hear Thor and Cooper yelling at each other in the backseat.

Not all that surprising that she seemed scared. I didn't know anyone who would be comfortable driving around in a car with Thor bellowing in the backseat.

By the time I got home, cleaned the many scrapes on my cheek, started the camcorder, and got into bed, I was exhausted. It was only an instant before I went into the white void that was my version of sleep. I hoped this Cooper guy made better choices in dreams than he did in friends.

From the moment when I felt the odd vibration that normally signalled I was about to enter my Dreamer's dream, I knew something was very wrong. Immediately, everything turned a solid, inky black. It was unlike any other dream I'd ever seen. It was deep and heavy...and it kept getting heavier.

The gloom pressed in, closing so tight around me I couldn't move. I could barely breathe...

And I couldn't escape.

THREE

When I finally woke up and was released from the hellish dream back into reality, my head threatened to explode with every beat of my heart. Even the light coming through my closed eyelids was like a knife slicing through my brain. The blankets I'd slept in, my pillow...even my bed was gone, and I was sprawled out on something very hard and cold. Whatever it was, it was not helping my horrific headache. My body ached everywhere and my stomach churned in my gut. Something smelled horrible, like a dusty old urinal. I raised my arm and shaded my eyes as I tried to open them. Peeking out between my fingers, I saw—flannel. Red flannel...and then it moved.

I sat straight up and my vision burst into violent white, like a light bulb had exploded behind my eyeballs. Then everything went dark, all but a pinpoint of glaring brightness in the center. Leaning back, I found what felt like a brick wall and rested against it, panting—and panicking.

All around me was confusing noise: a loud printer, a phone ringing in the distance, metal on metal, footsteps. And then, so close I could reach out and touch them, many people breathing: heavy breathing, light breathing, a cough here, a sniff over there. Someone laughed an emotionless, empty chuckle, but it echoed around me, through me, and I couldn't decide which direction it had come from.

This time I took it slower, parting my eyelids just enough to peek through and see a small slice of the room.

Everything around me was dingy white, with gray benches along all the walls. Other people sat or stood nearby—all men—and a few stared at me. I widened my eyelids a bit more and noticed the one detail that defined everything else. To my left, the white bricks I leaned against ended at a wall of gray bars.

Jail.

What the hell is going on?

My mind flew into a frenzy, trying to force the bars I was staring at into any kind of logic. To make them fit into one of the boxes I had that could make any sense—but I knew there was only one possible explanation.

Darkness had taken control.

I heard the low chuckle again and this time I recognized it... and which direction it had come from. Slowly, I turned my head to face the back corner of the room. There he was, arms folded as he leaned against the wall, giving me that cold smile that was all too familiar even though I hadn't seen him in months. He looked awful—one eye was swollen and bruised, knuckles caked with dried blood.

"You..." The word barely escaped my tight throat and wasteland of a mouth. My voice was a croaking thing that tried to bridge the gap between us and bring Darkness back into my mind where he belonged, where I could at least attempt to control him.

But nothing happened. Darkness even seemed amused by my pathetic effort and his cruel smile spread further across his face. He wasn't listening anymore, and at least for the moment, I couldn't make him.

Just like he'd promised, the last time he'd spoken to me the night before the fire, he'd gotten control again... and this time he'd made it a lot farther than Mia's old backyard. This time he'd managed to cause enough trouble to land me in jail.

"Well, looks like Sleeping Beauty is finally awake." The rough voice came from directly across the room. I struggled to open my eyes wider and shift my attention to the stranger. My right eyelid refused to cooperate and started to throb when I tried again. Reaching one hand up, I gingerly touched the swollen skin around it and realized I had a nasty black eye and banged-up knuckles to match the ones on Darkness. Perfect.

I groaned. Thor had scratched up my chin and cheek in the parking lot, but my eyes had been untouched. This was all new... gifts from my psychopathic alter ego.

Through my one good eye, I tried to locate the voice talking to me. Since everyone was staring, it was hard to tell who it was until a massive bald guy wearing a denim jacket spoke and I recognized the voice:

"Have sweet dreams, Princess?"

I laughed under my breath at the bitter irony of his choice of words and shook my head slightly. Just the one move sent my world spinning, and my stomach clenched down tight in pain. From the corner of my eye, I noticed Darkness wincing from our shared discomfort. He closed his eyes and slid down into a sitting position. The next instant, Baldy lifted me by my shirt and pinned me against the wall. My vision dimmed around the edges.

"Something funny?" he growled, his breath smelling like rotting meat. Someone outside the cell yelled for him to release me, but he didn't even seem to notice.

"No." My voice came out as scratchy and raw as before. "But if you don't put me down, I'm going to hurl on you and that might be a little funny."

Then I gagged, which added unintentional emphasis, and Baldy immediately dropped me, mumbling under his breath as he walked back to the other bench. I fell onto the floor and closed my eyes as I waited for the intense nausea to subside.

"Maybe you should stop angering the locals." Darkness's words were soft, but they carried as though on surround sound inside my head.

"Shut up." My growled words were unintelligible through my tight teeth, but I knew he'd understand me anyway.

"That's why I stopped drinking. Got real tired of wanting to die the morning after." A new voice spoke and I flinched away from it instinctively. "Easy now. I'd think, after last night, you'd at least know I wasn't going to hurt you. Of course, don't do me much good to stop drinking if I'm going to end up back in here anyway—but at least I'm feeling better than you."

Opening my eyes, I saw the older man in red flannel crouching over me. He extended a hand, and although he was missing half his teeth and I could see track marks up his arm, his face was kind. I gripped his hand tight and he helped me onto the bench.

"I have a hangover," I muttered, more as a question than a statement.

The man wheezed as he took a seat next to me. "Yeah, I'd bet you do. When they brought you in last night, you were more alcohol than human, I'd say. Tried to pick a fight with just about everyone in here, all with the guard watching. By the time your friend over there finally laid into you, everyone thought you deserved it."

"Sounds like I did." Between the bizarre suffocating dream and Darkness taking control, something had gone *really* wrong last night. The problem was...I had no idea what.

The old man looked at me sideways and raised an eyebrow. "Well, that's something I wasn't expecting—humility. Do yourself a favor, kid, and stop drinking. It brings out the monster in you."

"Tell me about it." I swallowed hard and ignored the barking laughter coming from Darkness's end of the room. There was no point arguing with or even responding to him when no one could see him but me. That kind of thing would get me locked away in a completely different room. "Where are we?"

"Newton City Jail." The man's eyes studied me with

pity now, and for a moment I was glad Darkness at least had given me the alcohol excuse. "You don't remember much about last night, then."

"Nothing." My brain felt sluggish, refusing to find the information I needed. I didn't expect to remember what had happened when Darkness was in control, but I couldn't even remember a nearby city named Newton. I gently probed my fingers against my throbbing face. "Umm... remind me where Newton is again?"

The stranger frowned and looked even more concerned. "About an hour south of Cedarville."

My mouth said "Ah, that's right" while my mind freaked out. Darkness had managed to get me drunk, thrown in jail, and beaten up *after* driving more than four hours from home and crossing state lines? How long was he in control? I'd gone to sleep by about eleven last night. I glanced through the bars and stared at the very plain silver clock hanging on the wall.

It was eleven thirty.

I turned and stared at the other me. He grinned and the pupil of his good eye shone almost black as he gave me a quick salute. Darkness had taken full control for more than half a day. And I had no idea how he'd done it.

I put my head in my hands and closed my eyes.

"Parker Chipp."

When I looked up, I saw an officer standing outside the cell looking at me.

"Ah, so that *is* your name." He folded his arms across

his chest. "You refused to answer to it last night. Happy to see you're coming to your senses."

"Yeah, sorry," I muttered, knowing this was probably just the beginning of the apologies I'd have to make. Starting with Mom. I winced just thinking about how upset she probably was.

The officer stared at me until I started to squirm. Finally he said, "You don't even seem like the same kid they brought in here last night."

I choked and then tried to swallow. "I'm sorry ... Sir."

"Your cousin is here to pick you up." He unlocked the door and slid it open, waiting for me to walk through it.

"My c-cousin?" At first I assumed it must be Finn, but he was still in Florida. Nothing made sense. I walked out of the cell and the guard closed it immediately. Darkness didn't make it out in time, so he just walked straight through the bars and the people like they weren't even there. As if this whole scenario wasn't bizarre enough without seeing that.

"Yeah, we got a call from your dad." The officer barely suppressed a laugh as I froze cold in place, my mind refusing to register anything but the words *your dad*. He continued, mistaking my reaction for fear. "I imagine you'll have a lot of explaining to do when you get home. As it should be, if you ask me. Parents are too soft these days."

"Parker."

Darkness and I turned slowly in place to face the new voice. My head was already spinning. When I finally got turned around, my eyes came to rest on an all-too-familiar emblem: a skull and two eye patches gleaming white on the arm of a black leather jacket. Blind Skull.

Jack.

Darkness disappeared from beside me before I could blink, but I didn't care. All I could see was the hesitant smile on Jack's face. I launched myself at him, but in my condition, it came across more like a stumble. He swooped under my swung fist so fast I felt like I was moving in slow motion. Grabbing my punching fist with his right hand, he tugged just slightly on it, spinning until my arm landed around his shoulder. I was left standing beside him, leaning against him while he propped up my weight and started shuffling me toward the door.

In only half a day, my world and mind had become a spinning, colliding mess, and I felt like I might never catch up. I fought against him, trying to free my wrist from the death grip he had it in.

He said, low enough that only I could hear, "If you want to stay in jail, keep it up."

Groaning, I stopped struggling and let him help me to the door.

"Thanks, Officer!" Jack grunted, smiling over his shoulder as he forced me out the door. "I'll make sure to keep him out of trouble."

Once safely outside, I jerked my arm away, promptly turned, and puked in the bushes. By the time I'd finished, not only was I shaky, weak, and absolutely exhausted, but Darkness had appeared near Jack and was looking as green as I felt, although a lot more composed. I leaned my forehead against the building, letting the cool stone soak into my skin and settle me a little.

I drew in deep breaths, trying to focus on anything but Darkness's newfound freedom. I'd have to deal with him later, but it was just too much to fix at once. For now, I'd just pretend Darkness was as nonexistent to me as he was to everyone around me.

Next to my head was a bulletin board where the police had posted all the Missing Persons alerts for the state. There were so many it shocked me. They took up too much room, layered on top of one another and making a wall of faces in black and white. One of the ones on top had been missing for a month. It was a sixty-seven-year-old African American woman named Delilah Jones. She'd disappeared while walking through a city park in broad daylight. There was a plea from her family, saying she was a grandma. Who kidnaps a random grandma from a park on a Sunday afternoon?

It looked like Oakville wasn't the only place where weird things were going on. People losing all their money in the middle of the night, strange disappearances, all kinds of crazy stuff.

Maybe it was spreading...

"I'm Jack. I take it you remember me?"

The hint of laughter in his tone made me want to stomp my foot hard into his face. I turned on him, more ready to face him than to think about the freaky questions the missing persons board raised. "What the hell do you think you're doing here?" I asked.

"I'm doing what I was told to do." Jack stared me down,

his brown eyes almost as cold and harsh as those belonging to Darkness, my other unwelcome companion. "And you're welcome."

Once my vision cleared a little, I saw that Jack's dark brown hair was slightly longer than it had been last time I saw him. His skin was tan, even though it wasn't technically summer yet. He had stubble across his face and his eyes looked tired. Up close, it surprised me how young he was. He looked older than me but not by much—a year, maybe—even though his mannerisms and the way he spoke made him seem much older.

"You're my cousin?" I pressed one hand against the side of my head and tried to make everything stop pounding.

"No." Jack gave me an acidic smile. "I lied."

"I saw you at my school... and then in the hospital... but then you disappeared." I tried to sort out what information he could actually provide now that he was here.

"Yeah. I don't do school much. I'm self-taught, mostly from books." He shrugged off the rest of my statement.

"You said my dad sent you." I moved away from the wall, feeling a little steadier with the fresh air across my face. "Take me to him."

He laughed, but there was another emotion beneath it... anger and pain. "No."

The familiar ache in my chest burned as I swallowed it back. My dad hadn't ever come back because he didn't need me in his life—well, I didn't need him either. "Fine."

Jack watched me for a minute, looking like he might say more. Instead he pulled a rumpled paper bag from under his jacket and tossed it to me. I caught it on instinct. Inside, I saw my keys, phone, and wallet. Sticking everything but the phone into my pockets, I threw the empty bag into a nearby garbage can. I squinted at the phone and pushed the power button. It was dead.

Jack sighed, reached in another pocket, and walked back to a vending machine just inside the police station. He came back with a cold can of Coke. "Better put this on your eye. Who did you want to call?"

"My mom. She's probably freaking out." I pressed the can against my eye and cursed. Darkness winced as the pressure sent pain through my already-throbbing head. He glared at me. In spite of the pain, it felt good to hurt him back a little after everything he'd done.

My good eye searched the parking lot for my car, but I didn't see it anywhere. Wait—had Darkness been driving after that much alcohol? I released a big puff of air. If so, my car was probably impounded. I could only assume he hadn't killed anyone or they wouldn't be letting me out this easy. Nausea rose up again and I put one clammy hand on the back of my neck.

"Oh, relax already..." Darkness muttered under his breath.

"Your mom's fine," Jack said. "When I saw you leave in the middle of the night, I snuck in and planted a note before following you." He shrugged. "She thinks you ran to Finn's house to get an assignment to turn in for him while he's gone."

Ignoring Darkness, I turned my attention fully on Jack. "You were watching me?"

He didn't answer.

"How did you have time to get in, plant a note, and still follow me?"

"You, uh … weren't the best driver. It took you ten minutes to get the car turned on and in the right gear."

"Oh … "

I glanced at Darkness, who rolled his eyes. "Watching you drive isn't the same as driving myself, okay?" he snapped.

"Come on." Jack turned and walked toward an old, dark green Volkswagen Bug parked up the block. "I'll take you to your car."

"Where is it?" My words barely came out between my gritted teeth. I had a million different questions for Jack, but I was still angry with him for disappearing like he had, and I couldn't decide how to force him to stay around to talk to me this time.

"Still parked behind the bar you got so wasted in." He pulled out some keys and unlocked the car, then hesitated before saying, "The other you isn't as bad as some I've seen. But you've got to get him under control."

My whole body burned hot and cold in sizzling waves of sensation as Jack's words echoed through my mind: *the other you.* I raised my head and stared at Darkness. He gave me a little shrug and looked almost bored, but behind his left eye I saw my own burning questions.

Jack climbed inside and unlocked my door. I pulled so

hard on the handle that my fingers hurt, but I didn't climb in, just bent down and gaped at him.

"What do you mean, 'the other me'?" My voice was low, quiet, and sounded dangerous.

"Come on. You're not the only one who's let it go too far." For the first time, I saw a hint of sympathy in Jack's eyes. "But your dad is right. You've got to get him under control before he ruins your life . . . or ends it."

I crumpled down on the curb beside the car door and tried to force my brain to catch up to my circumstances. Jack knew about Darkness. *Dad* knew about Darkness. I had no idea how, but they knew.

You're not the only one who's let it go too far.

"How do you know? What do you mean I'm not the only one? Let what go too far?" I watched Jack closely, forcing myself to let go of all the anger and frustration and ignore the fact that Darkness had appeared in the backseat, leaning intently forward between the front seats. For now, none of that mattered. I could let it all go if Jack could give me the one thing no one else had ever been able to provide: answers.

"Get in." Jack let out a slow breath, his expression grim as he put both hands on the wheel. "We have a lot to talk about."

FOUR

The inside of Jack's car was so spotless I felt like breathing on it might smudge something. I squirmed awkwardly in my seat. Spending the night in jail and then puking in the bushes hadn't exactly left me feeling squeaky-clean. Add to that the fact that my maniacal other half was busily biting his dirty nails and spitting them on the floor of the backseat, and I was more than a little outside my comfort zone.

"You can see him now?" Jack's eyes on me were piercing as he leaned forward to start the car.

I blinked . . . it was amazing how many times Jack's statements could leave me staggering in only a few minutes. "Y-yes—can you?"

"Of course not." Now he looked at me like I was crazy. "But the way you keep looking into the backseat with disgust is a pretty big giveaway."

43

"Oh, right." Turning, I looked straight out the front windshield as Jack started the car and drove out of the parking lot.

"I think you should start." Jack glanced at me from the corner of his eye.

"Start?"

"Yeah. You ask me questions. That way, I don't give you answers you aren't ready for yet."

"At this point, I'm ready for anything."

"Famous last words," he muttered as he flipped on his blinker and waited in the left hand turn lane.

"Fine." I decided to start with something simple... a question where the answer wouldn't scare me as much as the others. "What's up with the blind skull on your jacket? My dad had the same symbol on his wallet. Why?"

Jack looked down and touched it gently with his fingers. "It stands for seeing what other people don't. It's a symbol to help us identify other people like us. It started as the emblem of the Night Walkers, but for over a decade it's been more a symbol of the rebellion."

"Wha—rebellion?" There was way more information in that answer than I'd been expecting. "Wait... so, you're a Watcher? Like me?"

"Watcher..." Jack nodded slowly. "That isn't what we call it, but yeah, that works."

"What do you call it?"

"Like I said, Night Walkers. We're type 2, to be specific."

"Type 2?" I popped the knuckles of my left hand, struggling to grasp the concept that not only was I not alone in my curse, but there were different types? It felt like I was running behind a car going full speed with no hope of catching up. "How many types are there?"

"Three."

"Three?" I shook my head. "How are they different?

"Well, if we're Watchers, then type 3 would be the..." He thought for a few seconds before continuing. "Builders. They control dreams, and construct them. They're the key to our survival. They can build dreams directly for Watchers, to help us sleep. They can even make us stronger."

"Like Mia." I'd known all along there was something different about her. This was the first thing Jack had said that made perfect sense.

He released a short laugh. "No, not like Mia. You're lucky you've survived, even with her dreams. You caught a break, but she's no Builder."

"How do you know?"

"Because she dreamed what someone told her to with the self-hypnosis, right? And even then she often couldn't keep the nightmares away." He took a quick right down an alley. "A real Builder has much more control than that... once they know what they're doing."

"How do you know all this about Mia?"

Jack was quiet as he pulled into a parking lot behind a dirty old building with the name *The Trough* over the door in faded red letters. My blue Nissan sat in a back corner. Darkness let out a long, low whistle from just behind me but I kept ignoring him, hoping that if I pretended he wasn't there, then soon he wouldn't be. The bar's front windows were filled with old neon beer signs that were coated in about a decade's worth of dust. This was the place he'd gotten wasted last night? That Darkness…always keepin' it classy.

"I know about Mia because I know what I'm doing. Being a Watcher can be—an asset."

I gawked at Jack for a moment with my fingers around the door handle. I couldn't decide whether to scoff at him for calling it an "asset" or deck him for rubbing in the fact that he knew so much more than me—which was even worse because I suspected he'd learned it from my dad.

The man who should have been teaching me.

Before I had the chance to do something I'd regret, Jack put the car back in gear and drove across the street to a little diner.

"What are you doing?"

"You may be sobering up, but you don't look at all steady. I don't think you should be driving yet." Jack turned off the car and pulled the keys from the ignition. "We'll grab something to eat here first. Besides, I assume you have more questions."

I wanted to argue, but between Darkness hovering and the pounding in my ears, I knew Jack had a point. I'd been waiting for months for him to come back. I was going to get every answer I could before he got the chance to disappear again. Besides, my stomach had mostly stopped churning and felt achingly empty.

"I could eat."

The hostess sat us at a back corner table and I put down the now almost-warm can of Coke on the seat beside me. It had done its job, and I could actually open my eye a little wider now. Darkness glared at the spot with the can and then at me before hopping up on a barstool a few feet from the table. He seemed focused on leering at the waitress, but I could tell he was listening to every sound we made. I ordered the greasiest things I could find: fries and a grilled cheese sandwich.

My hands trembled as I drank some water, but I wasn't sure if it had more to do with a couple nights of no sleep or the hangover. Probably a combination of the two. I watched Jack across the table. He brought out a phone, typed into it for a moment, and then stuck it back in his pocket. Opening his straw slowly, he put it in his Coke and took a sip. He didn't look at me once.

"So, you going to ask questions or you learning enough by staring at me?"

"Did you just send a message to my dad?"

His eyes finally met mine and his jaw tightened. "No."

"I don't believe you."

"That's rough for you."

I grabbed the side of his jacket across the table and jerked him forward. "Tell me the truth."

Jack hammered one arm down across my wrist and broke my hold, sending shock waves of pain through every bone in my arm.

"I couldn't talk to Danny if I tried." His voice was a low snarl, but the instant the words were out he sat back against the seat, suddenly focused on the cars driving past.

My arms fell limp to my sides, all physical pain forgotten under the sudden onslaught of emotional ache.

The waitress showed up and placed our food in front

of us, and I thanked her out of habit. My body was on autopilot. Jack dove into his food, but I didn't touch mine. The strong salty smell of the fries made my stomach roll, and I considered rethinking the whole eating plan.

"Danny?" My dad's name was Daniel. It was where my middle name came from, but I'd never heard *anyone* call him Danny. Mom called him Dan and everyone else called him by his full name. Never *Danny*. "You call him Danny?"

"Sometimes." Jack swallowed his mouthful of burger before finishing. "So?"

"Nothing." I picked at my fries, trying to find one that looked less puke-inducing than the rest. The conversation really wasn't helping things. I might have my dad's blood, but this stranger knew Dad much better than I ever had.

I didn't realize Darkness had moved until I heard his voice from directly over my left shoulder. "You should pound him. He deserves it. I *know* you want to. I'd do it, but you have control ... for now."

Swallowing back the sharp and disturbing thrill I felt at the proposal, I forced myself to focus on the answers I needed. "What do you mean you can't talk to him?" I asked. "I thought you said he sent you."

"No, he sent me a few months ago." Jack's eyes were glued to his plate, and evasiveness seemed to ooze from his skin. "Today, I said I was doing as I was told."

"The officer said he called."

"That was me, too." Jack's voice shifted a bit lower and he sounded much older. "It's a skill I've picked up."

My heart sank and I wished I could rip it out and hurl

it away. Why could Dad still hurt me like this after so long? "So he didn't care enough to call? Or he doesn't know?"

"He doesn't know."

"Why not?"

Jack looked out the window but didn't answer me.

"Why tell me to ask questions and then be so freaking cryptic?" I glared at him. "Are you going to give me answers or aren't you?"

"Fine. Your dad was around more often last fall, when you were in your car accident and during the fire. He told me to keep an eye on you, to keep you hidd—to keep you out of trouble." His eyes had a hard glint to them. "It's been a bigger job than I thought."

"Why didn't you come back, like you said you would at the hospital?"

"You had Mia and Addie—and Finn. You didn't need my help yet and I had my hands full with other complications." He rolled his shoulders back and popped a piece of bun in his mouth. "Should've realized the second your friends left town everything would go to hell."

"I'll show you hell…" Darkness growled.

"Shut up!" I finally exploded. I whirled toward Darkness but he was gone, the booth and barstool empty… and now everyone in the diner was staring straight at me. I felt a little relieved until I heard Darkness's laugh echo inside my head. He hadn't gone far.

I shrunk down in my seat and took a long sip of water, waiting as the people around us slowly went back to whatever they'd been doing. Jack watched me, his brow lowered, but I didn't feel like giving him any answers when it had been so hard to get any from him.

"Just because I'm going to survive, now, doesn't mean my questions all go away," I grumbled.

After a minute, Jack spoke. "That's how we're doing this? We're just going to pretend your little outburst didn't happen?"

Drawing in another long sip, I scowled at him before completely ignoring his question. "So he's not around for you anymore either. Dad seems to be making a habit of disappearing when people are counting on him."

All the color drained from Jack's face and I could see anger in every muscle twitch, but when he spoke his voice was calm, soft. "You don't know *anything* about it."

"And whose fault is that?" My words were biting and hard.

He looked down and slid his plate aside, everything about him shifting from fury to sorrow and defeat. "Well then, let me educate you. Your dad is one of the bravest men I've ever known. He ran from you and your mom because he loved you enough to do anything to protect you, and there hasn't been a single day since that he hasn't talked about you."

Ever since Dad had left, anger and resentment had been the glue I'd used as I'd struggled to put my world back together, piece by piece. Jack's words shook me like an earthquake, cracking and shattering everything I'd built up and called truth. "Protect us?"

"Yes. He didn't want to leave you. He knew he had to get as far away from you as possible so the type 1s would believe he didn't care. The rebellion—it's against the type 1s. They've hurt, even killed, so many people, and he wanted to keep you safe. So he figured if he kept them busy chasing him, they wouldn't bother with you."

"Type 1s?"

"The first type of Night Walkers. They're different than the others. And there are twice as many of them as the rest of us put together. I'd call them Takers, because all they do is take. They're like type 2s—" He shook his head and spoke slower. "Sorry. I'm trying to use names that will make more sense to you. Takers are like Watchers in that they never sleep, but Builders can't help them like they can us. Takers' lifespans are very short due to this lack of sleep, and most of them have essentially become anarchists. Some infamous celebrities were Takers: James Dean, Kurt Cobain, Buddy Holly. They live hard and die young. The lucky ones live to their mid-twenties. They think of themselves as superior to all other humans because, as they put it, they live more in their shortened years than most people do in a hundred."

"Why can't Builders help them sleep?"

"Because Takers don't enter dreams once they reach maturity—ever."

I frowned, incredulous. "So, even their bodies always stay awake?"

"Not exactly." Jack leaned forward. "They make their connections with Dreamers just like Watchers do, through eye contact. But then their body enters a coma-like state and their minds take over the *bodies* of Dreamers. As long as the Taker's body is zoned out, the Taker controls the Dreamer—completely."

FIVE

I sat up straight, like someone had replaced my spine with a metal post. I'd thought Darkness was responsible for all the madness of the night before. Since he was so free today, it made sense, but maybe he wasn't... "Think a Taker might've taken me over last night?" I asked.

Jack smiled for the first time I could remember. I was so surprised, it put me even further on edge. "Not possible."

"Why not?" I gestured in the general direction of the jail. "Isn't this the exact kind of thing you said Takers could do?"

"Yes, and a Taker could be partly at fault... but this has to do with your own inner demons." Jack scratched his chin and took a long drink of his Coke. "It's impossible for a Taker to take over a Watcher. Just doesn't happen."

"Fine..." I nodded, extremely uncomfortable with his choice of the words *inner demons*, especially because today Darkness had been much more of an *outer demon* than anything. "What do you mean, 'partly at fault'?"

"From what I've seen, this other part of you hasn't gotten this kind of free rein before, right?"

I swallowed hard and shook my head. Even though Darkness was silent, it was like I could feel him listening. Yeah...he was definitely more present and free than he'd ever been.

And he wanted it to stay this way.

"Something backfires when a Taker and Watcher make eye contact and then go to sleep." Jack shrugged and his eyes got a little distant. "I've never experienced it, since I spend a lot of time avoiding Takers. Basically, I hear that you both get trapped in some kind of dark emptiness for the night...and, in cases like yours, your other side gets full control."

"Yes! That's what happened." I shuddered, remembering the inky suffocation. "It was so heavy I could barely breathe."

Jack's mouth pressed into a thin line, his expression grim at best. "I'd hoped you'd just lost control. Who is the Taker?"

"I don't know him, but his name is Cooper." I tried to remember anything that could help identify the guy, but he'd been pretty average in every respect. "He was with someone from my school. That's all I really know."

"You feel better?" Jack stood and dropped some cash on the table. "We've got to go."

I was much improved, but confused about the sudden rush. "Where? I still have questions."

"I know. Do you think your mom would mind if I stayed at your place for a while?" Jack started toward the door and didn't even check to make sure I was following him.

"No. She'll probably be happy that I know more people than just Finn and Addie."

Jack hesitated, throwing a wadded-up paper from his pocket into the garbage. "She might recognize me."

I remembered back in the hospital, when Jack had first introduced himself to Addie and me. My mom had looked at him funny even then. "How does she know you?"

"Your dad wanted to make sure you both were okay." Jack stared at the garbage can, his brown hair swinging forward a bit, then pivoted toward the door. "Before we discovered whether or not you were a Watcher, entering your dreams was too risky. We couldn't know what type of Night Walker you might be...and you've seen firsthand how bad it can suck getting stuck with a Taker. So I watched your mom's dreams off and on...asked her some questions occasionally."

"Weird."

"Tell me about it."

We reached the door, but I stopped as something occurred to me. "Why do you want to stay with us?"

"If there's a Taker in town, there's only one reason for it that I can think of." Jack pushed the door open. We walked out into the bright sunshine, but his words sent the chill of deep night through my body. "He's here for you—or your mom."

Jack didn't need to explain why my other questions had to wait. We ran to our cars and drove back to Oakville. Even if Cooper hadn't known I was a Watcher when we met last night in the parking lot, he sure knew now after being in that suffocating dream with me. And Thor only had to look through Oakville High's student directory to find out where I lived…where Mom lived.

The four-hour drive felt like the longest in my life. Darkness was strangely silent and subdued. I only knew he was still very present because every few minutes I had extremely violent thoughts and urges against Thor, Cooper…and, still, Jack.

I shuddered and turned the radio up, trying to switch my focus to anything else. My phone took a couple of minutes to power on once I'd plugged it in to the charger. At the first stoplight, I responded to numerous texts and two voicemails from Finn with a quick *I'm fine, just busy. Call me when your plane lands tomorrow.* And I called Mom six times with no answer. She was a realtor—she never went that long without answering her phone.

"We should kill him," Darkness muttered from the passenger seat. When I glanced over and met the icy hatred in my own eyes, I cringed. His words, spoken so clearly in my voice, sent a cold chill through me that no amount of heat could melt away. "Kill Cooper and maybe even kill Jack. Kill everyone who gets in the way."

Ignoring every word from Darkness, I focused hard on the part of me that was nothing like him. The part that cared only about those I loved. On that side, two thoughts rampaged through my head with every car I sped past on the way home.

First: Mom had to be okay. The Taker had found out about us because of me, because I was stupid and didn't want to watch Mom's nightmares again. I'd never forgive myself if she'd been hurt because of it. I'd do anything to keep the people I loved safe; I'd been willing to run away to prove that, back before the fire. I wouldn't hesitate to do it again if the Taker would chase me and leave her alone.

Second: did Dad feel like this when he'd run to keep us safe? If Jack was telling the truth, then we were facing the same enemy now. If so, for the first time in years, I felt like I could understand—that I *might* be able to forgive him.

By the time I pulled into the driveway, with Jack's green VW right behind me, I was in a full-on panic. My palms were so clammy it was hard to hold on to the steering wheel even when I gripped it so tight my knuckles ached. The radio had been blasting the entire drive, but the thrumming in my ears was so loud I couldn't name a single song that played. It wasn't quite five o'clock yet, but Mom's car was home already. Climbing out of my car, I pressed my hand to the metal of her car hood. It was cool—she'd been home awhile. That alone made my hair stand on end. My mom worked hard, long hours and only took time off when she was sicker than sick... or when I needed something.

I bolted toward the back door, but Jack caught my shoulder with a quick shake of his head before I could go crashing in. When I turned back to face him, I saw Darkness standing by the car, fists clenched tight by his sides and madness in his eyes. Seeing my darkest thoughts and desires played out on his face—my face—was really messing me up.

Jack walked around me and placed one steady hand on the knob. He turned it and silently opened the door. Music played, some of Mom's oldies, but I still felt on edge until I heard her laugh coming down the hall. Jack's shoulders relaxed, but he crept through the kitchen without a sound. I stuck close behind him; Darkness followed us like a shadow.

When we turned into the doorway of the living room, I saw Mom and Mr. Nelson dancing far closer than I'd ever wanted to witness. Intense relief tainted by a bit of revulsion smacked me across the face, and Darkness and I groaned in unison. When I gave him a startled look, he frowned and faded back into the shadows. Mom and my physics teacher spun to face us and Mom wiggled out of Mr. Nelson's arms, stepping awkwardly to one side.

"Hi, Parker." Her smile was half-apologetic, half-embarrassed, and she seemed to be looking at everything in the room but me. "I didn't realize you'd come home."

"Obviously," I muttered, watching Mr. Nelson smile, then frown, then put his hands in his pockets, then pull them out again. I decided to cut them some slack and let it blow over. At least Mom was okay. "Hi, Mr. Nelson."

"I already told you, Parker..." Mr. Nelson stuck the smile back on his face, but it fell again when his gaze settled on me. He leaned his head to one side with a slightly confused expression. "When we're not at school, you can call me Tom."

"Right—Tom—I'll work on it." I didn't mind the guy. There were definitely worse men my mom could be dating. I guess that would have to be enough for now. Turning back to Mom, I waved my hand for Jack to step forward, but she'd started looking at me odd, too. Then she gasped and rushed over.

"What happened to your face?" She stood on tiptoe and grabbed my chin, pulling it down so she could inspect the scratches I'd gotten from Thor in the parking lot, which ran up my left cheek, and the ugly black eye on the right side of my face. I'd almost forgotten about that. At least my mind found an explanation easy enough.

"It's nothing, Mom." I gently pushed her hands down and looked over her shoulder at Mr. Nelson. He was frowning and looked almost—angry? What was that about? "I was at the mall last night and some guys felt like having a chat about the school fire."

Unfortunately, this wasn't the first time I'd come home with a black eye. Some of the guys at school were pretty angry about Jeff's death. It was even worse because I'd dragged Mia and Finn out of the fire in time to save them, but I hadn't saved Jeff. Top that off with the fact that I'd blamed the whole thing on Jeff and yeah, they were angry and pretty vocal about it.

And by vocal, I mean they liked to talk a lot.

And by talk a lot, I mean they pinned me against a wall and punched me until I wasn't able to form words to disagree with them anymore.

"I thought you said that was over." Mom shook her head. "I'll go in Monday and talk to Principal Lint."

"No, it's just because Finn's out of town. He'll be back tomorrow. They're not as willing to attack when you travel in packs." Not exactly true. Finn had come home with a couple of black eyes himself, but Mom didn't have to know that. I smiled, but with the swelling in my eye only one side went up like normal. Mom clucked her tongue and I shifted my weight a bit, angling my body so my eye wasn't as obvious.

"Speaking of packs." I gestured behind me toward the one person in the room who I still didn't have a clue what to make of. "This is Jack. He's new at school. I wondered if he could hang out here for a couple days."

Jack stepped around me and smiled, extending his hand to Mom. She turned her attention to him but the more she stared, the more confused she looked. I stepped in to block her view and hooked my arm around her shoulder, breaking the spell as Jack turned and shook Mr. Nelson's hand.

"His parents are spending the weekend visiting a relative. He didn't want to go, but they weren't thrilled with the idea of him being home alone," I whispered in her ear. "Besides, I'm bored with Finn gone. You don't mind, do you?"

She looked up at me and shook her head. "No, that's fine. I think I've seen him around the school before. He looks familiar. Was he on the soccer team?"

"No, but he came to our last game, I think."

Mom winced. She knew firsthand how badly the championship had gone, and she also knew I didn't like to talk about it. She gave me a sympathetic squeeze, then scrunched up her nose and whispered. "You smell terrible, Parker. Did you take a run and not shower? Go clean up before anything else. I'll grab you some ibuprofen for your eye, okay?"

After the night I'd had, I was glad she thought I just smelled "terrible" and not, as my friendly neighborhood cellmate had described it, "more alcohol than human." Showering had been at the top of my agenda anyway. "Deal."

"I'm making dinner." Mom handed me the medicine and turned toward the kitchen. "Have you boys eaten yet?"

"Nope." I followed my mom into the kitchen as Jack jogged out the back door. He came back in with a backpack as I was checking out the delicious-looking roast in the oven. I tugged on his backpack strap, and he followed me toward my room as I shouted over my shoulder to my mom, "How long until dinner?"

"Go ahead and get settled." She waved us away. "About forty-five minutes. I'll call when it's done."

"Sounds good." I smiled and felt another intense surge of relief when she smiled back without even the slightest bit of suspicion or worry on her face. For the first time in a long time, she looked genuinely happy. She deserved to stay that way, and I'd do my best to make sure she could. "Thanks, Mom."

SIX

I'd never seen anyone eat like Jack…and Finn ate like a starving dog in a Purina factory, so that was really saying something. He dove in with such gusto that much of our meal was spent watching him, or waiting for him to take a breath so he could answer one of Mr. Nelson's many questions. I'm not sure if Mr. Nelson was trying to avoid awkward silences or was more suspicious of my new friend than I'd expected. Either way, he was more perceptive than I'd given him credit for.

"So you aren't taking Physics?" he asked.

Jack swallowed and took a sip of water. "No, but I'm getting my schedule sorted out for next year. Once I talk to the teacher, I think they'll put me in Advanced Chemistry."

I raised my eyebrows slightly at Jack, and he shrugged. I wondered if he was really planning to stick around that long.

Mr. Nelson nodded. "That's not an easy class. Very impressive."

A bitter wave hit me as I thought about the less-than-stellar grades I'd gotten in Chem last year. Dad had been a chemistry teacher, so it was no wonder Jack excelled at it. I fought back resentment, wondering what Mom would think if she knew Jack had spent so much time with her missing husband. But I squished the thought as soon as it surfaced. I was struggling enough with this situation and I didn't have a choice. I was a Watcher. I was part of this new world whether I wanted to be or not.

I'd keep Mom out of it, and the frustration and pain associated with it, as much as I could.

I felt my phone vibrate in my pocket and remembered I'd never called Finn back. When I tugged it out, though, it was Mia's smiling face that flashed across the screen. I opened her text and stopped chewing my food.

Had a bad nightmare last night. Miss you more than I thought I would. We should talk when I get back.

I stared at the message, trying to convince myself that Mia didn't mean it the way it sounded. Maybe the message was from Addie...actually, I hadn't heard from Addie since yesterday sometime. Maybe she'd lost her phone and was texting me using Mia's? Either way, it didn't make sense for Mia to mean it *that* way. It wasn't like that with us. It never had been.

"Parker, not at the table, please." The way Mom could combine a happy, lilting voice with eyes that shot daggers was impressive.

Stuffing the phone back in my pocket, I pushed all the new, unexpected questions out of my head. "Sorry."

Mr. Nelson smiled at my mom and I noticed Jack's gaze harden. What was that about? He had something against Mr. Nelson? This whole dinner situation was just getting weirder, and I was done trying to sort everything out. I ate my last bite and stood up.

"Thanks for dinner, Mom." I made certain to meet her gaze, knowing Jack hadn't told me yet what happened when Watchers got stuck together for the night. "You mind if Jack and I go outside and play basketball for a bit?"

"Nope, that's fine. Just please put your dishes in the dishwasher first?"

"Thank you for dinner," Jack said to Mom as he followed me into the kitchen.

"You're welcome," she responded, and then I could hear low murmurs as she and Mr. Nelson spoke softly to each other back at the table. After a moment, I heard another soft giggle from her and fought not to groan out loud.

Yes, getting out of here was a very good plan.

"I don't know how to play basketball." Jack's words were nearly drowned out by the water I was using to rinse my plate.

"We're not playing." I didn't look up. "Just taking a few shots."

"I don't really know how to do that either," he said, his voice still low but sounding strained.

"You've never shot a basketball?" Leaving the water running, I glanced at him over my shoulder but he kept his eyes down.

"No. I spent a lot of time out in the desert. Not exactly a lot of hoops out there."

The desert—so Dad had ended up there. He'd mentioned a few times that it was a great place to get away from people, out into nature. When I'd considered running away, I'd thought that would be a good place to start.

Turning off the water, I walked out the back door, dug the ball out of a cabinet we kept our sports equipment in, and tossed it at him. "Doesn't matter. Besides, this seems like a good time to try it out."

He caught the ball and held it out in front of him like it was something dangerous. I kept my gaze on the crisscrossing black lines of the ball to make sure I didn't accidentally look Jack in the eye.

"Just toss it up. Try to throw it in the hoop." I nodded toward the basketball stand and bent over to tie my shoes.

I heard the ball crash into the bushes ten feet behind the basket and Jack cursing under his breath. Then I noticed Darkness hovering in the shadows behind the hoop. He was leaning against a tree and watching us in silence. His mere presence set me on edge more than ever. It was like knowing the floor beneath me was electrified and at any moment someone could flip the switch and fry me.

Even worse, I was starting to wonder if I'd be stuck with this constant fear forever ... if Darkness would ever go away again.

"Maybe you shoot and I watch." Jack jogged back with the ball and tossed it to me as I stood back up.

I shrugged. "As long as you're still answering my questions, I don't care what you do."

"So ask." He sat on one of the wrought-iron benches and folded his arms over his chest.

The ball felt rough and cold in my hands. I knew what I wanted to ask next, especially after the violent thoughts Darkness kept pelting me with. I just wasn't completely sure I wanted the answer...but Jack might be the only one who could ever tell me for sure. Darkness shook his head from the shadows and I decided to go for it. "Is it possible to kill someone in a dream?"

From the corner of my eye, I saw Jack's eyebrows fly so far up they almost melded with his hair. "Why?"

"Just answer the question." My grip on the ball was so tight my knuckles hurt. I hurled it toward the basket and the collision made a clanging noise so loud it echoed back through the neighborhood around us.

Jack's shoulders hunched forward as he watched me, as if they could guard his secrets. The ball rolled across the pavement and came to rest at my feet, but I didn't pick it up. I just waited. It was a full minute before Jack responded. "I need to know you aren't going to use what I tell you to try to hurt anyone."

I swallowed hard and shook my head. It felt like someone had turned on a faucet and filled me from bottom to top with disgust. "That's not the problem."

Jack nodded. "Good. It's very difficult to do, almost

impossible—especially for someone like you, one of the Divided."

I didn't need to ask for clarification. I knew what he meant. "That's what you call it? Divided?"

"You have a better name?"

"No. That seems about right." I picked up the ball and rubbed my thumb along the seam. "How do people become...like this? And what does me being Divided have to do with the question?"

"It happens when a Watcher gets extremely sleep-deprived before finding a Builder to heal them." Jack gave me a look that almost held pity or regret before looking away and continuing. "There's a line somewhere that if you cross, you can't go back. Once you become Divided, a Builder can't fix it. They can still heal you, but you'll always be Divided. It's like your brain decided you couldn't handle the situation and it broke off a piece of you that only cares about survival."

Only survival. That sounded pretty accurate. I nodded but didn't speak. Then a thought bubbled to the surface that made me so angry it took several seconds before I could even form the words.

"You—and my dad—you both knew what was coming?" My tone dropped to a low and dangerous whisper. "And you just sat back and let it happen?"

"No!" Jack sounded so appalled it mollified my anger a bit. "We didn't even know for sure you were a Watcher. Let alone that it was this bad. It can vary widely—when or if someone develops into a Night Walker. We weren't sure."

I didn't respond, and Jack closed his eyes before finishing.

"You were good at covering your tracks, much better at continuing on with a normal life than we expected. I didn't even know for certain you were a Night Walker until I saw you screaming at the passenger seat in your car … just before your accident. At that point, you were already Divided." Opening his eyes again, he stared hard at me. "It was too late. *I* was too late. For that, I'm very sorry."

The sincerity of his statement was hard to argue with, but I was still too upset to admit to any forgiveness. So I sat, letting him squirm with discomfort while I tried to sort through the mountain of new information that every conversation with Jack deposited into my brain. Finally, he changed the subject.

"Anyway … back to your question. In order to do that kind of damage to a Dreamer, you have to mean it. You can't have any doubt or distraction. Your mind must be one hundred percent focused on destroying them. In the Divided, the two sides rarely have the same plan or goal in mind—so it doesn't really happen."

I'm not sure when my thumb stopped moving over the ball, but my body was completely still. When I'd attacked Dr. Freeburg in his dream, I'd felt no hesitation, no resistance. It could have been the one time Darkness and I acted together.

"Finally, you realize—" Darkness appeared right in front of me and I took a faltering step backward. With his back to the light, his face was hidden in shadow. The only thing I could see clearly was his cold smile. "You *should* be afraid of what I can do."

My hands were shaking, so I tried to dribble the ball, but

all sensation in my fingers seemed to have been cut off. After one bounce the ball hit my foot and flew over on to the grass. "I see."

I looked down and felt Jack's stare piercing through the side of my head. But when he finally spoke again all he said was, "Next question?"

Picking up the ball, I squeezed it between my fingers, grasping onto the first question that came to mind. "When you say a Builder can make you stronger, what do you mean?"

When he responded, his voice sounded like he was in a trance, like his mind was visiting some pleasant memory far away from the here and now. "They can craft a dream unlike anything you've ever experienced. Absolute peace. Everything else disappears. They can reconnect the breaks in your brain, repair the damage that all the missing sleep has done. Even build new connections where you had none before. Depending on what they focus on, they can improve your memory function, your coordination, your ability to think on your feet and brainstorm. Everything you can imagine and more. They make you whole again. Like I said, they can't fix a Divide like yours, but everything else is better—new and improved."

I sat down on the opposite side of the bench, working hard to ignore Darkness and everything wrong with me that he represented, and tried to picture what a dream with a Builder would be like. Truly turning my curse into something that could help me, something useful. It was hard to imagine. "I see the appeal."

Jack laughed. "Yeah."

"How do you find a Builder?"

Jack bent forward, resting his elbows on his knees and studying the cracks in the pavement below his feet. The sky was long past sunset now and I couldn't make out anything but his ears. His face was in shadow and his voice changed to match. "It's extremely hard. There are as many Builders as Watchers, but since their ability doesn't harm them in any way, most don't know about it. Night Walker traits run in families, so we try to find and watch the bloodlines, but it isn't easy or reliable. And even if you find a Builder, they're always in danger. Many Takers target suspected Builders as well as Watchers. They capture them—or kill them. They consider themselves superior and the rest of us defective. Why should other Night Walkers live normal lives when they can't? And if they wipe out the Builders..."

"The Watchers die with them." I watched Jack's shoulders as he drew in a shaky breath. "But still, why?"

I didn't know what else to say. This was a fight Jack had lived with for years and I'd just found out about today.

Jack rubbed his knuckles across the stubble on his chin. "As they go farther and farther down their sleep-deprived roads, Takers become less in touch with reality. Combining delusions and hallucinations with already sociopathic tendencies is not good. They can take over a Dreamer and kill their enemies without any trace of evidence leading back to them. They can walk into a police station, lie down on the benches in the waiting room, and kill someone while living inside the Dreamer's body. They are capable of iron-clad alibis and can get away with whatever they want. Even worse," he continued, "since Takers can't easily identify a Builder by their dreams the way a Watcher can, they just target anyone who known Watchers get close to."

I growled under my breath as images of my friends and my mom spun through my head like one of those picture carousels. "I'm really starting to hate Takers."

The muscle along his jaw tightened and he raised his face and stared hard at me. "That's a good instinct. Hold on to that."

SEVEN

The air around us seemed to have dropped twenty degrees in the fifteen minutes we'd been outside. I shivered as much from the chilling conversation as the temperature. Jack's voice dripped with pain, with truth. I was glad I'd never run into a Taker before last night.

Then his eyes met mine before I could think to look away. I flinched, but he didn't react at all.

I grasped for another question, anything to change the subject. It made me feel powerless just thinking about the Takers. Darkness was bad enough, but at least I'd been able to fight him off most of the time—and hopefully would again once Mia came back and I got a little more sleep. These Takers... they were new monsters in my world and already seemed more terrible than anything I'd ever witnessed in a nightmare. Monsters that I'd never even known existed until today.

"Okay, here's a question for you," I finally said. "What

did you mean when you said you couldn't get ahold of my dad if you tried?"

When Jack lurched back and immediately looked away, I realized I'd been asking the wrong questions all day. I'd assumed it wasn't that weird for Jack not to be able to get in touch with Dad. After all, I'd spent the last four years in that position. But from his reaction now, it was clear his situation was not the same.

"That doesn't matter right now," he said.

"Jack..." I leaned toward him across the bench. Darkness disappeared from where he'd been standing and my voice came out in a fierce snarl. "Where is my dad?"

Jack stood up and stretched, but he didn't give any further response. Jumping to my feet, I grabbed the front of his leather jacket and nearly jerked him off the ground.

He let out a surprised grunt and pushed against my chest, hard enough to break my grip. He stared at me like he was seeing me for the first time, and a low growl escaped his lips. "I *am not* your enemy."

"Uh... you guys want any dessert?" Mom's voice broke the heavy silence so unexpectedly we both spun to face her. Even from here, I could see she'd caught at least some of Jack's words. Even if she hadn't, our postures looked more like we were waiting for someone to ding a bell so we could attack each other than two new friends hanging out.

I stood up straight, knowing if I tried to play it off she'd be even more suspicious. "Yeah, we're just having a little disagreement. Give us a minute?"

Her expression looked torn between the desire to defend

me and the knowledge that she should trust me to handle my friendships on my own. After a few seconds she nodded and put on a fake smile. "Hurry. I'll dish it up."

When she went inside and closed the door, Jack's shoulders relaxed, but he didn't look any less wary.

"I don't need to know where he is," I said. "I need to know if Dad is in trouble. Tell me that much and I promise I'll leave the rest alone—for now."

Today had been too much, and the fatigue was abruptly closing in on me from every angle. Dad had been gone for years, but it was already obvious I didn't know the whole story. No matter his reason, I wasn't sure I could ever forgive him. Yet setting all that aside, he was still my dad. If he was in danger, I wanted to know about it.

"You'll only keep that promise if he *isn't* in trouble." Jack watched my feet as I backed slowly toward the house. "If he is, you'll immediately try to find him."

I froze mid-step and almost fell over. "He's in danger, then?"

Sighing, Jack closed his eyes and rubbed the back of his neck with his left hand. When he opened them again, he looked resigned. "Yes. You could definitely say that."

My legs felt shaky beneath me and I forced myself to stand up straight. "What kind of danger?"

"They have him, Parker." Jack walked closer to me and lowered his voice, checking the back door to make sure Mom wasn't there before he finished. "The Takers have finally caught up with your dad."

We struggled through an extremely awkward ice cream sundae where I fought hard not to look like an upset teenager pushing his melting rocky road around in circles instead of eating it. Mom still looked concerned, but Mr. Nelson—Tom—was a welcome distraction. When I said we were going to my room to play computer games, she didn't seem too worried.

"Make eye contact with your mom," Jack muttered as we were about to walk down the hall.

With a quick nod I went over to them, shook Tom's hand, and gave Mom a quick hug. "If we don't come out before noon tomorrow, send in Coke and Milk Duds."

She laughed and I met her eyes for a second or two before following Jack down the hall to my room.

Once the door was shut, I flipped on the small lamp by my bed. Then I grabbed my sunglasses from the dresser, tossing him the extra pair just to be safe. "What happens when two Watchers make eye contact?"

He pushed the glasses onto his nose and shook his head. "Same as when your Dreamer is awake. The empty space, except you're stuck in it together. I prefer dreams, though...the empty space is boring."

"Agreed." I grabbed my backpack and started dumping it on the bed. "How far away is he? We need to pack things up."

"Parker, this is why I didn't want to tell you." Jack plopped down on the chair in front of my computer. "We aren't going after your dad. Now is not the right time. To be more specific, *you* are not the right person."

I sat down on the bed and dragged the empty bag onto my lap. "What is *that* supposed to mean?"

"It means you inherited more than just your dad's blue eyes." Jack rested his elbows on my desk and bumped my mouse, making the screen light up. In the dim light of my room it cast an eerie shadow across half his face. "You have his temper, too. If you think for one second I'm taking the person he asked me to protect into the heart of everything he wanted to keep you safe from, you're even crazier than I thought."

Everything in me wanted to argue, wanted to pin him against the wall and force him to tell me where Dad was. I gripped the straps of my backpack so tight my fingertips went numb. Jack's spine stiffened, like he could feel me sizing him up. I had a few inches on him. Since I'd started getting more sleep after the fire, I'd put on some muscle. While Jack was thin and probably very fast, I was stronger. If I caught him off guard, I could do it. There were so many things in my room I could use as weapons. Whether I decided to just hurt him or kill him…

I stopped and my skin went icy-cold in an instant.

This wasn't me. This was everything I'd spent months fighting off. I mentally shoved Darkness back with all my strength. I couldn't help my father until I got control of him first.

My twisted half appeared again, looking furious as he leaned against the wall in the far corner of the room.

"Someday you'll understand. Not all my ideas are bad just because they don't come from you." And then Darkness dissolved back into the shadows.

His appearing and disappearing again and again was really getting exhausting. He created a war everywhere I went…in my house, my room, my head. How long could I keep fighting him off?

"What do you suggest we do?" I picked up my newly emptied backpack and took out my frustration by shoving everything back into the bag—hard. "What do they want from him?"

"They've been after him since he left you guys, but they've never caught him before." Jack's head shifted back and forth as he watched my motions. "We know for certain he's alive. They need him alive. For now. That has to be enough."

"Again…what do they want from him?" I was tired, scared for my dad, and getting *really* tired of repeating myself.

Jack leaned over and rested his forehead on the smooth wood of my desk, as if every piece of energy that kept him upright and animated had been sucked out by me asking the question again. "They want him to keep them alive— for a long, *long* time."

The bag slipped out of my hand and I barely caught it before all the contents fell out again. "W-what?"

Jack sat up straight and pivoted his chair toward me. "It's a complicated brain chemistry thing that I'm not even sure I understand, but here's the general idea. Your dad is a chemistry genius. The Takers want him to make them a magic drug that will let them take over Dreamers' bodies long-term. We aren't sure exactly how long, but from what I understand it could be indefinite. They call the drug Eclipse. In theory, it would allow a Taker's body to rest in perfect health for a much longer time period without moving or eating, which enables the Taker to just *stay* in the body and brain of a Dreamer. They'll run the Dreamer's body into the ground, the same way they do now, but when the body finally dies of sleep deprivation, the Taker will just switch to a new one. If your dad gets the formula right, Eclipse could enable Takers to survive—possessing bodies and never technically sleeping—for at least a normal human lifespan, maybe even longer."

I slouched down on my bed, trying to comprehend what I was hearing. "Are the Takers all crazy?"

"Yes."

"Why would they think he could make this drug? It's not even possible...is it?"

"Before he left your family, he was working on a drug to help the rebellion, to make Takers more like Watchers. He wanted to find a way to make them sleep somehow, so they could survive. He thought that if they could live longer by using his drug, then the rebellion could use it to get the Takers under control and stop the fighting. Instead, he ended up creating the prototype for Eclipse. His plan backfired, big time. The drug had major problems and wasn't safe, but still, the Takers were enthralled by the potential of what it *could* become. Your dad ran because they wanted him to keep working on it, trying to fix it." Jack shrugged. "Who knows if he can? But it doesn't matter because they *think* he can, and as long as they think he can, they need him alive."

Nodding, I didn't move. My entire world had turned upside down in under twenty-four hours and I felt like I was still trying to shake it around to make everything fall into place. Exhaustion pinned me down and every movement felt like a struggle. I missed Mia's dreams and real sleep. I missed Finn and his ability to make everything seem more manageable.

I missed Addie—how everything about her made me believe I could handle anything.

"What else haven't you told me?"

Jack turned in the chair and seemed very interested in a picture of Finn and me on the soccer team. "I told you everything I think I can trust you with—that's all I can do for now."

"You don't trust me?" I was oddly offended by this.

His head spun toward me and he squinted. "Can you think of a reason I should?"

"I can't think of a reason you shouldn't."

"The way I see it, you don't trust people until they earn your trust." Jack leaned forward and stared hard at me. "And for now, the simple fact that you're Divided is all the reason I need not to trust you completely." He scoffed, then muttered, "Hell, *you* don't even trust you completely."

I closed my mouth on any response I might have had. I didn't like it, but he had a point.

Jack picked up the camcorder from my desk, pushed a few buttons, and pointed it at the bed. I'd forgotten to check it when we got home, but I didn't need to. I knew what it would show, and I really didn't want to see Darkness controlling my body again. I'd already witnessed the results first hand. I reached up and gingerly touched the lump on the back of my head.

"You may not know anything about our world," Jack muttered as he adjusted the angle on the camera, "but even you have your good ideas. This was one of them."

"Uh … thanks." I didn't even try to hide my sarcasm.

"Come on, let's go to sleep." Jack shut down my computer and pulled the extra pillow off the bottom of my bed. "We have a lot of work to do."

Nodding without thought, I stood and pulled a sleeping bag out of the back of my closet before his words registered. "Wait—what do you mean, 'work'?"

He grabbed the sleeping bag and rolled it out on the floor against the wall. "Why do you think I had us both make eye contact with your mom last?"

"You did, too?" After watching him pull a toothbrush and an old pair of sweatpants out of his bag, I walked to my dresser and grabbed some flannel pajama pants to wear to bed. "Doesn't one of us cancel out the other or something?"

"No. The connection is set up on our end. It's the last person the Watcher makes eye contact with. Who the Dreamer makes eye contact with doesn't matter." Jack zipped his bag closed and looked up at me. "I thought you knew that."

"I guess I did … " I rubbed my fingers through my hair. My hangover headache—or maybe it was just an exhaustion headache now—was coming back with a vengeance. "I just never really thought about it."

"Anyway, we'll both watch your mom's dreams." Jack picked up his toothbrush and headed toward the bathroom. Just before he walked out, he turned back to me, his voice low, his expression serious. "Tonight, I'll start showing you what it means to be type 2—what it means to be a Watcher."

EIGHT

After everything that had happened that day, my brain churned for a while in spite of how tired I was. Jack was snoring softly long before I could relax enough to enter the white void—the place where my mind waited for my Dreamer to go to sleep.

But the void felt different as soon as I arrived in it. Everything about it appeared the same, but it was like the entire world was vibrating almost imperceptibly beneath it. Like two worlds were fighting to meld together. Now that I thought about it, that was probably exactly what was happening.

"You always have trouble coming in?" Jack was off to my right, lying down on the white nothingness with his eyes closed.

"You mean, falling asleep?"

"Well, we aren't exactly asleep. Are we?" He didn't open his eyes or even move. If he weren't talking, I'd wonder if he somehow got real sleep in the void.

"Right... is there a name for this?"

"We call it the Hollow."

"Okay, that works." I looked around. "No, I don't usually have a hard time. A lot happened today. I was thinking."

Jack finally opened his eyes and sat up. "Fair enough."

I shifted my weight to face him, but when I looked up, he was gone. "Jack?"

Where he'd been just an instant ago, there was now nothing. Nothing but me alone in what was apparently called the Hollow. I was starting to wonder if someone or something had woken him when he faded back in, right next to me. I jumped.

"First lesson." He lay back down. "You can control whether another person in the Hollow can see you. I could see you the entire time, but you couldn't see me. I'm betting it's the same with the Taker and his black hole of a mind that you got stuck in. He could probably see you the entire time, but you didn't see him at all, right?"

I shuddered at the memory. "I couldn't see anything."

"Your turn. Make yourself invisible." Jack closed his eyes.

I looked at my body, which felt just as real to me here as when I was awake, and then back at Jack's closed eyes. If he wanted to ask me to do stupid things without telling me how, then he should learn to expect stupid responses. "There. I'm invisible."

"You didn't even do anything."

"How do you know? Your eyes are closed." I leaned back on my elbows and looked at my legs, wondering how on earth I could make them disappear.

"Just focus on matching yourself to the Hollow. Picture yourself blending into it. It's constructed half by your mind, half by mine—and you're awake. You can control it and it shouldn't be that hard."

"No pressure." I stared at the black clothing I always had on in every dream I've ever been in. I'd never tried to change my appearance. Why would I? But it made sense that I should be able to. White clothes would be as real as these black ones. Neither actually existed, after all.

I pictured my clothes as white as everything around me. It only took a few seconds before I saw a slight flicker. Blinking a few times, I wasn't sure if I'd really seen it. When I tried again, immediately everything I had on turned as white as the Hollow.

"Good." Jack yawned, eyes still closed. "Now do it again."

The second he said the words, my clothes turned such a bright color of neon green it hurt my eyes. "What the ... did you do that?"

"Yep. Half your mind, half mine, remember?" Jack sat up and hooked one arm around his knee. "If you're in here with someone and they want to see you, you'll have to control your own mind and be stronger than theirs. Now do it—oh, too late—"

He squinted as he stared around the Hollow before finishing. "Here we go."

I tried to see what he was talking about, but nothing had changed. Then I felt it. The vibration had gotten stronger, like a third wavelength had joined the others. How had I never noticed this before? Maybe because there had never been another Watcher before? Then the very familiar sliding sensation came, and we both slipped into Mom's dream.

Relief lapped at my nerves just like the waves on the shore in Mom's dream. Not only did this one not feature any rotting corpses, but Mr. Nelson was nowhere in sight. She'd really outdone herself. The sand was creamy white, the water crystal-clear and so blue. I wondered if she'd ever actually been anywhere like this. We hadn't traveled at all since Dad left. Her idea of a vacation had become taking off a Saturday and spending it with me doing movie marathons at the Oakville Theater. One Saturday we'd stayed there from the first showing to the last. Funny movies, cartoons, scary ones, even a romantic comedy thrown in. I'd loved every minute of it.

Even those movie-cations, as Mom dubbed them, had only happened twice. The last time was over two years ago. Maybe I'd suggest we try a real vacation after we got everything with Jack and Dad sorted out. Maybe if I could save him from the Takers he'd want to come ba... no. I grabbed a fist full of warm sand and let it trickle slowly through my fingers.

I knew better than to hope for that anymore.

Jack waded through the waves for a minute and walked back as I got on my feet. "Next lesson. You can alter the dreams."

I frowned. "I've tried that. It didn't work."

"Watch." Jack walked over to where Mom lounged in

a chair, sunglasses pushed back on her head and her eyes closed. She had earbuds in and was humming along to some song I didn't recognize. Leaning down, Jack reached out his hand and stretched his fingers experimentally, and then shoved his hand right through the side of her head.

I leaned back in surprise, but she didn't move, didn't even open her eyes. Nothing had changed for her.

Jack's eyes closed, and then the dream started to change. Storm clouds approached in the distance and the lapping waves got bigger and bigger. Mom opened her eyes and watched the horizon, her brow furrowed.

"You did that?" I watched the storm across the now-choppy blue surface. It continued to build and move closer every second. Wind kicked up water in a wet gust and knocked Mom's drink over.

"I just planted the seed that a storm was coming. This was a tiny change, and now she's running with it. How far it goes, how bad it becomes—her brain is controlling that." Jack sat down on the now-empty beach chair as Mom scrambled around trying to gather her stuff in a bag before it blew away. Sand stung her eyes and her broad white hat blew out into the ocean. The sky darkened and the waves crashed farther and farther up the beach. This was happening faster than it could in real life, but this was a dream storm. It could do anything her brain conjured up.

And Jack had just set it loose on Mom's peaceful beach.

"I've seen enough nightmares, thanks. Can you stop it?" My voice was soft, almost carried away by the wild and whipping wind.

"That's harder to do once the Dreamer's mind takes hold like this. It's better to plant a new seed that changes everything." Jack climbed out of the chair and walked over to where Mom was frantically trying to stuff her towel into a bag. Every time she got it in, it would somehow fall out again. Tears of fear and frustration filled her eyes as she kept glancing up at the storm.

Jack extended his fingers again and I braced myself for when he put them into her head. His eyes closed, and then I saw the difference. In the distance, a massive black Hummer barreled up the beach towards us. A small smile crossed Jack's lips as he stepped back and pulled his hand away.

The Hummer came to a stop a short way from us and I saw a man climb out of the driver's side. All I saw was a glimpse of brown hair, only a bit shorter than mine, whipping around his head before he hopped out and disappeared around the other side of the vehicle. Holding his hand up to block his face from the blowing sand, the figure jogged toward us. Everything inside me buckled and I fell to my knees as I watched my dad run up to my mom.

The moment she recognized him, Mom dropped her bag, her towel … everything. The wind still blew at its frenetic pace, but she didn't care anymore. She stopped noticing the wind, the storm, the beach, the waves—everything faded into a low background murmur as her brain focused all its attention on her long-lost husband.

Only it wasn't him. It wasn't the man we remembered. This man was muscular and tan. My dad, the chemistry professor, had never been tan in his life—or, it seemed, the life I knew. My father had short hair, always trimmed and neat, not the wavy flopping mess that fell across this stranger's bearded face.

But his eyes … his eyes were my eyes, exactly the same in every detail. When he smiled, I recognized the smile, even though it had been years and everything else about his face seemed so different. I still knew him, and my chest felt like it was ready to explode with the strangest combination of resentment and happiness I'd ever experienced.

Even when every aspect of him was different, somehow he was still a part of me.

Mom fell into his arms, sobbing, her words unintelligible. Dad pulled her in so tight she almost disappeared against his chest. The voice I hadn't heard in years whispered words I couldn't quite make out as he kissed her forehead. After a moment I heard the nickname I'd almost forgotten, even though it was the only name I'd ever heard him call her: "I miss you, Milly."

Milly—Dad's shortened version of my mom's name, Emily. I choked back my own emotions, reminding myself over and over again that this wasn't real. It was just a dream. I looked over and found Jack's eyes on me. He looked pale, and I could see the realization of what he'd done in his face.

"Stop this." My voice came out so heavy and rough it felt like each word that rolled off my tongue had physical weight. In spite of my attempts to keep myself under control, every time I looked back toward my parents' embrace my eyes burned.

I glared at Jack. After the last few hours, the anger I'd felt at him for disappearing after the fire had started to fade. Not anymore.

"*This*"—I gestured toward my parents over my shoulder—"is cruel."

Jack looked from my parents back to me, but he made no move to stop it.

"We didn't know him like this. *She* never knew him like this." I got to my feet and took a step toward Jack. Every piece of me was so filled with pain and newfound fury that my bones ached to release it. "Why would you do this?"

"This is how I know him! How he is now . . ." Jack shook his head. "I implanted this image because you both need to see him this way. Your mom n-needs to recognize him, to know him."

"No! We remember him just fine without you forcing this on us!" I roared, and the dream around us seemed to literally shake in response.

"Parker—" Jack took a faltering step away. "Do not give in to him."

His words made no sense. To who? My body and head throbbed with a strange feeling of strength. I felt full . . . I felt powerful. The sensation was both familiar and new at the same time. My thoughts felt clearer, my emotion purer.

Jack took another step back, eyes stretched wide, his gaze glued to my face. He looked . . . afraid. Good. He should be afraid. Every time I caught a glimpse of my parents out of the corner of my eyes, I felt a fresh wave of maddening rage course through my body. Everything in our lives was destroyed when Dad left, and just when we had started to put the pieces back together, Jack was here to remind us of what we'd lost.

"Why this?" I shouted. The words came out so hard and loud they were like barbed wire, tearing at the soft flesh of my throat as they passed.

"Because he asked me to!" Jack yelled back. His breath came out in sporadic gushing bursts. I froze in place, thrown off balance by the anguish I saw reflected back at me. "Do you think he wants you to forget him? All these years, he's still hoped that someday he could lea—come back. You've both always been everything he ever wanted. You were the hole no one else could fill no matter how hard they tried. You two are the *only* thing he ever wanted."

His voice trailed off and he looked away, at the water, the ground—anything but me. I recognized the empty pain in his eyes ... but my rage burned ever hotter in spite of it. My fingers clenched and unclenched at my sides, aching to take action. I could almost imagine punching Jack. Hitting him again and again and again. I could take all those years of pain and frustration I'd built up and just let go.

And it would feel *so good* to let all that go.

I wanted to hurt him and end the pain he was causing. For daring to act wounded that he hadn't been able to fully take my place the way he'd so obviously wanted to, to punish him for doing this to me—and to Mom.

Simultaneously, somewhere deep inside my head a crevice formed, a tiny line with new cracks splitting off it as I began to question. A brief flash of clarity told me I should feel sympathy. Jack seemed angry and bitter that my dad would choose someone else instead of him. That he would leave him for us if given the chance. As wrong as that emotion sounded to me, how many times had I had the same thought? I knew Jack's pain, even if I didn't believe he had a right to feel it about *my* father.

I kicked my toe hard into the sand in front of me. It flew up into the air and Jack sputtered, rubbing it out of his eyes. He'd be such an easy target. A growl escaped my chest, but it felt strange—foreign. My left hand reached out, grasping for Jack's shirt. He disappeared . . . just like he said he could. I focused and made him visible again with my mind. It was so much easier now, like flipping a switch. His eyes went wide and I grabbed him again and forced him to stay put. Why was I getting angrier even now? Something didn't make sense . . . I stared at my right hand, now so tightly clenched it seemed to have a mind of its own. Then Jack's words echoed through my head again, and I abruptly understood what he meant.

Do not give in to him.

I'd never felt so complete. Part of me had always seemed empty—I'd thought it was fear and exhaustion causing it, but even when I'd been happy and rested from Mia's dreams, the hole was still there. I'd wondered if it could be from missing Dad, but it was none of those things. I felt strong now in spite of the exhaustion that had begun building up again this week, and I knew now what was causing this raw feeling of power. I knew the source of my rage.

As Jack had said, I was Divided, and this was how it felt to be whole again—to become one with Darkness.

It felt fantastic.

My hand clenched as I lowered it to my side. I took one more step forward and Jack tripped backward into the sand, breaking my hold on his shirt. A slow smile slid across my face like a shadow at the end of day... until I remembered.

There was a reason this feeling was familiar. I'd felt this way before—only once. Only one time ever, but now that I felt it again, I couldn't deny it anymore. I had been one with Darkness in Dr. Freeburg's dream.

There was no more room for doubt. I had killed Dr. Freeburg—I had murdered him.

The confirmation of my greatest fear broke me. It sapped my strength like a vacuum, tore my soul in two. Two pieces like it had been, like it should be, like it should *always* stay.

Because when I became whole—people died.

Do not give in to him.

NINE

Darkness screamed so loud in my head it felt like I was being shredded. I crouched over in the sand, shoving my hands against my ears in a futile attempt to muffle something that wasn't real. I heard a curse from Jack as he climbed to his feet and walked to my mom. I assumed he did one of his Watcher tricks because within a few moments I could hear Mom talking to one of her coworkers and the sand I'd been resting on turned into the carpet of her office.

I focused on the air filling my chest, in and out... repeated endlessly. Until Darkness stopped trying to make our brain explode, it was all I could do. Most of my anger had been ripped away with him, and the sound that echoed inside my head wasn't one of anger. He was in horrible agony. Separating into two again had caused Darkness physical pain. It was exhausting. I once again felt the gaping hole of being Divided—but the separation didn't hurt me the way it did him.

After a few moments, Darkness's cries softened to whimpers. When he finally spoke, his words were separated by panting breaths, his anguish replaced by sorrow and confusion.

"You see—I know you do." He coughed and sputtered for a moment before continuing. "We are stronger—together—why can't you let me stay?"

"No idea you have is ever a good one." I closed my eyes and shook my head. My voice came out like whispers muffled against the carpet. "I can't trust you or control you. It's too easy to lose track of right and wrong when you...when you're part of me."

He didn't respond, but I felt his sadness turn into the familiar resentment I'd grown to know so well.

"Parker?" Jack's voice was more than hesitant. It was tense, afraid.

"Yeah." The throbbing in my head from Darkness's screams had dulled and I sat back on my knees. The dream had changed, like I'd thought. Dad was gone, the beach, the Hummer. Everything was settled back into Mom's office and she hummed as she sorted through a stack of files on the desk in front of her.

"You okay?" Jack took a couple steps toward me, but stayed far enough away that I couldn't reach him.

"Yeah, but you're lucky you still are." I climbed to my feet and glared at him. "I almost—what were you thinking? Bringing *him* into the dream?"

Jack relaxed a little and his gaze went back and forth between Mom and me. "I didn't realize. I didn't think about how seeing him how he is now would affect either of you."

My eyes were on Mom, but in my head I kept seeing her sobbing in my dad's arms. "Will she remember?"

"Hard to say. She shouldn't." Jack rolled his shoulders back and then pinched the bridge of his nose between his fingers. "I tried to bury it in as many other dream layers as I could, but you never know."

I nodded, but my voice was ice cold when I said, "Fine."

"Any questions?"

Turning my back, I studied the office, trying to focus on the dream and not my anger. "What's the point?"

"Um … what are we talking about now?" Jack sounded hesitant.

"Being able to bury something in dreams, being a Watcher … all of it."

"The point?" Jack's expression was incredulous. "We don't even know for sure what our limits are yet. So many of the early Watchers died so young. We can uncover secrets, make someone forget something, change their minds—even alter emotions and feelings about things. We're like spies of the mind. Takers can manipulate Dreamers' bodies, but we are able to manipulate thoughts, feelings, personalities … anything."

I pivoted to face him, the ramifications both fascinating and appalling me. "And you do all that?"

"No." Jack's expression was grim. "We try not to. The rule we follow is simple: we try not to harm anyone. Otherwise, we'd be no better than the Takers."

I nodded, but knowing we had that kind of power was unsettling … no matter how it was used.

"Now, you need to test your limits and try it. That was the point of this whole dream." Jack sighed. "Sorry I got us off track, but my mistake is a good lesson. You can't be sure where the Dreamer will take something or how they will respond. You might think you're helping them by changing a bad nightmare or something, but you have to be careful when you're messing around inside someone's head."

"You think?" I muttered under my breath. As much as I liked the idea of having some control over whatever dream I got stuck watching every night, Jack's mistake had already made it crystal clear that it wasn't something to be taken lightly. "What do you want me to do?"

He acted like he hadn't heard my first words, but I was pretty sure he had. "You can touch Dreamers now, right?"

I nodded.

"Try to go back to what it was like when you first became a Watcher, before you fully developed. You could pass through the Dreamer. You need to be like that again. Try to picture yourself more as part of the dream, and then reach into her mind."

"Officially the weirdest thing anyone has ever said to me." I shook my arms out by my side and took a few steps closer to Mom. I tried to think of the office as real and that I was coming to visit her. Walking to her side, I reached my fingers out and pictured them passing through her hair. At first there was a little resistance, and she froze in the middle of searching through a folder. I tried harder to blend in, pictured her going back to what she'd been working on, and she did. Then my fingers passed through easily.

The second they did, my mind was filled with her thoughts: *Where did I put the Kellers' contract? Did they schedule the time for closing? I need to hurry or I'll never finish all this up in time to make it home for dinner with Parker.*

She sighed, closed the file she was working on, and counted the ones in her stack again: *Eleven. We had dinner together the other day. He'd understand me missing tonight, right? I need to make another sale this month to make the house payment. The Stevensons are so close . . .*

Even as she thought all of this, her intense feeling of guilt swept over me. I jerked my hand back. The emotions I felt in a dream were always powerful, but this was even stronger. It was like the new connection had amplified the emotions.

"It worked? You heard her?" Jack had taken a seat in the chair across the desk from Mom.

"Yeah. It worked." I felt a little shaken by the stronger emotions, but it had actually been easier than I expected.

"Good. Now do it again and try to alter the dream. Start small, nothing big."

I leveled my stare at him. "Right—I saw how well you did that."

Jack's jaw closed with a click and he looked down but didn't respond.

Taking a deep breath, I focused, and my fingers passed into Mom's head with no resistance. I felt nothing but a slight tingling sensation at my fingertips. Ignoring her thoughts, I came up with something small, something I'd seen her do every time I'd stopped by her office for a visit. Then I tried to mingle my thought with hers and send them back to her: *Coffee sounds really good right now.*

Mom kept flipping through her papers, but after a moment, she reached out and punched a button on her phone. "Cindy? Could you grab me a coffee?"

Cindy's voice came back through the phone. "Sure, no problem."

I dropped my hand back to my side and faced Jack as the ramifications sank in. "So I can alter any dream that way? I can make someone switch from a nightmare to a good dream? Make my mom stop making out with Mr. Nelson? Anything I want?"

"Mostly." Jack shrugged. "Some dreamers are more resistant, and sometimes you'll do more harm than good … like you saw before." He winced, then continued. "Again—I'm sorry about that, really."

I nodded. "Okay. I get that it wasn't intentional."

"Sometimes I just think … " Jack hesitated and then hurried on. "There's so much that you don't understand about him and his life."

I held out my hands. "Like?"

Jack's face flushed with anger. "Like that he lived with other Night Walkers before he met your mom. He was involved with a Builder there. Her name was Sarah."

I stared at him for a minute. "So?"

"So she loved him and chose him to be with, to dream with. She made him stronger. He never loved her, though, and she knew that, but they were happy together. Until he met your mom. Then he left."

"Left the Builder?"

"Left everyone." Jack popped his neck on one side and watched me. "He was important to the cause, a leader in starting the rebellion against the Takers. Then, a year in, he met your mom and left all of that—along with his chances for a long life—to be with her. And then to be with you."

My hands fell to my side, but my jaw twitched with anger. "What am I supposed to say? I'm sorry? Well, I am. I'm sorry he's unreliable. The only thing this history lesson teaches me is that he's had years of experience at leaving people he's supposed to care about."

"Oh, poor, poor Parker." Jack spat out my name as he stood and started pacing back and forth on the other side of my mom's desk. "You can be so selfish sometimes. I don't know how I'm supposed to trust you with information when you don't understand so much about our world. So many like us have sacrificed, have been murdered. The Takers became monsters, so we rebelled. Even after your dad left the rebellion, he still worked on the drug to help us beat them. But that failed spectacularly, and he stopped making it the moment he realized what it actually did. Now we're nearing the end—either they win and force him to make Eclipse, or we find a way to defeat them once and for all."

Stopping, he pressed the palms of his hands flat on Mom's desk and stared up at me with wild eyes. "This isn't about being happy, Parker. Screw being happy. For us it's about survival. But your dad—he risked survival for happiness. He sacrificed everything, left everything and everyone he knew and called family, all to make a new family with your mom.

The only thing that forced him to leave you two was when he found out the Takers intended to hurt you to get to him."

I didn't know what to say to any of this. It was so much information that I still couldn't really understand. I knew nothing of their world, of their code. And I didn't appreciate the way Jack acted like I didn't have a right to my own emotions anymore. My breath came out slow and choppy. "Do you have a point?"

Jack groaned and flopped back in a chair. "My point is that you barely knew your dad, and you know nothing about our kind, let alone this entire world you've been thrust into. You, Parker, are in over your head with all this, and you're going to have to learn to trust me a little until you can discover the truths for yourself."

"Fine!" I barely kept from shouting my response. We stood in silence, watching each other as our anger dimmed. "Did he go back to her?"

Jack flinched, but immediately acted like he hadn't. "Who?"

"The Builder. How has my dad survived as long as he has without one?"

"He used to visit her to be healed when he could, but he hasn't gone back to see … to see Sarah since he left you." Jack pivoted the chair away and gazed out the window at nothing. Mom's attention wasn't focused there, so outside the window there was nothing at all.

"Why not?" I watched him close. His jaw twitched and there was the slightest tremble in his hands.

When he finally turned to face me, his expression

betrayed no emotion. "Because the Takers killed her when they came looking for him."

I closed my eyes tight. "You knew her?"

"Yeah." He was facing the window again when I opened my eyes. "She was my sister. I was twelve. They said it was to get even because your dad had stopped working on their drug."

Rubbing my left arm with my opposite hand, I felt abruptly cold. I relived everything I'd ever said to Jack. He and I hadn't ever gotten along, but I'd never really given him a chance.

"I'm really sorry," I said.

"He left you and your mom as soon as he heard about Sarah. He was terrified the same thing would happen to you." Jack shrugged, and the motion seemed to ripple all the way down his body. It was silent for almost a full minute before he spoke again. "We should get back to the training before we waste the whole night

He cleared his throat, but emotion was still evident in his tone as he went on. "The same way you just altered your mom's dream, you can send the Dreamer's mind on tangents. Bury something in dream layers. It all depends on how specific you are and how hard you push."

He leaned toward Mom's desk, his eyes searching an old picture that sat near the edge. I'd almost forgotten she had it. It was from my eighth birthday. Dad was in it, smiling wide, one arm around each of us. When Jack sat back again, he said, "This is all going to come with practice. I can't really teach you in one dream. Now that you know how to do it, you just need to use it and figure it out."

"I can do that." I stepped back around the desk, but Jack stood up and pointed to the chair next to him. When I took the seat, he stepped around to Mom's side of the desk and looked at me.

"That was just step one. This is step two." He raised his hands and leaned toward my mom.

"Wait!"

He dropped his hands to his sides and raised one eyebrow at me.

"Just, nothing to do with my dad this time, okay?"

Jack inclined his head and then lifted his hands back to Mom again. This time he physically touched her, like I'd done with Addie and Mia in their dreams before. She turned to look at him, not at all as surprised to see him there as I'd expected.

"Do you trust me?"

"I don't know yet."

"How can I make you trust me?"

"Take care of Parker." Her eyes were honest; there was nothing hidden. It was so much like when I'd talked to Addie in her dreams. They were so vulnerable in here.

"You can trust me now. I have already helped Parker."

"Okay."

"I'm welcome to stay in your house as long as I want," Jack continued, and Mom nodded before he'd even finished his sentence. "You want me to stay. You don't even want to ask about it."

"Yes. You should stay." Mom smiled and I fought the

urge to push Jack away, to make him stop manipulating her. *He's not hurting her. He's not.* I repeated it a few times in my head. This was harmless.

Jack smiled. "Go back to your work now. You don't remember me being here."

Mom nodded and turned back to her desk as Jack removed his hands. It was like nothing had happened. She even picked up the same page she'd been working on before and went right back to it.

"Dreaming is the ultimate truth serum. No one ever learns to lie in them. There isn't a need." Jack stood up straight. "I can find out anything I want to know and often make people believe what I want them to believe. And so can you, as long as you use it carefully."

"She remembered you when you met, though. How many times have you done this to her?" I couldn't decide how to feel about this information. It was so huge it scared me. I was beginning to see what Jack had said. This thing that I'd always believed was a curse could help me wield an enormous amount of power ... of control.

"I don't keep track." Jack turned his back to me and studied some of the shelves on the walls. "Your dad asked me to make sure you both stayed safe. Since you didn't encounter your first Taker until yesterday, I think I've done a pretty good job."

"If she recognized you, doesn't that mean your little trick didn't work?" Even knowing that Jack was trying to help, my voice came out a little bitter.

"No. You meet someone's eyes enough times around town

and they're bound to start looking familiar." Jack rubbed the back of his neck with his right hand. "To be honest, staying with you, actually meeting her—it compromises my position. I can't bump into her at the end of the day on a regular basis once I leave your house without her being suspicious. It will make it more difficult for me to keep everyone safe."

I hadn't thought of it like that. "I can protect her. I don't need you for that."

From the corner of my eye, I thought I saw Jack shake his head, but he didn't comment. "Your turn. Try it now."

"I've done this before with Addie." I rested my elbows on my knees and leaned forward. "It wasn't intentional, but I touched her in a dream and asked her to talk to me when I came to her the next day."

He raised his eyebrows but didn't comment. "Making them forget you is the hardest part. Have you done that?"

With a frown, I stood up, but Jack held up a hand. "When you focus on making her forget you, try to picture the entire dream without you in it and put that in her thoughts. Be gentle."

I walked over to Mom's side and touched her shoulder. She looked up at me and smiled. "Hi, Parker."

"Hi, Mom." Her emotions were happy and full, proud when she looked at me. Even after everything else, she was still proud of me. I honestly didn't know how to feel about that. "Do you trust me?"

"Yes." No hesitation, not even for an instant.

"Do you still think I do drugs?"

"No." Feelings of guilt and sadness hit me like a punch

in the gut. She still felt bad for all the times she'd searched my room and accused me.

"You shouldn't feel bad about that. I understand."

She looked uncertain and her eyes filled with tears. I hadn't understood how much it had upset her. How bad she'd felt.

"Don't feel bad. I forgive you."

She nodded and blinked away her tears. "Okay."

"Go back to work now. You don't remember seeing me here." I spoke each word slowly, picturing everything about the dream around us without me or Jack in it.

Mom turned back to her work and I let go. I felt drained. It was much like I felt when fighting with Darkness. Like every person I tried to control stole bits of me. I didn't know how I could use these abilities on a regular basis if this was the result.

Jack was sitting in one of the chairs, and his eyes followed me as I flopped down in the other.

"And that's where Builders come in."

I rolled my head to the side and looked at him. "What?"

"Builders' dreams replenish everything this drains from us, and more."

"Well, that doesn't do me a whole lot of good, Jack." I closed my eyes and took a few deep breaths. "Since you're so sure Mia's not one, and sleeping during her self-hypnosis is just a fluke, apparently I don't know any Builders."

Jack laughed, slow and quiet. I peeked at him. "Think that's funny?"

"Watchers across the world spend their lives looking for

Builders. In communities of Night Walkers, they're often shared by the Watchers. So everyone can survive. This isn't a new thing." He leaned his head against his fist.

"Yeah, I see what you mean." My voice dripped with sarcasm. "That's hilarious."

"No, Parker. It's ironic." Jack's words carried a hard, cutting edge. I felt the dream around us shift. Mom was waking up. "*So ironic*—because you've known a Builder almost your entire life and you don't even know it."

TEN

I woke to the sun peeking past my curtains. From the pale tint, I could tell that it was still fairly early. My clock read eight a.m. and I groaned. I always tried to sleep in later than this on weekends. I didn't always wake up when my Dreamer did; mostly I'd just shift into my void, or, as Jack called it, the Hollow. But for some reason when Mom woke up that morning, so did I. Jack was still out cold in his sleeping bag.

What did he mean, I'd known a Builder almost my whole life?

Tossing my blankets off, I put my feet on the floor, then casually reached out and nudged Jack with my toes. He didn't even twitch. I pushed him a little harder and he rolled from his side onto his stomach, but still didn't wake up. I yawned, stretched, and shuffled to the bathroom. If he didn't wake up by the time I got back, I'd try again.

I looked in the mirror above the sink as I washed my

hands and splashed some cold water on my face. I leaned in for a closer look. Lately, I'd started to look more normal. The dark circles under my eyes had lightened, although this week they'd started getting darker again. My right eye was less swollen than it was yesterday, even though the entire eyelid—top and bottom—was now an angry purple bruise. My cheeks, beneath the healing asphalt scratches, were fleshed out a bit.

More than once over the last couple of months, Addie had said I was "starting to look human." I figured she might not feel the same way when she saw me now.

Their flight back from Florida was supposed to land by noon, and knowing my friends, they'd head over here as soon as they got home. I was glad. Judging by the last few days, my life tended to fall apart when they weren't around.

Leaning back from the mirror, I jumped when I saw Darkness standing behind me.

"Stop doing that," I snapped.

He smiled as I turned to face him, but once again it didn't reach all the way to his eyes. "What else am I supposed to do?"

"Go away."

"Why don't you?" His smile fell away and his gaze was icier than an early morning in January. "We've both always been here. Why do I have to disappear and you get to stay?"

I opened my mouth . . . then closed it again. I didn't know how to respond to that question.

"That's what I thought." He smirked and leaned against the wall again. "I'm not going anywhere."

"You are evil, and I'll keep fighting you. I won't let you have control again."

His voice mocked me. "Right and wrong, evil and good. Not everything is so easily defined. You don't have a clue what this is like for me. I'm not as simple as you think."

"Complex or not, every time you have any bit of power everything goes horribly wrong. That ends now." I spit out the words before walking out and leaving him in the bathroom.

"Maybe I need to let you *see* exactly what it's like to be me."

His words made me spin back around, but he was already gone again.

Stepping over Jack's still sleeping form, I went back to my bed. I reached over onto the desk, grabbed my phone, and re-read Mia's text:

Had a bad nightmare last night. Miss you more than I thought I would. We should talk when I get back.

What did she want to talk about? I hoped "Miss you more than I thought I would" had just came out wrong. I figured that in a few hours, I'd find out. Instead of replying, I sent a new text to all three of them:

Some stuff happened yesterday and Jack is back. Come to my house as soon as you can.

I didn't really want to get into any more detail right then. Would telling them about the Takers just scare them? But if one of them knew something about that Cooper guy, that could help. Could I tell them I'd ended up in jail? Addie was the only one who knew about Darkness. Could I tell the others? Tell them I wasn't always myself...

Tell them I'd killed Dr. Freeburg?

Picking up a glass of water from my nightstand, I dipped my fingers in it and stood over Jack. I shook a few drips onto his neck and face. He gasped and bolted straight up, wild eyes blinking fast and holding both hands above his head.

"What? Wh—what?" he sputtered, and I would have made fun of him if he hadn't looked so terrified.

"It's just a few drops of water." I kept my voice low, not sure if I'd just heard my mom in the kitchen or not. "Calm down."

Jack took a deep breath, but I think he was trying to burn a hole through my forehead with his eyes. "I've lived half my life in the desert. A couple of drops could lead to a flash flood in minutes. Not so funny."

"Okay, okay... I'm sorry."

In the silence that followed, Jack lay back down on his pillow and stretched. "That's something you'll have to learn to avoid. Getting too attached to the Dreamer."

"What do you mean?"

"You woke up when your mom did because in *your* head somewhere, you doubted what we did in that dream. You convinced her that everything was okay, but now you need to believe it yourself. We didn't hurt her. She isn't at risk because of what we did. If you can't stop worrying and separate yourself from Dreamers, you run the risk of undoing all or part of the things you said to her. She could forget the stuff you said about the drug suspicions, she could forget that you told her not to remember you, or she could forget everything."

"Okay, Obi-Wan. I'll try not to doubt myself." I scratched my elbow. "So who is it?"

"What?" He tilted his head to look at me.

"Who is the Builder you said I know?"

"Oh." He closed his eyes and relaxed back into the pillow before finally answering. "It's Addie."

I watched him for a minute, waiting for the joke … the punch line that had to follow. Addie couldn't be a Builder. It made no sense. I shook my head. "No, she tried to control her dreams once, back before the fire. She couldn't do it. Not enough for me to sleep."

"You're kidding." Jack didn't open his eyes, but a sarcastic smirk snuck across his face. "A Builder with no training couldn't control her dreams? That's unbelievable."

"I've seen her dreams. There wasn't anything obvious. How can you tell?" Jack was really rubbing me the wrong way, and I'd spent less than twenty-four hours with him.

"It isn't very easy to tell, but it has to do with her amount of control. She can change dreams when she wants to. She doesn't get stuck in nightmares like normal people would." Jack spoke with absolute certainty, but was frowning when he continued. "I knew for sure when I watched a nightmare she had about Finn dying, and by choice turned it into a memory of them having a snowball fight. Normal people can't do that."

"Yeah, I've noticed she has more control … I just didn't realize what it meant." I picked up my running shoes and grabbed some socks from my drawer. If Addie was a Builder...an entire wonderful future seemed to open up before me, but I closed it before I could consider taking even the first step. There was a lot to consider here. I wanted to be with Addie because of who she was...not what she could do for me. I shouldn't get ahead of myself. "So how does she learn, then?"

"I'll teach her." A small smile curved up the corner of Jack's mouth, but it disappeared when he opened his eyes and found me glaring at him.

"How?" I asked, even though I knew what the obvious answer was. I hoped I was wrong. Jealousy flared inside me at the idea of Jack spending time with Addie in her dreams.

"The same way I taught you." Jack stared straight back at me and I could almost believe he didn't notice that this bothered me. "I'll start tonight."

But then that damn smile popped up at the corner of his mouth again.

"Don't you have a Builder already?"

"Yes, but Libby is shared between several of us..." He let the insinuation hang in the air.

My voice came out more like a growl than I'd intended. "Why don't you go back to *your* Builder and let Addie practice on her own?"

He lowered his chin and frowned. "Because being left on your own worked so well for you?"

My hands clenched into fists at my sides as I struggled to control my rising anger. "But...don't you have more to teach me?"

"No. For right now, you should focus on practicing what I've taught you so far." Jack sat up. "Mia should be the perfect person to practice on. Plus, you can catch up a bit on whatever form of sleep she offers you."

Every word out of his mouth was making me angrier: Jack spending time in Addie's dreams, acting like Mia was some sort of lesser person just because she wasn't a Night Walker. I tugged my shoes on harder than necessary and threw on a sweatjacket. "I'm going for a run."

As I grabbed the door handle, I heard Jack's voice behind me. "Try not to bump into any Takers this time."

"I'd probably prefer them to you," I muttered as I pulled my bedroom door shut and walked to the kitchen. Mom sat with her coffee at the kitchen table. I stared at it, wondering if her desire for it this morning might go back to what I'd said to her in her dream last night. I didn't like the idea of controlling people that way. I'd have to be very careful with my newfound power.

"Good morning, honey." Mom smiled and looked down at my shoes. "Going for a run?"

"Yeah…" I thought for a moment before asking the question on my mind. "How did you sleep last night?"

"Pretty well, I think." She took another sip and then gave me a knowing look. "Don't worry. I haven't had any more middle-of-the-night breakdowns."

I winced at the memory of her sobbing on the beach. She didn't *remember* any breakdowns, anyway. I tried to cover it with a grin. "That makes two of us."

"Good. Oh, I was wondering, I had a few appointments

added to my schedule this morning. Could you run a few errands for me when you're done?" She handed me a paper with a list scribbled on it. "Pretty please?"

"Sure, Mom." Stuffing it in my pocket, I jogged out the front door into the still-cool morning air.

ELEVEN

Between running like my life depended on it for an hour straight, then hopping in my car and doing the errands Mom gave me, it was after noon by the time I got home. Finn's text had said they were on their way over, but I wasn't sure if he'd texted from his house or the airport. Either way, they would probably beat me to my house.

I was caked in dried sweat and starving by the time I turned back onto my street. The only thing that could make me smile at that point was sitting parked at the curb in front of my house—Mia's purple pick-up truck.

I parked in the garage. When I climbed out of my car, I heard something that made me stop and listen. Even from out here, the sound of Addie's laugh made me smile. It had been a long time since I'd heard her laugh like that. It sounded like some time with Mickey might have helped a few things after all.

"I'm not kidding. This is really the cheese."

I stood in the doorway for a few extra seconds...there was no way I'd heard that right.

Pushing the door open silently, I walked the few steps toward the kitchen and peeked around the corner. I saw Finn first. He sat at the counter, his face scrunched up as he stared at the television set. It was tuned to the news. My stomach dropped as I caught the tail end of a piece about a couple more people who had been reported missing. Then it moved on to a story about some guy who'd pled innocent to charges of killing a complete stranger. There was something about the smug smile on the district attorney's face that told me he felt like he'd won his case already.

Now that I knew what Takers could do, I couldn't help but wonder how much of this might be caused by Cooper or others like him. And what they might do next.

Mia sat next to Finn, biting her lip as she twisted back and forth on her barstool. The movement snapped me out of my dark train of thought. "I'm still confused, Jack," she was saying. "You're here because you're helping Parker now? Since when? And when will he be back?"

"It's kind of complicated. I think he'd rather tell you, but he should be back soon." Jack's voice came from around the corner, and I moved one step closer so I could see him.

He was standing with Addie over a box of mac and cheese. He'd cleaned up and was wearing a dark red shirt, his brown hair smoothed back out of his face. He was standing way closer to her than I wanted him to. Darkness flared inside me, and it took everything in me to hold still and not let loose. I took a deep breath and counted: 1–2–3.

Mia froze on her stool, and when I glanced at her, she grinned and hopped to her feet. "Parker!"

She jogged across the space in an instant and threw her arms around me. It was unexpected and jarring. Not that she'd never hugged me or anything; she'd gotten more and more comfortable over the months that I'd been sharing her dreams. But something about it felt different after reading the text sent from her phone—and I didn't know if it was her or me that was causing it.

"Hi, Mia." I started to extract myself from her arms, suddenly aware I hadn't taken a shower yet, but then Finn stood up and I saw his shirt: *The Voices in My Head are Telling Me to Kill You.*

For once, it was just too much. The visuals I'd been avoiding all day pelted me from all directions: Dr. Freeburg's dream, his body, the bloody paperweight I'd swung at his head, the unity I'd felt with Darkness at that moment … then that same wholeness when I'd gone after Jack. I knew now that I'd killed Freeburg. I had no proof—there was none— but I was sure all the same.

My skin felt hot and icy cold and I stood, staring, with Mia hugging me and everyone's eyes on me. Finn's expression was oddly blank. Addie's mouth dropped open in a cute little "o" of surprise that warmed me a bit in spite of all the other emotions fighting for control.

"Wow, what happened to your eye?" Mia asked, but I

didn't want to get into all that until I'd taken a minute to calm down.

"I see you all got acquainted." My voice was soft and flat.

When I saw Jack step forward and place a hand on Addie's shoulder, I felt that familiar fury bubbling inside and knew I had to get away—I had to calm down. Right now, before I ended up hurting someone else.

Grabbing Mia's hands, I pushed them firmly down to her sides. She took a quick step back in surprise.

"Sorry, guys. Just finished my run, need to grab a quick shower." I backed down the hall toward my room. "Be right back."

Instead of my familiar routine of a cold shower to keep me awake, I turned the water as hot as I could stand it and leaned my head against the tile, letting the steaming water run over my shoulders and down my back. Everything in my world felt changed since my friends had left a week ago. I wasn't even sure where to start.

Darkness still growled low and dark in a corner of my mind. Something primal in him had reacted to seeing Jack touch Addie. He had a jealous streak, but now, knowing Addie was a Builder and could help me, his need for her was stronger than ever. I felt it to my bones, and half of me wanted to let him loose. It might feel good to teach Jack a lesson. But I still needed Jack's help.

More than that, I knew Addie. She'd be less than impressed ... in fact, there was a good chance she'd never talk to me again for doing something to Jack. And I would deserve it.

"Shut up." My whisper was impossible to hear over the water pounding down on me. "Your instincts are not going to help here."

Darkness growled louder for a moment, then said, "Fine." And my head was silent for the first time all day.

I was so shocked I sat there, waiting for one minute—two. Then I grabbed the soap and scrubbed my body, getting out every inch of frustration and resentment Darkness had left in his wake. I didn't know how long he'd be gone...but I wasn't going to waste the time.

I hurried out and got dressed in five minutes flat. As I came back into the kitchen and plastered a large, happy smile on my face, my hair was still dripping down the back of my neck.

"Welcome back!" I went to where Mia sat on her barstool first, feeling bad about the way I'd pushed her away before, and gave her a quick squeeze. "Hopefully I smell better this time."

She laughed and I knew all was forgiven. "Thank God."

I walked around her to Finn. His smile was back... although something seemed off behind his eyes. I clapped him on the back in one of our customary man-hugs.

Then, putting on my best fake-mobster accent like we'd done for an entire evening the last time we'd watched *The Godfather*, I said, "Did Mickey take care of yous all like he promised?"

Finn's smile blossomed into a full-on grin. "Well, he didn't make us swim with the fishes like yous was afraid of."

"Oh please, not this again." Addie laughed behind me.

I turned toward the other side of the kitchen island where she was scooping mac and cheese into bowls with Jack hovering directly behind her. I took all my frustration and ignored him, focusing on her. She smiled wider than I'd seen in a long time. At least Disney World seemed to have done the trick for her. In that case, everything I'd gone through this week was completely worth it.

Walking around the counter, I wrapped her in a tight hug and lifted her off the floor. "Don't yous dames give us no lip, ya hear?"

She giggled right into my ear and my heart thudded so loud and hard against my chest I swear she had to be able to feel it. It was an incredible feeling, knowing I still had the ability to make her happy like that. I needed to do it more often.

Making them happy made me happy. I didn't know where I'd lost sight of that, but I felt so much better in that instant than I'd felt in a long time. It made one truth suddenly, stunningly clear. I'd been doing everything wrong. I needed to do everything I was doing in this moment more often. Be with my friends, make them happy, and hug Addie.

Which made another truth clear ... I really needed to tell Finn how I felt about Addie, and soon. I was done waiting, and he would understand. I had to make him understand somehow. For a second I considered using my new Watcher ability to *make* him understand in a dream, but I immediately shoved the thought away in disgust. He was my friend and he deserved to be able to make his own decisions. I didn't want to manipulate him. I just hoped more than anything that he'd take it well.

But all of this wasn't something to worry about at the moment, not with so many witnesses and so many other pressing things to discuss. It needed to be a private conversation. Besides, I'd hate to have Addie feel like she needed to make her brother stop punching me...that would be awkward.

I lowered Addie to the ground, gently taking her hands down from around my neck, and reached for a spoonful of the mac and cheese. When I looked back, her cheeks were a little flushed and the last bits of her smile had dissolved from her face. Like she'd been a little girl floating high in the sky and I'd suddenly popped all her balloons and brought her back to reality. It started a burning pain in my chest to see it.

So I did the only thing I could with all these people around watching us...I pretended I couldn't see what was written so clearly on her face. "We eating lunch? I have a lot to catch you guys up on."

Addie nodded and looked over her shoulder at Jack. He was glaring daggers at me, and Addie looked as surprised as I was by his anger. An instant later it was gone and he said, "I'll grab spoons and bowls."

TWELVE

We all gathered around the table, eating mac and cheese as I filled them in on some of the things that had happened while they were gone. I told them about the run-in with Cooper—none of them knew him, either—and Jack explained that Cooper was a Taker, that he could take over peoples' bodies while they were sleeping, and all the happy history of the people they kill. He also explained about my dad being a Watcher. He was about to leave off the fact that the Takers had captured him, but I really wanted things to be better, to be different. I needed to be as honest with my friends as I could from now on.

I'd learned, last time, that secrets were more likely to hurt the people I cared about than the truth was. All of Dad's secrets coming out now only reinforced this fact. My mom was the only possible exception to my new approach, and I was even beginning to doubt that as well.

"My dad has been captured by the Takers," I blurted out, as Jack looked like he was about to take the conversation another direction.

"What?" Finn stood up from the table and knocked his bowl over … luckily, he was Finn, so it was already empty. "Where? Can we help him?"

"Thanks, man." I set his bowl upright as he sat back down. "But it sounds like it's a little more complicated than that."

Addie and Mia's faces were pale, and I felt Addie's hand squeeze my knee before everyone turned their expectant eyes on Jack. He groaned and leaned back in his chair.

"It is more complicated. Parker's dad left because he was trying to protect him and his mom, and he sent me here to watch over them. If we took Parker into the heart of the Takers, well, we might just be in more danger from his dad than from the Takers." Jack leaned forward like this was all we needed to know and we were crazy if we didn't agree.

Finn nodded, steepled his fingers in front of him, and seemed to have calmed down. But I knew him; this conversation was far from over.

"Right, right … but, uh … *so what?*" He leaned across the table until he was so close that Jack looked uncomfortable. Finn didn't raise his voice, but his tone made it clear that he thought this was the stupidest argument ever heard by mankind. "We're not going to help his dad because he'll be mad? Parents are mad at their kids all the time! It's like … their jobs!"

"We're also not going to get him because Jack won't tell me where they have him," I said softly, sitting back in my chair. I'd promised I'd leave it alone if Jack told me if my dad was in danger. Finn had not made the same promise.

"Going into the Taker stronghold with Parker would be like handing them a giant weapon to use against his dad." Jack was fuming but he kept his voice level. "Why don't we bring his mom along while we're at it?"

He obviously didn't like being cornered like this, but if it was the only way to get full answers, then I didn't mind doing it.

Finn leaned back in his chair so hard it almost fell over, but before he could speak again, Mia whispered, "We can't risk his mom in any way . . . are the Takers after her?" She swallowed around the obvious emotion in her voice. "One parent is better than none—I promise."

Addie reached over and wrapped an arm around her.

I'd felt the unbearable loss of one parent. I couldn't risk anything happening to Mom. "She's right. Whatever we do, we have to keep my mom safe."

"That's why we wait." Jack nodded. Everything about him had become subdued. "We need to figure out what's going on with this Cooper guy. Is he the only Taker here? We need to watch, wait for them to make a move, and keep Parker and his mom safe. Once we have those answers, then we can decide if and how to help Danny."

Everyone at the table seemed to stutter on the name "Danny." As always, Finn was the one to ask about it.

"Danny?" He looked to me instead of Jack for the explanation. He knew my dad's name, and he knew that was who Jack was talking about. He just wanted to know why.

"Yeah ... I'm still getting used to it too." I rubbed my hand through my now almost-dry hair.

Jack shook his head and got to his feet. "Sorry. You'd prefer Daniel? Or Mr. Chipp, perhaps?"

I shrugged. The pain I felt at knowing how much better Jack knew my own dad wasn't going to be eased by him calling him something different.

"Yeah. That would probably be an improvement." Finn seemed ready to fight; Jack had rubbed him the wrong way.

"Finn, it's not worth arguing about." I grabbed his shoulder, but he turned and jerked away. For the first time, I started to wonder whether Finn was angry at Jack or me.

"You okay, man?"

Finn mumbled something, nodded, and took his bowl to the sink. I watched him scrub at his fork like it had offended him greatly. How had I managed to tick him off already?

"Oh, there is one more thing." Jack raised his head and smiled at Addie. It felt like my intestines had turned to ice. "You should know that there are three types of Night Walkers. You know about the Watchers—" He gestured to me and then to himself. "And now you know about the Takers."

Addie shuddered, slid her chair out from the table, and got to her feet, placing her spoon inside her bowl. "And the third?"

Jack reached out and took her bowl with a small smile. "You are the third."

Addie blinked at him, then looked at me, then at Mia. "I think you have me confused with her ... I'm not the one with the cool dreams."

Jack laughed, put the dishes in the sink, and came back. "You are definitely the one. You're what we call a Builder, Addie." He winked at her and leaned in like he was sharing a secret. "And I can help you learn how to build dreams that will let you help Watchers."

Darkness popped up suddenly right beside Addie and Jack. His hands were clenched into useless fists in front of him. The only sounds escaping his mouth at the moment were growls. He was like the embodiment of all the anger and frustration I'd become so good at burying. Watching him was... well, it was bizarre. There was no other way to put it.

In some ways, it helped me to recognize the emotion as not helpful and cool down faster, but Darkness didn't look any calmer as he shouted across them to me.

"How can you just sit here and watch this?" He turned his back, took a breath, and walked toward me. "Together we're stronger than him. Much stronger. We could *make him* leave her alone."

"Shh..." I whispered, and I think Mia was the only one who heard me. She glanced my way, but what Jack was saying was far more interesting, so her gaze only lingered for an instant.

Not that his suggestion sounded like a half-bad idea, but I was done paying attention to Darkness. I was watching the emotions on Addie's face as she processed everything Jack was saying. Even if it wasn't clear to Jack, it was very obvious to me that she didn't need me to jump in and keep him away.

I whispered one word so soft I knew that no one but the person I shared my brain with would be able to hear it. "Wait."

"And how do *you* know I'm a Builder and Mia isn't?" Addie's voice was soft. Her lips curved in a sweet smile.

"Because I've watched your dreams. A lot of them, actually. Mia has been great for Parker, and the self-hypnosis has made it so she can help him a little. That's great, but it's not at all the same as what you can do. Not everyone"—he pointed at me over his shoulder—"can tell a Builder when they see one. But you don't need to worry. I'm sure about this."

"Well, that's a relief. One question, though . . ." Then Addie's tone got harder with every word and she stood up on tiptoe. "Who exactly invited you into my head?"

Jack's eyes grew wide and he took a step back. I could almost hear his brain backpedaling, and Mia hid a giggle behind her hand. "I—uh . . . I didn't think . . . I'm sorry."

"No." Addie lowered back down to flat feet. "You didn't think. I accept your apology, but I don't want you in my dreams again until I invite you. Okay?"

Jack nodded reluctantly, and when he spoke again he was significantly less confident in his approach. "Being a Builder is cool, though. I can teach you to control your dreams in every way. They become a canvas, and you can create anything you want."

Mia flinched beside me at the word "canvas." Everything about this conversation seemed to be upsetting someone. I walked closer, put my hand on her shoulder, and whispered, "You okay?"

She nodded but looked up at me. Her dark blue eyes, which used to be fearful, were now wide and trusting. I hoped I'd earned her trust now as much as I'd earned her fear before.

The way she started twisting her fingers together, though, clearly spoke of nerves. I made her nervous?

"When this conversation is done, I need to talk to you— alone," she said.

Her text…right. I'd almost convinced myself it had come from Addie. I hid my discomfort with a nod and turned back to face Addie and Jack. He was busy explaining everything a Builder could do to help a Watcher heal, improve, and generally have a full life. She was looking less offended and more interested in Jack by the second. Perfect.

"But…how did I become a Builder? What made you and Parker into Watchers? What happened to us?"

I froze and all my attention shifted straight to Jack. Of course Addie would think of the one question I hadn't even thought to ask. My brain must have been even more exhausted than I'd thought.

"It's a long story. The gist of it is that a few years prior to 1900, there was a team of Russian scientists that worked with Marie de Manacéine. She was studying sleep deprivation and its effects on animals. During the first World War, some of the scientists decided to do something useful with what they learned."

"This started in World War I?" My words came out low and hushed. Everyone else in the room was absolutely silent, including Darkness. I tried to ignore his presence, but at the moment it felt like I was standing next to a mirror. He stood directly beside me with all his attention on Jack. Exactly like me. I shuddered.

"Yeah." Jack shook his head. "They figured that if they

could mix up a few chemicals and end up with an army that didn't need to sleep, that would be a pretty huge asset. They tested a drug and it worked, so it was distributed to select units within the armies of all Russian allies. Only after distributing it widely did they realize that it only helped most soldiers stay awake and alert for about a month before they started collapsing. It ended up killing one in ten people that took it, within a year. The majority woke up with no other effects... until a few of their kids, or grandkids, or great-grandkids started having strange sleep issues."

He was silent for a few seconds before Addie sighed and said, "Why do greedy people always screw up everything?"

"How has it been kept a secret this long?" Mia took a step closer. Her expression was worried and she couldn't seem to decide whether to look at Addie, Jack, or me. The result was that her eyes kept darting between all three of us.

"The scientists were still alive when the first Takers popped up. There were Watchers and Builders first, but no one had identified the Builders and no one really believed the Watchers. But when it comes to someone who can take over the body of a scientist and go have a conversation with another scientist, proving their claim... well, that's a lot harder to argue with. So they moved into an old bomb shelter and started the NWS. I guess since they were studying the effects of their own mistakes, they kept it all a secret. They wanted to help. To fix the problem they'd created, but they died before they could find a cure. Others like us took up searching where the scientists left off. Rather than become the government's lab rats, the NWS has run things this way ever since."

"NWS?" Addie's eyes were locked on me even though her question was clearly for Jack. We were joined in more ways than we'd ever expected.

"I had no idea the National Weather Service was involved in big secret projects." Finn peered around me to grin at Mia, and she laughed.

"Night Walker Society." The bitterness in Jack's voice cut off Mia's laughter and forced both my and Addie's eyes back to him. "It was founded to help our kind, but in the last twenty years it's pretty much become the Takers' thug club. It took two full years of their behavior getting worse and worse before the other Night Walkers rebelled. The NWS is the group that has Parker's dad."

I leaned back against the table and tried to digest all this new information. The people who were supposed to be looking for a way to help Night Walkers like me were the same ones who'd captured Dad? They were the reason he'd left us in the first place? Who could we trust if we couldn't trust the group that was formed to save us?

Mia walked right through Darkness and he faded like nothing more than smoke. She rested a hand on my shoulder and I flinched before I heard her voice asking if I was okay. I raised my eyes and met Addie's hazel gaze. She looked worried, upset...and something else that I hadn't seen on her in a long while. Was she jealous? I took a small step to one side and Mia dropped her hand, wringing them both in front of her.

"I'm fine. Thanks, Mia." I straightened my shoulders and looked around at the whole group. "At least now I know who we're up against."

Finn stood off to my right, and I could tell from his angry breathing and his stance that he wasn't happy either. It was nice to know he'd always be there to back me up. But I faltered back a step when I saw that his glare wasn't directed at the idea of the NWS or even at Jack…it was at me.

"Something wrong?"

He scoffed and walked past me out into the backyard.

Darkness had appeared again, next to the back door. He chuckled as he leaned against the wall. "You sure know how to make a mess out of every situation, don't you?"

I stared at the ground and rubbed the back of my neck as I tried to sort out where I'd gone wrong with Finn. "I'm guessing that's a yes…"

Mia looked from me to the back door in confusion.

"You don't know what's going on either?" I asked.

She shook her head. "He's been acting weird since yesterday."

"So maybe it's not just me…that's hopeful. I'll go talk to him." I walked outside but couldn't see Finn anywhere. Then I heard Mia's truck start up. I was so shocked, it took me a minute to process the only possibility that made sense. By the time I'd run around to the front, Finn had peeled out and was driving, alone, down the street.

Addie, Mia, and Jack ran out the front door and stood beside me. We all watched in silence as the back of Mia's truck disappeared around the corner.

"Does he always act like this?" Jack glanced at Addie, but all three of us answered in unison:

"No."

Then I added, "Finn never acts like this."

THIRTEEN

Driving Addie and Mia home was more than a little awkward. Especially because Jack insisted on riding with Addie in the backseat so they could talk more about her training. Mia tried to chat with me a couple of times, but between worrying about what was going on with Finn, thinking about my dad and the NWS, and eavesdropping on Addie and Jack's chat, I wasn't the best at keeping up my part of the conversation. My only consolation was that at least Darkness didn't feel the need to appear on anyone's lap or anything.

By the time we got to the Patricks' house, I was dying for just a couple of minutes with Addie. I parked the car and we all got out. I saw her pull Mia aside for a couple of words that I couldn't quite make out. Mia didn't look all that thrilled, but finally she nodded and walked over.

"Jack, I was wondering if you could come help me find Finn for a minute. I wanted to ask you a few questions about my dreams, and you seem to be the local authority."

Jack looked reluctant to leave Addie's side, but he nodded. He spoke over his shoulder to Addie as he followed Mia toward the house. "Remember, though. Think about it, at least?"

Addie nodded and leaned against my car without any word of explanation.

The moment they were out of sight, I grabbed her hand, pulled her into the shadow of a big oak tree, and wrapped my arms around her. Tangling my fingers in her hair, I inhaled the fresh citrus smell that always reminded me of her.

I murmured by her ear, "Thank you for sending them away. I missed you."

She reached her right hand up and around my neck, pulling me closer...then, slowly, she placed her left hand against my chest and pushed me away with a groan.

"We need to talk."

"Or...we could do other things instead." I leaned down and kissed her forehead, her nose, her cheek. I curled one arm around her back and trailed kisses down toward her lips. I could see in her eyes that she was serious, but I could also see that she didn't really want to talk.

I kissed her lightly at first, tempting, teasing her...pushing to see just how important this conversation was. Addie sighed and gave in quickly, wrapping both arms around my neck and kissing me back the way I'd hoped she would and more. She pulled me in tight, scratching the back of my neck lightly and twisting the calf of one leg playfully around mine.

She was the perfect mix of everything I wanted, everything I needed. She was sweet and sexy, truth and trust, unwavering loyalty, a friend and so much more.

Then Addie pushed me gently back, her breath coming in erratic gasps that matched my pounding heart. "I missed you too ... *now*, we have to talk."

"Okay." I smiled reluctantly and checked to make sure no one had come back out of the house. I cradled one of her hands between both of mine.

She looked a lot more hesitant now than she had before the kiss. I felt suddenly wary.

"Jack asked me on a date."

My skin went cold, and Darkness appeared so close behind her it was like she was in a Parker sandwich. I felt sick and furious and extremely sad, all at the same time. Jack and I weren't friends—we'd never been friends—but still, him making this move on Addie surprised me. I'd make sure not to underestimate or trust him again.

And if I couldn't trust him, then he shouldn't be able to trust me. My free hand clenched by my side.

But Addie was my bigger focus at the moment. While we'd never agreed not to date anyone else, never even talked about it, it hadn't been an issue before. Darkness looked so angry it was terrifying, and as upset as I was, I didn't want to look like he did. I didn't want to scare her. I counted to ten slowly in my head before responding.

"That's what you agreed to think about?"

"That's all you have to say?" Darkness practically screeched, releasing his pent-up frustration.

"Yeah..." She nodded, but her eyes fired sparks when I tried to release her hand. "This is really your call though, Parker. It's been your decision all along, and I've been pretty patient."

I stopped, my teeth making a strange noise as I ground them together, and I held her hand tightly in mine. "Okay, then I say, NO."

"It isn't that simple." Now Addie tugged her fingers free. "You don't get to pretend you don't care about me when everyone is looking and then tell me what to do."

My voice was full of emotion, and I felt weak that she could hurt me so easily. "Then don't tell me it's my decision."

"I meant you need to decide whether you want to be with me, out in the open where everyone knows about it." She folded her arms across her chest and the light from a nearby streetlamp reflected back at me accusingly in the tears I hadn't realized were falling down her cheeks. "I need...I deserve better, Parker. I—I shouldn't have to be someone's secret."

"I know, Addie." I hated that she would ever feel like that. I hated even more that it was my fault. Reaching out, I brushed the tears off her cheek with my thumb. "I've been thinking about this, and I've already decided we should tell everyone. I'll tell Finn..."

She froze, waiting and listening with the slightest glimmer of hope in her eyes. I flinched when my next words appeared to snuff it out completely.

"But I think, with the way he's acting right now..."

"No, Parker." She took a step back and my hand fell to my side. "There will always be a reason not to. This isn't a threat. It's a fact. No more secrets. I hate them—I hate that I've become one of your many. I don't want to be with anyone else, but I can't be happy with the way things are anymore."

"So, what? You're just going to go hook up with Jack? The next guy to come along?" My words and voice were beyond bitter, and I regretted what I'd said the instant it rolled off my tongue.

The slight gasp I heard from her cut deeper than any of her words could. I hated myself for hurting her. Especially when I knew everything she was saying was true.

"I guess that's none of your business anymore." She turned and ran to the front door.

"Addie," I called after her, in a voice even I could barely hear. I crumpled onto the curb and tried to sort out how to fix things with her without making things with Finn—and possibly Mia—irreparable.

The moment I sat down, the exhaustion hit. Everything else had me running on pure adrenaline...now, facing everything that had just happened with Addie, I felt like a deflated balloon after a party. Empty, wasted, and left in the gutter by the side of the street. It had been days now—and rough ones at that—since I'd slept, and all the effects were creeping back up on me.

"That wasn't pretty...but I can't say you didn't deserve it."

"Oh, will you just shut up and go away for once?" I snarled, wishing I could physically punch only the part of my brain he lived in.

"Fine." Finn stepped out from the shadows on the side of the house. I had to blink for a minute to decide whether or not he was real. He'd sounded just like Darkness—or at least my tired brain thought he did. Was he another hallucination? I watched, waiting for him to dissolve or disappear the way Darkness did.

But he didn't. He was real, and from what he'd just said, he'd heard part if not all of my conversation with Addie.

Shaking his head, Finn turned toward the house as I stood staring at him.

"No, wait! I'm sorry. I thought you were someone else."

He didn't respond as he stomped toward his front door, and I barely caught up with him before he climbed the stairs. He brushed past me and pushed through the door just as Mia and Jack were opening it to come out.

They both looked from Finn to me with wide eyes. I just shook my head. I didn't know how I'd managed to lose both of my best friends within a few hours of them coming home, but it was clear that I had.

"I know you wanted to talk to me, Mia." My hands and voice shook with a terrible cocktail of exhaustion and frustration. "Can it wait?"

She bit her lip and then nodded. "Sure."

"Let's go back to your house, Parker." Jack's face was unreadable, but as he walked back inside to grab his jacket, I heard Addie's voice.

"You … you can start teaching me tonight." She sounded upset even from here, and it felt like a punch to my gut. I didn't know how I was supposed to fix all this, but I would. I forced a breath of air out as hard as I could and tried to push away the emotion. Even if it made me sick to think of them going on a date, it was still just one date. They'd have one date, and Addie and I would have years. She was too angry right now. I'd give her a night to cool off, and then I'd figure it out. After a full night of sleep, hopefully my brain would be ready to help me out.

After one last, long look at Mia's dark blue eyes, I plodded back to my car. Jack and I drove home in frigid silence, and I barely made it to bed before everything went dark.

FOURTEEN

Mia's dream started with the touch of soft leaves beneath my hands, the salty-tang of ocean in the air, and the sound of waves crashing far below us. Every sense was as crisp and clear as reality. I wasn't sure how long I'd been in the Hollow, as Jack called it, before entering Mia's dream. Everything had felt so hazy there, and my head was throbbing in a rhythmic pattern. Nothing made sense. My brain couldn't sort anything out through this new agony.

I cupped my palms over my temples in a futile attempt to ease the pain. The only thing I wanted, the only thing I could think about, was getting some sleep. Mia showed up in her white dress in front of the canvas and picked up her paintbrush—and a jar of red paint. I stared, all thought of sleep vanishing as I climbed quickly to my feet. I'd seen the canvas and paintbrush dozens of times... but the jar of red paint was absolutely new.

Mia used to paint all the time. She'd wanted to become an artist. But after watching her parents burn in a house fire along with all her paintings, she hadn't been able to touch a brush to canvas since. In every dream, she stood before a blank canvas in frustration. The addition of red paint felt like a massive step forward.

I stopped a few feet away and watched Mia dip her paintbrush into the red … but when she pulled it out, she froze in place. The paint moved on the brush almost in slow motion, filling up the tip until a single drop of blood-red paint fell onto the skirt of her white dress—then another, and another. The brush seemed to have an endless supply. It spattered her dress and then fell on her bare foot. Mia might be making progress, but she still couldn't make that final leap to painting.

… or maybe she could.

I inched forward, trying to remember everything Jack had taught me. I focused on being part of the dream. It was harder than I expected. Everything here was manufactured through the self-hypnosis methods Mia had learned from Dr. Freeburg. Since Mia had created it, it was much harder for me to blend into than Mom's dreams. I tried again, pushing aside my aching head and focusing all my energy on being part of my surroundings. I pictured myself doing the only thing Mia knew I did in her dreams. Somewhere in her brain, she knew I slept here … so that was worth a try. Relaxing onto the ground next to her feet, I took a deep breath, and suddenly I could feel myself sinking into the dream the same way I had with Mom's. It had worked.

Moving slowly, I reached out my hand and pushed my

fingers through her ankle. Instantly, all the air was shoved out of my lungs like the wind had been sucked right out of me. It was as if that one movement broke open a dam and spilled image after image from Mia's mind into mine. I saw gorgeous paintings stacked against the walls of a room. There was one of her mom and dad looking at each other. Mostly, though, there were stunning landscapes: a beautiful valley with mountains and a stream, a lush green forest … even the lighthouse across from the cliff we were now standing on. Every scene that had filled her dreams was beautifully depicted on the canvases across the room.

And then they started burning.

The flames started with a candle that was left too close to a curtain, and then it spread quickly across every painting and toward the stairs. I saw Mia dash from her room on the lower floor, tripping as she flew out the back door and rolled onto the backyard. A few scrapes marked her cheek and she had a bruise forming on her forehead as she made her way around to the front lawn and waited in tears for the parents, who would never make it out.

I watched her parents start down the stairs, only to find them already blocked by flames. The fire moved so fast it felt unreal, chasing them like a living, breathing monster back up to their room. In an instant they were trapped, so they went to the window, but it was stuck and wouldn't open. The room filled with smoke so fast; they were coughing and pounding on the window … then something happened that I'd never seen in her nightmares before. Mia ran up to the front door, but it was locked and when she grasped the knob it was so hot it burned her hand. She screamed and grabbed it again, then kicked and pounded on the door before running back out to the front and watching her parents through their window. Her mom looked out at Mia, placing one palm flat against the glass. I could see her mouth moving, forming the words that were so important for Mia to see before the flames stole them away forever.

"We love you."

Then her dad wrapped his arms around her mom and pulled her away from the window. There were a couple of muted crashes as he tried to break the window. It cracked with the last hit, but the fire moved so fast, and then there was only silence. Silence followed by the crackle of the flames as they burned away everything Mia had ever loved.

I pulled my hand free of her ankle. The memories stopped, and I rolled face-down into the groundcover and inhaled the strong scent of dirt and life. I let it soak into my skin and my brain and tried to wash away Mia's pain…but you can't forget or leave behind something like that.

Something wet fell onto the palm of my hand, and I looked up at the paint still dripping from Mia's brush. I pulled in a long slow breath and reached for her ankle again.

This time I saw Dr. Freeburg and my breath stopped in my throat. He ushered her into his office and she lay back on the couch as he hypnotized her. As he scooted his ottoman closer, I didn't dare even breathe. I didn't want to interrupt him. I needed to see inside Mia's mind, to know for sure if he'd actually done the things I'd killed him for.

Dr. Freeburg sat perfectly still and closed his own eyes as

they spoke. He moved his hands over her, but unlike in his dream, he never actually touched her. No wonder Mia had never remembered anything he'd done to her. He hadn't done it at all. In his dream, and in his mind, he'd abused Mia—but in reality, he'd stayed an inch away.

That inch gap was what separated his memory from his fantasy. That's why it had felt so real. It almost was real...

And yet, it wasn't. Pulling my hand free, I pushed aside the sudden sickening knowledge that Dr. Freeburg hadn't acted on his impulses, and I had. The understanding that he'd been innocent, at least with Mia, and I'd murdered him made my stomach clench and roll with waves of nausea.

I shouldn't have watched this. It had been a mistake. I didn't want to know, and I could never take back what I'd already done.

Lying perfectly still, I felt the paint drip on the back of my hand. Drip—drip—drip—I didn't care. It could paint me red; the color of blood was fitting. It fit me. I was a monster and no matter how hard I tried, it seemed I couldn't change it.

If anything, it was changing me.

Another drip landed on my hand, but this one felt colder. I looked up and saw that Mia was crying. Mia was my friend— I was right here beside her, and I'd be damned if I couldn't try harder to do something to help her.

I probably was damned ... but I'd try anyway.

Pressing my fingers back into her ankle, I tried to ignore the barrage of thoughts and memories and instead focus on the side of Mia's mind that was keeping them all at bay with the hypnosis. Her thoughts were in heavy conflict. She missed painting with a fierceness that surprised me, but she hated herself because a fireman had told her that all the paint and canvas in the house had allowed the fire to spread quicker than normal.

And it had been Mia's candle accidentally left burning in the living room. The candle that had smelled like the sea and let her really envision the setting for her latest canvas. The candle that her dad had reminded her twice to blow out... and she'd still forgotten.

I felt my stomach clench at everything she'd had to deal with. No wonder she'd stopped painting.

Gathering all my energy, I focused on one thought and mingled it like a balm in the midst of all her own accusations: *It's not my fault.*

The single seed seemed to take hold and spread slowly, smothering the other thoughts one by one until everything stilled. I withdrew my fingers from her ankle and looked up to see Mia leaning in toward the canvas as her hand flicked the paintbrush deftly this way and that.

I'd done it.

With a small smile, I climbed to my feet. Resting my hands on my knees, I drew in a deep slow breath. It might not happen the first time every time, but I *could* help. I needed to help, to make up for all the times when I'd done anything but.

My spine straightened as I stood up the rest of the way and I took a step forward to see the painting. Mia's expression stopped me before I got there, and my stomach dropped. An entire table full of supplies had appeared next to her now and she was painting with broad, violent strokes as tears fell in a torrent down her cheeks.

I walked around, almost afraid of what I'd see. The clouds in her dream cracked with thunder and the wind around us kicked up. On the canvas was a horrifying image of fire and death. Angry flames with maniacal faces licked across skeletons in the midst of heaps of ash and twisted metal.

Reaching out, I gripped Mia's shoulder and pulled her into my arms. She fought against me for a moment, so I whispered, "Shh...it's me, Mia. Everything is okay." And she folded into me. Her brush dripped red against my black shirt, and my shoulder was wet with her tears.

"I wanted to tell you..." Her voice shook, weighed down by emotion, by pain. "About the paint."

"I saw." It was all I could say. I'd learned nothing from watching what Jack did to Mom and me—I'd done the same thing to Mia. I'd pushed too far, and she wasn't ready.

"What do you think it means?"

I pulled back enough to look her in the eyes and focused on everything in the dream around me. Using the second lesson Jack had taught me, about how to repair the damage I'd done, I pictured the easel behind her wiped clean. I pictured all the paints gone but the red one. I used every ounce of my strength to push my thoughts into her own, burying the pain I felt with what she should be feeling: pride at her new step forward.

"I think it means you're getting closer," I told her. "This is amazing, Mia. You're doing really great."

Pushing through her self-hypnosis drained me until it

felt like she was holding me up, but I had to finish. "You are starting to understand that it wasn't your fault…because it wasn't, Mia. Nothing that happened was your fault."

Fresh tears flowed down her cheeks, but she nodded and a new emotion flowed with the pain…relief. She kept nodding, and I saw the easel behind her fade to white and all the paints disappear but the red one. It had worked. I'd finally used my ability to help her instead of hurt her.

She hugged me again and then spoke. "I really missed you."

"I missed you too." I felt guilty and hoped she wouldn't take my words to mean something they didn't, but I wasn't going to hurt her again at that point. And after the extreme effort it took to change her dream, I could barely keep my eyes open in the only place I'd been able to sleep.

"Are you okay if I go to sleep now?" I asked. "I don't want you to remember any of this. Okay? Just a peaceful night of sleep that you don't remember."

Mia smiled and wiped the tears off her cheek. "Yes. You go sleep."

"Thanks, Mia." I released her arm and she immediately turned back to her canvas. She still didn't paint, but she picked up the paint and swished the brush through it as the rumbling in the sky overhead quieted.

I watched her as I lay down on the ground. The last thought I had before falling asleep was that it was the first time her face had ever looked peaceful in a dream.

FIFTEEN

The world around me was all undulating haze and shadows. No pure light or complete dark, just spinning shades of gray. The gloom moved around me...no, I moved through it. My arms and legs tingled with the chill of night. As the haze of my vision cleared, I found myself walking down a street on a shady side of town. I heard music coming from a nearby alley, and I kicked aside an empty beer bottle as my body turned of its own volition and walked toward the music.

This is a very strange dream.

"Wakey wakey, Dr. Jekyll." My voice spoke, but it wasn't me.

Darkness? I don't see him in dreams usually...what's going on here?

"It may take a minute to adjust." He chuckled softly. "That's normal."

Making a conscious effort to control my body and

this dream, I visualized myself stopping. I tried to lock up my legs, but they just keep walking—sauntering, even. I finally stopped in front of the door with the music. A very drunk bouncer nodded at me, without a second glance, as I opened the door and entered a dark pub. There was a long bar down the right side of the room and a dance floor to the left. Walking around the edge of the room, I slid into a booth in the corner. The wall across from me had a cracked mirror and I saw my face smiling back at me. My hair hung in a messy sheet in front of one eye, and my mouth curved into a half smile as I stared at myself.

Oh my God... this is real.

"Of course, I kept my promise." His smile widened into a dark grin. "I said I'd let you *see* what it was like to be me."

"Is this seat taken? Or are you just here to chat with yourself?" A blonde with a ton of makeup and much less clothing—if a blue halter top, unbelievably tiny shorts, and a pair of red heels count as clothing—slid into the booth next to me.

"Oh, I'd much rather talk to you." My voice was low and smooth and I raised my arm to drape it across the seat behind her.

Leave. Now.

He ignored me, so I gathered all my strength and tried to bring my arm back down. After getting a little sleep in Mia's dream before Darkness had woken me up, I was feeling stronger than I had in a few days. I pushed and prodded, but it was like ramming my head into a stone wall. It didn't have a lot of effect, and it really gave me a headache.

Finally, after a few minutes, I felt my arm budge, but all I'd succeeded in doing was dropping my arm forward so that now it was around the girl's shoulders instead—really not what I was going for.

Darkness's expression in the mirror showed a flicker of surprise before he looked like he was about to start laughing.

"That's what I thought." She giggled, but somehow it sounded almost husky. "What's your name?"

Darkness laughed and glanced up at the mirror. "What do you think it is?"

"I don't know ... Joey?"

"Wow. You're good." My head nodded and I felt sick. "You got it right. I'm Joey.

"I'm Jasmine."

"Of course you are." He grinned and moved his face into her hair, smelling it, which made my lungs itch to cough from the chemicals. She placed her hand on my leg and slid it up and down over my knee. Everything about this, everything that was happening—it all felt so wrong.

And I couldn't do anything about it.

The booth shifted a little and I saw a dark form slide into the other seat. As hard as I tried, I couldn't get Darkness to turn his head and look. Who was it? It could be Cooper, or another Taker. It could be Jasmine's boyfriend.

If you're going to get my face pounded, you might as well let me see who is going to do it.

Darkness waited just long enough to prove he was still in absolute control before lifting my face out of Jasmine's cloud of hair. He turned, and my eyes settled on Jack's tired face.

"What do you think you're doing?"

"I'm getting tired of you playing my shadow." Darkness's anger spiked. He was definitely not pleased that Jack had followed him again. "You should leave now, while you still can."

"Ooh, that's hot." Jasmine moved her hand farther up my leg and kissed my ear. I shuddered mentally, but my body didn't. Focusing, I tried to close my eyes. Tried to pretend some girl wasn't touching me. Tried to pretend Darkness wasn't running my fingers across her shoulder and along the edge of the tie on her halter top. I didn't want this . . . I might have screwed things up with Addie, but she was still the only one I wanted.

"Ugh, that's what I was afraid of." Jack sighed and leaned back. Waving a waitress over, he ordered two waters. "Okay, bad guy, you go ahead and have your fun. I can't stop you, but I'm not leaving you."

"Um . . . he's not your ex or something, is he?" Jasmine whispered, her breath smelling like alcohol and mint gum.

"No." Darkness laughed loud. "You want me to prove it?"

She fluttered her eyelashes and put both arms around my neck before nodding. And then I was kissing her. It was wild and hectic and kind of awful. Jasmine had her lips on my neck, ear, shoulder, mouth. And Darkness was more than a willing participant.

I fought and pushed and pulled and nothing happened. I couldn't stop it, so I tried to retreat. I tried to go back to Mia's dream. I struggled to find a dark corner of my mind and hide from this sense of powerlessness. It was horrifying. I felt like

I was betraying everything I cared about. I was powerless in every sense of the word.

What are you trying to prove? I asked.

I didn't expect Darkness to respond, since he was busy using my mouth to give Jasmine a hickey. But he did:

That it's worse than you imagine.

What is?

Being me.

I'm convinced. Now stop.

I'm not quite done...

My hand reached into my pocket and pulled out my phone. Stretching it out as far as I could, I snapped a picture of me and Jasmine making out. Then Darkness came up for air just long enough to punch a few buttons...

No. Please, no. Don't do this!

And send it to Addie.

Jack grabbed the phone from my hand just an instant too late. When he saw what Darkness had done, he winced and shook his head before sticking the phone in his jacket pocket. "That really wasn't cool."

I felt myself growing smaller and smaller in my own mind. I was disappearing with everything he did to hurt me, to hurt those I cared so much about. It was a prison where I had no voice, no words, no ability to fight back.

Jasmine snuggled into my neck and nibbled on my ear. "You want to go somewhere? Away from your, uh—friend?"

"Sure." I felt myself smile wide and then followed Jasmine out of the booth and toward the door. Jack was right behind us and I begged, pleaded, and prayed that he would do something to stop me.

As soon as we were outside, Jack tapped me on the shoulder and I turned to face him.

"Yeah, hate to break all this romance up, but this..." He gestured toward Jasmine and me before finishing. "I can't let this happen."

Darkness smiled. Then, before I could even see it coming, I hauled back and slammed my fist into Jack's face so hard I felt the shockwave up through my shoulder. He fell back against the building, but only for a second before he leapt forward with a punch to my jaw that made my eye sockets feel like they might collapse in on themselves. I fell flat on my back, the wind knocked out of me. The world tilted, swam, and spun. I was certain I'd hit him hard, but he'd hit me *much* harder.

I'd have to thank him for that later.

The last thing I heard before I lost consciousness was Jasmine's red heels clicking on the pavement as she ran down the street.

"Good morning, Parker."

I blinked and coughed at the water that was dropping in my eyes and mouth. "Wha—what is...?"

Jack stopped and watched me sit up in my bed. "Not so fun, is it?"

Rubbing my hands across my face, I brushed all the water off. The knuckles on my right hand were sore and I couldn't make my brain work well enough to tell me why. My head was all fire and pain. It felt like miniature fireworks were going off behind my eyeballs.

"You … uh … are Parker, right?" Jack took a step back and stared hard at me. He'd obviously been up for a while. He was showered and had his black leather jacket on with the symbol for the NWS on it.

"I'm myself." My throat felt like I'd spent the night screaming. I stretched out my legs, intentionally resting my feet on Jack's pillow.

He kicked my legs off and moved his bedding against the wall, out of my reach. "After last night, I wasn't sure."

I rubbed one hand through my hair, and then bits and pieces of what had happened with Darkness came back. I froze. Looking down at my hands, I stretched them and moved them back and forth. They responded to every command. Getting to my feet, I walked to the mirror on the back of my door and was filled with relief when it was only me staring back. Me with a massive bruise from my chin to my ear … but nonetheless, me.

Jack turned and squinted at me. "You don't know—" At my expression, he stopped. "Huh. What exactly do you remember?" With his last words, his expression got more concerned.

"He showed me. Wanted me to know what it was like." I went back to my bed and slumped down onto the edge. I needed to shower—for a long time. The more I remembered, the more I realized it was possible that there wasn't enough hot water in the world.

"What hooking up in a sleazy bar was like?" Jack tilted his head to one side. "He seemed to enjoy it."

"No...what it's like to be trapped inside with no control. Just watching." I fell back on my pillow and stared at my ceiling. "It's horrible."

"I tried to keep him from getting into too much trouble." Jack winced, and I realized he had a bruise on one cheekbone. "He didn't appreciate it."

"Yeah...well, I do. Thank you." Saying those words to Jack felt wrong, but I owed him that much.

He shrugged it off and looked away. I was surprised he'd tried so hard to protect me, and after seeing the bruise, I felt a little guilty. "So you brought me back here after you knocked me out?"

"Yeah...sorry about your jaw." His brow lowered as he studied me. "You sure you're completely in charge again?"

"Yes, completely." I stared at my hands again and shrugged. "I just wish I understood how it worked, how to control him. What he wants from me. I've never understood why he does the things he does."

"Most of the Divided are ruled by the Id...but your situation seems more complicated than that."

It took a full five seconds for me to process everything he'd said and come to the conclusion that my confusion had nothing to do with just waking up. He really hadn't made any sense.

"What?"

"The Id." Jack looked at me in surprise. "Ever heard of Freud?"

"He's an old psychologist or something...right?"

"He's a dead neurologist, but close enough." Jack sighed and sat on the edge of my desk. "He studied the different aspects of the personality. The part that was controlled by instinct and need—that paid no attention to morality—is what he called the Id."

"That sounds about right." I closed my eyes and leaned back against my pillow before a new problem occurred to me. "Hey, I wasn't stuck with a Taker last night. I was in Mia's dream."

Jack straightened the front of his jacket and looked bored. "Yeah, so?"

"So how did he get that much control?"

"I don't know." Jack walked to my door and put his fingers on the handle. "For some reason, last night you were weak and he was strong. You're the one who's Divided. You figure it out."

"Gee, thanks." But even as I said it, I remembered the time Darkness had gotten enough control to go to the tree in Mia's backyard. That hadn't started with eye contact with a Taker either. Although it did seem like the Takers made Darkness stronger.

"There's only so much I can do. I'm not like you, and I don't get it any more than you do." Jack didn't look all that sympathetic, and I started enjoying the memory of Darkness punching him just a little bit more than I should have. Then there was a tentative knock on the front door.

"That's for me. I'll see you later." Jack opened my bedroom door and was halfway down the hall before I followed him.

"Hey," I called, "where do you think you're go—"

As I rounded the corner, he pulled open the front door and my words caught in my throat. Addie was standing on the porch. She looked at me and her eyes hardened so fast I thought I might get whiplash. I fell a step backward. The memory of the photo Darkness sent her last night hit me so hard and fast it sent my brain reeling.

"Addie." My voice was tentative. I wished Jack would give us some privacy. I didn't like the idea of him watching this. "I need to explain..."

She didn't respond, just turned her sweet smile on Jack and placed her hand on his arm. "You ready to go?"

My heart dropped with a thud and my chest hurt so bad I couldn't breathe. "You—you came for him?"

"Yes, but don't worry. I'm sure the girl from last night still has time for you." She looked at me and her eyes flashed, but then she visibly paled. "Y-you still have her lipstick on your mouth."

I rubbed the back of my arm hard across my mouth, but I didn't say anything. I couldn't find words with which to defend myself.

Her eyes filled with tears and her voice dripped pain. "Just stay away from me." Then she turned and jogged down the steps.

Jack started to walk after her, but I grabbed the sleeve of his jacket and jerked him back inside.

"Where are you going with Addie? Why are you doing this?" Knowing that they planned to go on a date at some point was very different from actually seeing them leave together. This was moving too fast, and I hadn't had time to fix things with Addie yet.

I pinned Jack against the wall, but in two moves he was out and had my wrist bent behind my back. It didn't hurt unless I struggled ... but that didn't stop me.

"You obviously need to get your life together, and I'm sorry if you can't handle it, but I'm not going to stand aside unless she asks me to. She deserves better." Jack's voice was soft and firm, but I could see something in his eyes that I recognized—guilt.

I stopped fighting and stared him down. "Well, how very convenient that is for you."

He flinched and released my arm. "What?"

"After we met, you never came back to help me like you said you would. And now you're saying I'm not good enough because my life is too complicated?" My voice was gruff and low. "You don't even know Addie. You're just using her because of what she is."

"No—I'm not." Jack stepped toward me and even though I was taller, I had to fight not to back away from the anger in his eyes.

"You said Watchers spend their whole lives looking for a Builder. And you got tired of sharing the one you have. Well, here's another one. And because you grabbed that phone last night a second too late, Addie is furious with me. How do I know you didn't *want* me to send that picture?"

"This is what I get for trying to help you? I didn't make you kiss that girl." Jack shook his head, his laughter bitter and hard. "Even with all this, you still don't get it. Addie isn't just a

Builder. She's *everything*. I've been watching her almost as long as I've been watching you. You're an idiot, Parker. She wanted you and all you did was mess it up over and over again."

His words hit me harder than his fist could have, the truth of every word sinking in and branding me to the bone.

"You'll have to forgive me if I finally got tired of standing in the background and watching you walk all over the most amazing girl—Builder or otherwise—that I've ever met." Then he walked out and slammed the door behind him.

SIXTEEN

I'd never felt so wrong. I stumbled to the bathroom and splashed some cold water on my face. My skin felt prickly and hot. It fit me perfectly. I hurt everyone who got close enough to touch me. Looking up in the mirror, I saw Darkness in my own expression. A small smirk and then it was gone. I leaned closer, studying my face. Addie was right; I had smudges of red lipstick on the skin just above my mouth.

I couldn't have hurt her worse if I'd tried.

My heart ached so bad it felt like someone had ripped it out and placed a black hole in its place. It sucked at pieces of me, trying to make everything else I had left disappear along with it.

I took a shower, then another, and another. I washed my face until my skin was raw, scrubbing until long after all traces of the lipstick was gone. Wandering down the hall, I went into my room, flopped down on my bed, and pulled out my phone. There were several pictures from last night, but the one Darkness sent to Addie featured Jasmine on my lap. Jasmine wasn't even very pretty. Not that it mattered; nothing was worth what this photo had cost me.

Yes, Addie had already agreed to this date with Jack, but I knew her. She didn't move fast, and normally it would have taken a while for her to agree to an actual date and time. The picture had hurt her, and she was hurting me back. Addie and I had fought, but if I'd had time, I could have fixed it.

Now I didn't think she would even give me the chance.

Now I knew she probably shouldn't.

I deleted the pictures, tossed my phone onto my desk, and pulled my pillow on top of my head. My dad was being held prisoner. I couldn't help him. My best friend was mad at me. Addie hated me. And I agreed with her.

This week was already tied for Worst Week Ever with the one when Jeff had tried to set me on fire, and it was only Monday. Super.

There was a light knock on my open door. I grunted but didn't remove the pillow.

"Can I come in?" Mom's voice sounded concerned.

"Yeah." My voice was muffled, but I felt the bed shift when she sat on the edge of it a minute later.

"Did I see Jack leave this morning with Addie?"

I tried to force the emotion out of my voice when I answered. "Yep."

Her hand landed on my knee and squeezed. "You want to talk about it?"

"Not really." I pulled the pillow off my head and sat up.

"But all I seem to do is mess things up lately. Maybe if I let someone else tell me what to do, that might change."

Mom was dressed for work, but she sat against the end of my bed and acted like she had all the time in the world. "Let's give it a try."

"Addie is ... well ... " This was more awkward than I'd expected.

"You like her and she likes you," Mom stated without any doubt.

"Yeah ... " I tilted my head. "How long have you ... "

"A long time." She smiled. "Probably longer than you. Moms notice these things. It's part of the job."

"Guess so ... well, I did some things, not intentionally, that really hurt her." I ran my right hand through my hair. "Now she's hurt and angry, and I don't think I can fix it. I'm not even sure if I should."

"Why not?" Now she looked surprised.

"Maybe she's better off?" I shrugged and looked down at Jack's pillow. At least he could control his own actions. At least he could be trusted.

Mom didn't respond until I looked up at her. She had a sad smile on her face. "Your dad hurt me a lot when he left. I know he hurt you, too."

This conversation had taken an unexpected turn. I nodded, trying not to let the secrets I held about Dad show on my face.

"Still, I wouldn't trade a minute I had with him to take all the pain away." She reached out and squeezed my hand. "I've seen the way Addie looks at you, Parker. She doesn't look at Jack like that. Give her a reason to forgive you, say you're sorry, and don't make the same mistake again."

The only thing I could think was, what if I can't make that promise? But I said, "Thanks, Mom."

She smiled and stood up. "I'm going to work. Don't waste your day. Go fix things with your friends...fix things with Addie."

I gave her a crooked grin. "Why are you trying to help me make up with her? Aren't you supposed to want me to stay single forever?"

Mom ruffled my hair and this time I didn't pull away. "I'm supposed to want my son to be happy. You're happy around Addie. It's simple."

She was right. Addie made me happy. And Jack was right, too. Addie was amazing *and* she deserved better. As Mom walked out and shut the door, I knew there was only one thing left to do.

I would *be* better.

————

Time felt like it slowed down as I got ready and drove to Finn's house. I'd let Addie and Jack go on their date. I wouldn't get in their way. Instead, I'd tell Finn how I felt about his sister and see if I could do anything to fix whatever had pissed him off.

Then...I'd talk to Mia and hope that I was wrong about what she wanted to tell me.

Darkness appeared in the passenger seat and it took all

my strength not to try to smash his nonexistent face through the windshield. He didn't say anything, but he looked pretty pleased with himself.

"Why?" It was the only word I trusted myself to speak.

"You know why I let you watch. As for the rest ... I'm helping you. You said I always ruin things and so this time I decided to help." He smiled, and there was a touch of acid behind it. "You're welcome."

"How on earth did this help?" Every word scratched my throat with raw anger.

"You were stuck in between. Even after the fight, Addie might have forgiven you and ditched Jack, and things would have gone back to the way they were. You were hoping that." He stared at me hard and then gave a little nod. "Now she won't. No more sitting on the fence. You're all in or you're out in the cold. It's better this way."

"How is this better and why do you even care?"

"You're stronger with your friends, but you're weaker when your secrets keep you trapped in the middle." His mouth pressed into a firm line. "The less Divided we are when going after the NWS, the better. I'm *really* not sure about you, but I like surviving."

I pulled up to the curb in front of Finn's house, getting more confused by the minute. "First—in case you didn't notice, we don't even know where the NWS is, let alone how to go after them. Second—if this is how you do it, please stop trying to help me!"

Turning off the car, I jumped out before he could try to argue any further, but when I stepped out he was right in front of me. Fury drove me forward and I swung at him, knowing it would do no good. I fell back against the car and he crossed his arms over his chest.

"Well, that was stupid."

I leaned my head back against the car. "All I want in the world is for you to shut up and leave me alone. Just stop all this."

"It's good to want things..." He gave me a lazy grin, positively reveling in my frustration. "But as I was saying, we don't have to know where the NWS is. We know who the Taker is. All we have to do is ask, and I'm sure he'll take us to whoever has Dad. We just need to know how to get back out."

I blinked at the absolute conviction in my own eyes. "You are crazy."

"If Jack won't tell us, it's the only way."

"Why *should* we go after Dad?" My mind filled with acrid resentment. I knew Jack said he was trying to protect me and Mom, but Dad could have let us know he was okay if he'd wanted to. He never even cared enough to drop a post card in the mail.

"Your bitterness rules you."

I stared at Darkness in utter confusion. "Says the king of revenge body snatching! You make absolutely no sense!"

He shook his head and opened his mouth to speak again when I heard Finn's voice behind me.

"Who are you talking to?" Finn sounded worried, but when I turned to face him, he took a step back. What I read on his face was more than worry; it was fear.

"It's kind of a long story." I wanted to kick myself for

not being more careful. Addie was the only one I'd ever told about Darkness. I'd kept Finn out of it. When would I learn that keeping my friends in the dark never paid off?

I would learn it now—right now. "But I'll tell you everything," I added. "If you'll let me."

SEVENTEEN

We sat on a low garden wall behind Finn's house, across from the basketball hoop. He'd agreed to listen, but he wouldn't look at me and the muscle in his jaw kept twitching. His shirt of the day read, *You'll Regret Reading This Shirt When the Sketch Artist Asks You to Describe My Face.*

I really wasn't sure where to begin, but I figured the best option would be to start with the secret I'd been hiding the longest. That way it would be harder to chicken out.

"I like Addie." I forced the words out as quick and straightforward as I could. "I don't know how much of our conversation you heard yesterday, but I'm guessing at least that much."

Finn didn't look up, but he picked the basketball up from between his feet.

"We've ... liked each other for a while, but I didn't tell you because I didn't want to make you angry after all your bro-code talk."

Finn laughed, cold as ice, and shook his head. "You should've just told me when it started."

"I know. I'm sorry."

"I'm not the one you should be saying you're sorry to." His fingers tightened on the ball until I thought it might pop.

"I'll be doing that next." I couldn't get a feel for how this conversation was going. Finn almost seemed to be getting angrier. "You should know that I'd never intentionally hurt Addie."

"Well, intentionally or not, you sure have been hurting a lot of people lately." Finn stood up and threw the ball up so hard the backboard vibrated loudly for what felt like minutes.

"I get why Addie is mad at me, and I really deserve it." Standing up, I stretched, then walked around Finn and looked him in the eye. "But why are you? You've seemed mad since you got back."

"Because I'm tired of watching you hurt people I care about. What were you thinking, Parker? That you could just toy with them both and it would be fine?" Finn's fist kept clenching and unclenching at his side. If he didn't have super-human levels of restraint, I was pretty sure he would have punched me already.

"Wait, toy with who?"

Finn scoffed. "Oh that's right, you haven't confessed to that part of it yet. Are you going to or do you just want to keep the secrets that are convenient for you?"

I shook my head. "I don't know what you're talking about."

"The fact that you've been messing around with Mia and Addie at the same time. It was bad enough knowing you were making out with my sister every time I turned my back, but then I found out you had something going with Mia, too. It's just too much, man."

"Whoa, what? I don't understand..." My mind whirled trying to keep up with everything he'd said. I took a step forward, but when I put my hand on his shoulder, Finn jerked back and shoved my arm away. I looked him straight in the eye and spoke slowly, emphasizing every word. "Listen to me—I have *never* had anything going on with Mia."

Finn looked at me, his conviction wavering for a second, then said, "And if I'd asked you a week ago, would you have said the same thing about Addie?"

I hesitated. He had me on that one, and I wasn't going to lie about it. I couldn't believe he'd known all along. "Probably... but I'm telling the truth about Mia. Where did you even get the idea there was something going on between us?"

Finn walked back to the wall and sat down, looking confused. "When we were on vacation, she asked me to go get her phone and a text from you came in. When I pulled it up, I saw the text about her missing you and wanting to talk to you and everything. Did I read it wrong?"

Slumping down beside him, I pushed one hand through my hair, tugging on the strands. "I don't know... to be honest, that message freaked me out a little, too."

He turned to face me and I could see defeat written on his face. "So there hasn't been anything going on, but she wants there to be?"

"I don't know, Finn, and honestly it doesn't matter. I

want to be with Addie and as much as you deny it, I know you like Mia."

His cheeks flushed red all the way up to his hairline, but he didn't argue.

"I might bend your bro-code with the sister rule, but I wouldn't stomp all over it like that." I grinned, got up, and jogged over to the basketball. When I came back, Finn was on his feet and had a small smile on his face. He looked like the normal Finn for the first time since he'd gotten back from Disney World.

"No more vacations." I tossed him the ball and he gave me a confused look. "They change you, man."

He laughed, then jogged to the hoop and made a layup. When I ran up next to him, he passed me the ball and looked hesitant for a second.

"When you do find out what's going on with Mia..." His words came out fast and uncomfortable. Finn had always talked big about the cheerleaders and girls he'd gone out with, but I could tell pretty early on that Mia was different.

"I'll tell you as soon as I know." I dribbled the ball, and then looked up. "How long have you known about Addie and me?"

"Since the day of the fire at the school." Finn frowned. "You should've heard her voice when she called and asked me to go after you. It was obvious. After that, well... you guys just aren't as sneaky as you think you are."

My mouth dropped open. "Why didn't you ever tell us that you knew?"

He shrugged and looked a little uncomfortable. "It was

nice to keep it a secret. I was afraid that if you knew that I knew, then everything would change. With the fire and you being a Watcher—I just felt like enough had changed already. I decided to wait until you told me. I just didn't think it would take this long."

I nodded. "I'm sorry. I've screwed a lot of things up."

"It's okay." He looked serious, but I could see him holding back a smile. "It's kind of what you do."

"Sad but true." I put up a shot and made it.

"Do me a favor, though?" Finn caught the ball, dribbled it out to the three-point line, and made the shot.

"Yeah?"

"Whether I'm okay with it or not, don't make out with my sister in front of me. Just the few seconds I saw yesterday gave me nightmares."

"Yeah, that isn't something you need to worry about."

"Oh, but it is." He shuddered and missed his first shot all day.

"I doubt it. She said yes to a date with Jack because I was stupid. And then their date happened today because I was even more stupid. She's angry at me, Finn, and she has several very good reasons to be." I groaned. Just thinking about what Addie and Jack could be doing right now made me feel ill. How could I have screwed up this bad?

"Jack's a hoser." Finn stopped bouncing the ball and palmed it in his right hand. "Why is he going after her?"

"He basically thinks she's the thing he's been looking for since he became a Watcher. Oh, and that I don't deserve her," I muttered, kicking a small rock into the garden. "It doesn't help that I agree with him."

"Don't be an idiot."

"Too late." I sat back down on the wall. "Remember how you asked who I was talking to, over by the car? Well, I've done a lot worse things than talk to myself. You sure you want to hear all of it?"

"One question." Finn grabbed the basketball, sat next to me, and spun it on one finger. "Am I going to need popcorn for this?"

———

It took about a half an hour and a whole lot of discussion to explain everything to Finn. I told him about Darkness and how he sometimes took control, and what Jack had said about being Divided. I talked about how making eye contact with Cooper had somehow landed me in jail, the picture Darkness sent Addie, the painting episode from Mia's dream last night, even Dr. Freeburg. I told him everything I'd been wanting to, plus a whole lot of things I wished I never had to tell anyone.

Finn asked some questions at the end: about split personalities, multiple personalities, and why I was pretty sure this wasn't some kind of demonic possession. Finally he shook his head and stopped asking questions. He didn't look horrified, disgusted, or—what I'd feared most—afraid of me.

He sat for a little while in silence, then tugged on his ear before saying, "Well, you sure know how to keep things interesting."

"I guess so."

"So you have an alternate personality type thing that likes to cause massive amounts of trouble, you may have killed some old geezer in his dreams..."

"Probably—"

"*Maybe*—I'm with Addie on this one. You don't know for certain and believe me, the rest is bad enough as it is." Finn stared at me hard, his face unreadable. "You've been thrown in jail," he continued, "made out with random girls you don't know, are a proven stalker, have a history of screwing everything up whenever you try to help—and you want to date my little sister."

I couldn't meet his stare any longer. Every detail was absolutely true.

He shrugged and stood up, stretching his back. "I guess she could do worse."

A startled laugh burst from my chest and I studied his face. Finn gave me a sideways grin, then picked up the ball and headed for the house.

"How could she possibly do worse?" I followed, a little stunned, in his wake.

"I don't know. You could be a terrorist, or..." He turned and gave me a horrified expression. "Someone who can't appreciate old kung-fu movies."

I laughed. "I'm surprised I met your high expectations."

"Don't get me wrong. I'm worried about what's going on with you, and if you hurt her I will kill you in both my dreams and reality." He held open the back door, his face serious as he waited for me to catch up. "But I've known you my whole life. You're a good guy. I know that... and so does Addie."

"Thanks, man." I ducked past him out of the bright sunlight and into the dark kitchen—and ran straight into Mia. I had to grab her arms to keep her upright.

"Sorry, Mia!"

Finn came in behind me and I quickly jerked my hands back. Mia nearly lost her balance with the sudden movement. Finn gave me a small smile, and Mia glanced between us in confusion before turning to me.

"I've been looking for you. Do you have a second to talk to me now?"

I sat down at the kitchen table. "Sure. Go ahead."

Finn grabbed us each a bottled water from the fridge and tossed one over Mia's shoulder, straight into my hand.

She flinched. "Uh, can we go outside where there are less..." She glanced toward Finn. "Flying objects?"

I looked at Finn. His face fell, but he nodded slightly and spoke up. "It's fine. I was going to go watch some TV anyway."

He walked past us with a wave and down the hall. I heard the TV turn on, but I wondered if he was actually watching it.

Pivoting in my seat, I kicked the chair across from me out and Mia slid into it. Her long brown hair was pulled back from her face and it made her eyes look even bigger than normal. She was really pretty, but even so, I just didn't feel that way about her. She was more like a sister to me, one that I alternated between tormenting and wanting to protect—*a lot* like a sister, actually. At least, what I'd think it would be like to have one. Now, I just hoped I didn't have to hurt her more than I already had.

"What did you want to talk about?"

She smiled. "Did you get my text while I was in Florida?"

I hesitated. "Yes."

"You know which one?"

"I think so..."

"And you were in my dream last night?" She looked at me intently.

"Yes."

"Why didn't you talk to me?"

"I w—was really tired." What was I supposed to say? I did talk to you, but it went so horribly wrong I was afraid I'd damaged you for life so I made you forget it all? Yeah... better not.

"Oh." She looked disappointed. She'd wanted me to talk to her about this in her dream? Why?

"Listen, Mia, you're amazing." I really had no idea how to let someone down gently. I usually just avoided them until they got tired of trying. That wasn't exactly an option with Mia. The irony of the fact that she'd spent the first couple of months we knew each other trying like hell to avoid me was not lost on me. "I am so happy that we've gotten to be *friends*."

"Uh...yeah, me too." She looked uncertain, confused. "But did you notice anything different?"

"Why would we want anything different than friends?" I could tell this was going downhill from the deep frown that spread across Mia's face.

"Parker...why are you acting so weird?"

"I'm not." My words came out a little too quickly. "I just

really think you're great…that what we have, as friends, is great."

Mia's eyebrows shot up sky high. "Are you…do you think that…I like you?"

"Uh…" I abruptly suspected that the answer to this question was a big, resounding "no."

Then she started laughing…really hard. And one more balloon of tension released in my chest.

"You dork." Mia shook her head, wiping a tear away from her eye. "Is that why you've been avoiding me?"

"I, uh…" My cheeks felt like they were on fire; there was no denying it. "I'm apparently not capable of coherent speech anymore."

"Aww, and you were trying to let me down easy? How cute." She smiled broadly at me.

I grumbled. "All right, all right, Parker is an idiot. We get it. So what is all this about, if not that?"

"It's about my dreams. You see them clearer than I do. I wanted your help and advice. Did you notice the difference in my dream? The red paint?" She leaned forward and lowered her voice like she was telling me some kind of secret. "You saw it, right?"

I swallowed and nodded, forcing a smile as I remembered vividly all the images of her parents in the fire. "I saw it."

"What do you think it means?" She shook loose one long strand of brown hair and wrapped it around her pinkie finger. "Do you think it's a good thing?"

This time my smile was not forced. "I think it's a really

good thing. I don't think you should rush it, but I think when you feel ready to paint, you should."

She looked at me but her mind was somewhere else, somewhere distant. "I really loved it once."

The back door opened and Mr. Patrick came in with a bag of groceries in each arm.

"Hi Mia! Hi Parker!" He grinned and tried to wrap his fingers around the door handle without dropping the bags. We both stood immediately. I took both bags and put them on the counter, and Mia closed the door. Mr. Patrick laughed. "Who needs to pay servants when you can just feed teenagers?"

Finn popped his head around the doorframe. "Did I hear you say 'feed teenagers'?"

"Exactly."

While Mr. Patrick went to the living room to make a phone call, Finn and Mia unpacked the groceries together. When she wasn't looking, Finn raised one eyebrow in my direction. I shook my head and mouthed the words, "all yours" to him. He grinned widely and stole one of the boxes from her hands to slide onto the top shelf. She laughed and swatted his hands away when he tried to steal her other box. Mia definitely treated Finn differently than she did me. It was subtle, and I wasn't sure if she even realized it, but it was definitely there. I'd seen Addie look at me that way before.

"I think I'm going to vomit." Darkness appeared right next to me, staring at Finn and Mia.

"I think I'm going to leave." I stood up and moved toward the back door. Finn and Mia both looked at me.

"You aren't staying for dinner?"

"No. I'm going to go home and work out a few things. Please...do the protective big brother bit when Addie gets home?" I looked at Finn, and Mia's eyes widened.

"Sure." Finn nodded. "And if Jack shows up with her, I'll kick him out."

Mia looked confused, but I left it to Finn to tell her whatever he wanted to. I trusted him to decide how much Mia needed to know.

EIGHTEEN

I called Finn first thing the next morning. "You up for some more detective work? Your suspect lists were pretty spectacular last fall."

"Um ... do you even need to ask?"

We agreed to meet after school, and before we even got off the phone, Mia had asked to join in. They were waiting at my car by the time I got out to the parking lot. I didn't know where Addie was. I figured it probably had something to do with Jack, and I really didn't want to know.

"So what's up, Sherlock?" Finn hopped in the backseat after opening the front passenger door for Mia. "By the way, do not take this to mean that you *must* call me Watson ... I'll also take Professor Plum, Colonel Mustard, Scooby Doo, or Batman. You'll have to be Robin. He's kind of a tool."

"Then who am I?" Mia grinned.

"Miss Scarlet? Daphne, maybe?"

"Okay, Watson … are you interested in what the plan is? Or should we spend the night on the Internet searching for cool nicknames?" Resting my elbow on the back of my seat, I turned back to face him and wasn't at all surprised to see him muttering to himself as though seriously weighing the merits of these two options.

When Finn saw me watching him, he nodded firmly. "Let's investigate. What are we investigating?"

I clicked my seat belt into place. "With people disappearing and other people doing bizarre things while they think they're asleep, I've wondered whether it's related to Takers. But I didn't know what to do to find out more. Then I got an idea about how to get some information."

"How?" Mia faced forward in her seat and pulled her seat belt on.

"We're going to the police station."

"Why?" they both asked in unison.

"I'm thinking maybe we can pick up clues about whether the police have discovered anything new. Jack wants me to wait on investigating the Takers until they make a move, show their hand, but so far, nothing's happening and I've got nothing. But if the Takers are involved with the weird incidents, then maybe we can learn something about their plan for my dad. Besides, Jack and I aren't exactly friendly at the moment. He isn't going to tell me anything more about the Takers." I started the car and turned the wheel toward the parking lot exit. "And I'm not done asking questions."

———

The Oakville police station seemed surprisingly busy for our relatively small town. There were officers walking people in cuffs this way and that, while others filled out paperwork or asked people questions at desks. I saw a holding cell at the back that contained even more people than had been in mine. Some of them looked like they'd been sleeping on the street, while a couple of others were in expensive-looking business suits. That seemed odd...

I rubbed the back of my neck with one hand. Apparently I was getting far too familiar with police stations.

Darkness appeared, sitting in the middle of the floor in front of me. "Don't look at me. You came here of your own free will this time."

"I'm not sure I have such a thing anymore." I breathed the words, but not soft enough for my friends not to hear.

"What did you say?" Mia leaned closer, like the reason she hadn't heard me was the noise level.

"Nothing," I answered, and Finn squinted at me like he might be able to figure out how to fix me if he looked close enough. I wished he could, but I was still relieved when he looked away. Everything with Darkness was getting so real lately that it was hard to remember when to speak out loud and when to keep my answers in my head. Of course, ignoring him was the best option... but he was making that increasingly difficult to do.

"You sure this is where you want to start?" Mia asked me as she shuffled two steps to one side, putting herself in the perfect position to block Finn's gaze. Which was now focused on what was most likely a prostitute sitting next to a cop in a chair against the far wall. She was so subtle, I almost wondered if I was imagining it.

"Yes. Just not sure exactly why … " An officer walked in with a chubby older man wearing what could only be described as clown pants, suspenders, and no shirt or shoes. He walked the man to a bench.

"Sit here while I get the paperwork. Don't move or I'll cuff you to the chair." The officer turned toward a nearby counter with a clerk behind it and said, "Got another one."

"Let's start there." I pointed to clown-man and walked right through Darkness on my way over. When the man saw us coming, he moved his hands like he was trying to cover up his shirtless chest.

"Oh great," Finn muttered behind me. "I hate clowns."

"I don't think that guy is a clown … " Mia whispered back.

"What happened to you?" I took a seat one spot away from him and picked up a magazine, pretending to look through it.

"Me?" He had red lipstick smeared from his chin to one earlobe.

I looked over at him and nodded, then took off my hoodie and handed it to him.

The man-clown nearly broke down as he pulled it over his head and tried to make his shaking fingers zip it all the way up. "I have no idea. I went to bed and woke up like this! In a … " He looked around him like he was afraid someone might hear. "A strip club … on the stage. I don't even—I don't know—Margie is going to kill me."

Finn leaned around me. "I take it clown stripping isn't your usual Tuesday evening activity?"

The man shuddered and vehemently shook his head. "I'm a pediatrician. I could lose my patients, my practice, if people saw me like this."

"Come on, buddy." The officer came back. "Enough chit-chat. Let's go call your lawyer."

The man got to his feet, then pointed to my hoodie and started to unzip it.

"Keep it."

"Thank you." He pulled the hood up over his head and looked like he was trying to hide from his entire life.

"That was my favorite jacket..." Darkness's voice spoke from directly behind my ear. It took all my restraint not to whirl around to face him. *Ignore him... just ignore him.*

"Well, that was interesting." Mia watched clown-man until he went into an office on the opposite side of the station.

"Drunk?" Finn asked, his fingers tugging on his ear.

"Maybe... he smelled like booze." I rubbed my knuckles against each other and then shook my head. "But he didn't seem out of it. He seemed genuinely panicked... scared."

Scanning the room, I spotted something I'd been hoping to find here. A sign with all the Missing Persons fliers. There was someone standing in front of it, so I'd almost missed it. "Over here."

Finn and Mia followed me over, but I stood back a few feet so as not to crowd the guy already there. I didn't realize he wasn't real until Mia walked right through him.

Darkness.

I went cold inside and out. How much further could he take this? As soon as I thought the question, I wanted to take it back. The last thing I needed was for him to take it as some sort of challenge.

"You have to accept it. Ignoring me won't work." He pivoted in place. Mia still stood merged with his entire left side. "Otherwise—I haven't even skimmed the surface of the kind of things I could make you see."

I swallowed hard and nodded. And sent him a thought loud and clear: *You win. Stop messing with my head like this and I won't ignore you anymore.*

"That's all I want...for now." Then he disappeared. Darkness really had a flair for the dramatic.

Shaking off his ominous departure, I stepped up next to Finn and Mia and examined the board. There were at least as many fliers here as there'd been at the Newton City Jail.

"What are we looking for?" Finn whispered next to me, then looked around like someone trying to steal a car.

"I don't know..." My eyes scanned the faces, but I really had no clue what I thought I could learn from this. "A pattern, maybe?"

"Can I help you kids with something?" A female officer walked up behind us with a wary smile. Her badge said *Officer Sweeney*.

"Is this a normal amount of missing people?"

She gave me an odd look but answered my question. "I would hope zero would be a normal amount...but we've definitely had a bit of an uptick over the last couple of months. Are you doing an article for the school paper or something?"

"Yes," Mia answered at the same time Finn said "No."

I put my hands on their shoulders. "She is. He isn't."

Officer Sweeney slowly nodded, then turned to Mia. "Any other questions?"

"You said it's increased ... is there anything else weird about it?"

"Well, many of the missing aren't considered individuals with high-risk lifestyles ... which is odd, as most disappearances fall under that category." She rubbed the ends of her fingers together and studied the fliers.

"Did a lot of them go missing at night?" I asked.

"Some ... why?" Sweeney focused on me for the first time, her eyes narrowing.

"Just wondering."

"Oh ... kay." The officer raised one eyebrow, then turned back to Mia. "I'll be over there if you think of anything else. Good luck with your report."

"Thanks."

We stood beside the board for a few more minutes before Finn groaned and said, "I've got nothing. "You guys?"

"Excuse me, please." A male officer spoke from directly behind Finn, and he jumped to one side.

This officer—his nametag read *Jensen*—walked up to the board, opened the plastic case, and put up a new flier. With one forearm, he lifted up the bottom row of papers to reveal a state map that hadn't been visible before. Then he lifted a red pin from a small tray below the board. With a frown, he checked something on the new flier and pushed a pin into an empty spot on the map. Another missing person.

There were *so many* red pins...I tried to count them, but I only got to twelve and was nowhere near done when Jensen dropped the fliers and the map was hidden away from sight again. As he closed and locked the case, my gaze landed on the new flier. Audrey Martin—blond hair, brown eyes, last seen coming home from school today by the school crossing guard. She was seven years old. The picture of her showed a missing front tooth. She was holding out a flower.

Finn, Mia, and I stared at it in silence as the officer pulled his key out and walked away. Then I heard soft sobbing coming from nearby. I searched the room and found a couple seated at a desk opposite Officer Jensen. The woman had short blond hair and her eyes were red and swollen, her shoulders trembling. The man beside her rubbed his hand across her back over and over until I wondered if he might take off skin. She seemed numb to it. They were wearing nice clothes, were obviously wealthy...and they looked absolutely powerless.

The man stared hard at the officer. "What do you mean, 'all you can do for now'?"

"Sir, we've sent Audrey's picture everywhere. I told you we have officers combing the area. We've sent out alerts statewide. We're investigating where she was last seen, asking around the neighborhood. If you'd like to call family, it might be good to have a support system right now."

"A support system? We don't need support. We need you to stop asking us questions and figure out who has her. Someone took her. We need to find her!" He slammed his fist down on the desk.

"Sir, I know this is difficult, but you need to try to stay calm and be patient. We're trying to help you. Let us do that."

The woman leaned her head against her husband's chest and clutched her fingers in his shirt. He wrapped his arms around her and kissed the top of her head as he murmured something to her.

Jensen cleared his throat and stood up. "I'll give you a minute."

I was next to the desk without even thinking. "I—I just saw your daughter's picture. I'm so sorry."

My heart broke for them. This scene was bringing back memories of when we'd reported Dad missing: Mom breaking down every time she thought I wasn't watching, everyone acting like he was probably dead. They didn't know…they couldn't know. And it turned out, they'd been wrong.

The man nodded but didn't speak.

I felt like there was more I should say…but I couldn't figure out what it was, so I just stood there.

"Come on, Parker." Mia put her hand on my elbow and started to pull me away.

"M-my dad disappeared a few years ago."

The woman pulled back from her husband's chest and now they both were looking up at me. Waiting to hear whether my story had ended the way they'd hoped theirs would.

"Did they find him?" Her words were hushed, raw with hope and misery.

Darkness appeared behind them and smirked. "Now what, genius?"

"Yeah…" My voice cracked on the lie. "Yeah, he's fine. I'm sure your daughter will be, too."

They hugged each other again, but this time there seemed to be a little more hope and a little less despair. The man said, "Thank you."

Neither Finn nor Mia spoke as they followed me out the front door of the police station. I felt defeated, deflated. No one at the police station had helped me learn anything, because none of them *knew* anything. I'd discovered nothing except that the world still sucked just as bad as I thought it did. And I didn't know how I would be able to learn more.

When we got in the car, Finn spoke first. "So I get the clown guy. There could be a Taker messing with his head… not cool, but I get it."

"Right…" I turned on my blinker and pulled into the left turn lane, then looked at Finn in the rearview mirror. He was rubbing his forehead with his fingertips.

"But why are people completely disappearing? Why kidnap that little girl?" he asked.

"I don't know. That might not even be related to the Takers." The light turned green and I turned, putting my foot on the gas a little harder than necessary. My thoughts went to Addie, and my stomach clenched down hard with fear before I continued. "But Jack said they capture other Night Walkers… that they kill people they even suspect might be Builders. If they're kidnapping regular people, too, there could be a million reasons why that we'll never understand."

My friends didn't respond, but I felt Mia place one hand on my arm for a second. Frustration bubbled under my skin and I felt Darkness agreeing with me. This was always a concern, but this time I didn't fight it. I didn't think I wanted to be patient about this anymore, waiting for Jack to tell me everything I needed to know. I felt like a tiger locked in a cage. It was too tight, too constrictive. I had the will. I wanted to help... to fight... but no one would release me, and I couldn't figure out how to undo the lock myself.

———

I ate dinner with Finn and Mia at the Patricks' house. Mom was on a date with Mr. Nelson and I didn't feel like heating up whatever leftovers I could find. We talked about TV shows, movies, the weird things Finn had done in Disney World... anything but the police station or the fact that Addie was probably out on another date with Jack.

My appetite disappeared every time I thought about that, so by the time I'd finished half my plate, I was ready to leave.

"Thanks for going with me today, guys," I said to Finn and Mia as they walked me down the hall toward the front door. "Sorry it didn't give us more info."

"That's okay." Finn gave me a crooked smile. "It's hard to accomplish much without firm aliases established beforehand. Rookie mistake. Next time we'll be better prepared. I'm still pushing to be Batman, though."

"As long as I don't have to wear a cape or tights, I'm in." I turned and opened the door, and then every organ in my body dropped into my shoes when I saw Jack kissing Addie on the front porch.

NINETEEN

Power surged through me. I had Jack off of Addie and pinned against the brick wall of the house in less than a second. My hands moved to his throat and tightened. His eyes bulged out and he brought his arm down across mine with all his strength, but I didn't budge. It was like I was made of steel. He couldn't hurt me. He was nothing.

Addie pulled on my shoulder and then I heard Finn by my ear.

"Let Jack go." His voice lowered. "Don't let the other— don't let *him* take over. Don't make me change my mind about who you really are."

Jack's face was red, and I could feel his pulse beneath my fingers. It beat one—two—three times. I drew in a slow, deep breath and loosened my grip until he dropped to the ground. Addie was beating against my shoulder, yelling. All I could think about was having my hands on Jack's throat again. It was what I wanted, what I needed. Why had I let him go? I couldn't make out Addie's words. Jack gasped on the porch steps, his eyes staring daggers through me.

"You...are..." He drew in a deep ragged breath before finishing. "A monster."

Darkness laughed in my head. "You have no idea."

I didn't realize I'd said the words out loud until I heard Mia gasp behind me.

"I'm—sorry. That wasn't me." I looked down at Jack, and even though I could see that he knew what I meant, there was only anger and fear in his face.

Addie stood furious in the corner. "Everyone. Go inside. I need to talk to Parker."

Finn's expression was shaken, but I still saw loyalty in his eyes. He put one hand on my shoulder as he walked past. "Good luck, man."

"Thanks."

Jack didn't leave. "Addie, I don't think—"

"Please go." She didn't take her eyes from me, but I couldn't meet them for long. There was so much pain, betrayal, and anger there. It was agonizing to see.

Jack got up and went inside, but I could hear from the way his footsteps stopped that he was just inside the door. That was fine. If Darkness took over, I wanted someone to be there to stop me. I'd never recover if he hurt her...any more than he already had.

"I know that you need to visit Mia, and I want you to survive," Addie said, her voice trembling under the weight of her emotion. "But I don't want to see you anymore, Parker."

"Addie…" I reached out and tugged on the bottom of her fingers, but she jerked her hand away as though I'd burned her. "Please, can you let me explain?"

She leaned against the house, and in the fading evening light her hair seemed to glow like a sheet of dark flame around her. "I don't see the point, but go ahead."

"The picture, and the girl I kissed." She physically recoiled when I said the words. "You remember how I told you about the other part of me? About Darkness?"

She inclined her head slightly and I continued.

"Ever since I made eye contact with the Taker, for some reason Darkness has had more control. Whenever I'm a little weak or tired, maybe, he can take over." I shuddered just thinking about how awful it had been to watch Darkness have total control. "That was him in that bar… not me. I'd never—I couldn't do that to you."

Her expression softened a little, but when she spoke a tear rolled down her cheek. "It's not enough."

I rushed ahead, desperate to say anything that might help. "Yesterday I told Finn everything. I told him that I wanted to be with you."

I stepped closer and tentatively raised my hand, brushing the single tear away with my knuckles. "I—I love you, Addie. You have to know that I've been in love with you for longer than I can remember. You've always been the only one I could ever imagine being with. Please tell me how to fix this, because I can't lose you. You're the only one who believes in me even when I don't. Please—" I lifted her chin until I could see those beautiful hazel eyes that kept her secrets from me.

Now the secrets were gone, replaced by pain, betrayal, and tears. My voice shook and I couldn't help the pleading tone that crept in. "Please don't give up on me now."

She closed her eyes, and as the tears rolled down her cheeks a soft sob escaped her lips. "It doesn't matter. Not unless you can prove that you haven't become the monster."

My entire body went cold. "How?"

"Just now ... was that you or Darkness who grabbed Jack and nearly choked the life out of him?" Her words floated across the space between us, making the inches feel like canyons, the breaths like galaxies.

I closed my eyes tight, learning my lesson too late as always. I told her the truth, even though I knew the lie could make everything better. I told her the truth that I knew would send her inside to where Jack was waiting, the truth that would steal her away from me forever. "It was both of us."

She slid across the wall and away from me. "We all have to fight to do the right thing, Parker. You just have to fight harder than the rest of us."

I crumpled down into a heap on the steps as she opened the door. "I'll send Jack out and you should go home. Please don't hurt anyone anymore—including yourself."

Then she walked inside and closed the door behind her.

———

The next morning I felt rested from Mia's dream, but it did nothing to heal all the fresh wounds left by Addie. My only consolation was that I had a plan for school that day. I wasn't always a big fan of school, but for now, despite the fact that I had to get out of bed, I could only see upside of it. School would be out for summer soon and I needed to use this time to find that Cooper kid, if he went to school with us. Plus, I had several classes with Finn, none with Addie, and I didn't have to see Jack at all.

I'd considered kicking Jack out, but since he was the only link I had left to my dad, I resisted. Still, it was extremely uncomfortable. He seemed to be avoiding me—not that I minded. And I had to give Mom a couple of extra excuses for why he was still staying with us, which I'm not entirely certain whether she was buying.

When we got home last night, I'd moved all of Jack's bedding and his backpack to the couch in the den. Darkness followed me every step of the way, yelling all the things I should say and do to Jack. I couldn't say I disagreed with all of his suggestions, but I tried not to encourage him.

When I got to school, Finn was standing by his locker. I opened my locker and threw a couple of books onto the shelf. Finn jumped and looked over at me, his eyes wide and bloodshot.

"Wow … you look more like me than like you." I leaned back and took in the dark circles under his eyes. His shirt was solid black with a wide white stripe across the middle. No-slogan days were never good days. "Have a rough night?"

Finn's laugh came out high-pitched and uncomfortable. He cleared his throat and tried again, with a plastered-on smile this time. "No, it's fine." Then he reached into the locker and seemed very intent on sorting through the mess at the bottom.

"Okay…" After grabbing the things I needed for English, our first class, I closed my locker and waited for him. He kept watching me out of the corner of his eye like he was waiting for me to leave. Finally, he groaned and leaned his head against his locker.

"Do you remember what we're supposed to be working on in class today?" he asked.

I shrugged and glanced down at my book. "I think we're still doing Shakespeare."

"That's right." Finn reached under the pile and pulled out his book before closing the locker. Then he bent over and straightened his shoe as I started walking backward toward our class. The bell was about to ring and I'd been trying to bring up my grades this semester, now that Mia was helping me sleep and I had a chance at a future.

"You're slow today." I laughed as Finn caught up with me. "You trying to get out of school or something?"

"Maybe." He shrugged. "It's not like it really matters."

I stared at him. Finn goofed off a lot, but he'd always been very serious about school, grades, college, and everything that went with that. "Are you sure you're feeling okay?"

"I'm fine. Just seeing things more clearly today, that's all." He walked into the class as the bell rang and made his way to the empty desk in the back row. There weren't assigned seats in here, but it was where I usually sat. I raised my eyebrows as I took the seat in front of him, but he just stared back at me—more challenge in his gaze than any kind of answer. I wondered whether something at the police station yesterday was bothering him.

Or maybe I'd freaked him out even more than I thought when I went after Jack. I could only hope he didn't think I'd passed the point of no return, like it seemed Addie did. I blew out a lungful of air and tried to convince myself that it wasn't a possibility.

Either way, I would wait until Finn wanted to tell me. I'd certainly had my share of days when I'd acted weird. I guessed it was probably his turn. He'd been struggling ever since the fire—maybe it was all starting to catch up to him. After everything Finn had done for me, the least I could do was be a little patient. I'd be here for him when he was ready to talk.

Just like he was for me.

After English, Finn took off and wasn't at his locker when I got there. Maybe he really wasn't feeling well and had gone home. I was just pulling out my books when I looked up and felt like I'd been kicked in the gut. Addie and Mia were rounding the corner, and Addie froze in place. Her hair moved around her the way it always did, and I had a vivid flashback to how amazing it smelled. Then she pivoted on one foot and walked off in the other direction. Mia sighed and crossed the hall to me.

"Well, today is sucking pretty hard for me." She leaned against Finn's locker and then gave me an apologetic smile. "I'm guessing it's worse for you."

I rested my head against my locker and banged it softly a few times before answering. "Yeah, I'm not a fan."

"Addie will get over it—I think." Mia winced and stood upright. "Walk me to class?"

"Sure." I strolled beside her in silence, still stunned by the fact that one Addie sighting could make me want to drive home and crawl back into bed... or break things. Breaking things sounded good.

"Finn doesn't seem to be doing great either." Mia lowered her voice when we spotted Finn walking halfway up the hall ahead of us. "Is he mad at you and Addie? You wait this long to tell him about dating her, and then you guys break up the same day? Does he think he has to pick sides?"

"I don't think it's about me and Addie. He didn't seem mad when I talked to him about it." I kept my voice low. "And what happened with Addie the last couple of days... that wasn't my choice."

Mia sighed. "Right. Sorry."

"Besides, Finn doesn't have to pick a side. It isn't like that. No one is asking him to." I glanced down and noticed Mia biting her lip. "And you don't have to worry about that either."

The section of the school we were walking through had mirrors along one wall. Most of the hall was empty now and Finn had disappeared. When I glanced over, I saw two of me walking next to Mia. My pulse sped up for a moment. Then I blinked, and he was gone.

Darkness was enjoying his newfound freedom a little too much. He really enjoyed messing with my head.

Again ... I was not a fan.

"See you later, Parker." Mia ducked into her class with a little wave, and I walked around the corner to my Physics classes. I made it through the door just after the bell rang, and Mr. Nelson gestured for me to take my seat with a slight smile.

I smiled right back ... not so much as a lecture for being late? At least there were a few perks to the teacher dating my mom.

TWENTY

I drove home from school alone, for the first time since the Patricks had gotten back from vacation. Mia had given Addie and Jack a ride and I couldn't find Finn anywhere. It was starting to worry me, but Mia said she thought he might have left early. I really hoped all this wasn't because of my attack on Jack, because if it was, then I felt even worse. I didn't want to be hoping Finn was sick or something, but at this point, I was crossing my fingers that the problem was something temporary like that. Nothing serious ... just a minor flu or bad allergies.

The next couple days of school were flat-out depressing. I missed my friends. I missed Addie more than I ever thought I could. And the idea of her spending her free time—and her dreams—with Jack made me want to pull my hair out one strand at a time and shred each piece into tiny bits.

It was possible that this line of thinking was not healthy,

but as long as I kept myself from acting on it, I called it a win.

On Friday, I sat at my kitchen counter after the final day of the school year, flipping through channel after channel of public interest stories about what kind of "sizzling summer sales" would be starting next week. Upside: no school for three months. Downside: I didn't even want to think about how crazy I was going to go with all that downtime and no friends. I glanced across the counter at Darkness—my only consistent company these days. That was even more depressing. I was becoming less afraid of him. Every day he seemed less like a threat and more like... a psychopathic toddler with no respect for morals or societal values. Admittedly, not a huge improvement. And since I didn't trust him at all, it made me nervous that he was seeming less like a monster to me. Did that mean he was becoming more like me—or that I was becoming more like him?

He glared at the remote control. It drove him crazy that I could touch it and he couldn't. "Would you turn it up— please?" he growled.

With a loud sigh, I pushed the volume button, got up, and started searching around in the cupboard for something to eat. The cupboards were bare. Even though Jack spent most of his awake time somewhere else—I didn't even want to think about where—Mom still hadn't figured out how to shop for two teenage boys in the house. I'd had to make a couple of extra trips to the grocery store so she wouldn't get annoyed and decide Jack wasn't welcome here anymore. I definitely wasn't Jack's biggest fan these days, but he was still my only source for answers about my dad, even if he'd stopped giving me any.

The point was, we needed food, and at the moment I was bored out of my mind.

Picking up my phone, I called Finn for the third time that afternoon. It went straight to voicemail. Either Finn was still avoiding me or he'd dropped his phone in the toilet—*again*. I decided it was time to find out exactly what was wrong.

I pushed the power button and the TV cut off in the middle of a story about a police commissioner's surprising resignation.

"Hey, I was watching that!" Darkness followed me to the door to the garage. When I slammed it in his face, he just appeared on the opposite side of my car. "Where are we going?"

I climbed in. I'd been working hard the last few days on not responding out loud, which only seemed to make him angrier. It totally counted as a perk.

Driving through the neighborhood, I stopped at a stop sign and turned up the radio in an effort to drown out Darkness's chatter. Then I looked up and saw Addie and Jack come to a stop on the road to the right. She was laughing and he was shaking his head. Neither of them had seen me, and now that my gut was folded up into a ball of pain, I preferred to keep it that way.

I drove through the intersection and pulled over, turning off the car. The radio cut off and everything went immediately silent. Even Darkness had stopped talking, though I could feel his fury fuming inside me. He looked over and I stared into my own eyes.

Then everything faded away.

When I regained awareness, I was still sitting behind the wheel of my car but it was much later in the day. The sun had set and the sky had faded to the hazy violet of twilight. Darkness seethed in the passenger seat, obviously unhappy to have lost control. I did a quick check of my clothes and looked in the mirror. No lipstick, no black eye. I took a deep breath... I didn't feel like I'd been drinking. I dug my phone out of my pocket and scrolled through the recent history. No texts, pictures, or calls had occurred in the last couple of hours.

I looked back at Darkness, who had a hard smirk on his face. "Yeah, yeah... don't get sappy. You can repay me later."

"Why didn't you make me watch this time?"

He didn't respond for a while and when he did, his voice was gruff. "No one deserves that... not even you."

I squinted over the steering wheel and out the front window at the house Darkness was watching. It was run down and in a rough neighborhood I'd never been in before. I tried to make out the last name on the mailbox. It was too dark and most of the letters were missing—but it started with a T. The bushes in the front of the house were so high and overgrown they probably blocked out any sun that tried to creep in through the windows. Gray paint that probably used to be a different color peeled on every surface. The house's roof looked like it had been patched a few times, very ineffectively.

"Where are we?"

"You didn't listen, so I decided to bring us here on my own."

A chill ran down my spine at the cold satisfaction in his voice, but before I could ask Darkness to clarify, I saw the front door open and Finn walked out. Through the open door I could have sworn I saw the hulking form of Thor before it quickly closed.

T … for Thornton. I glanced at Darkness, but his jaw was hanging open wide. He may have come to check up on Thor, but it was clear he was just as surprised as I was to see Finn here.

We watched Finn jump into his old crappy car, which was parked about a block away. After two attempts it started up and he pulled away from the curb. I started my car, too, and stayed back a few blocks. Darkness seemed at least curious because he didn't argue—and as a general rule, he argued with everything I said, did, or thought.

I followed Finn through a few cross streets and finally back to his house. He went inside, and I sat in my car trying to decide what to do next. Darkness disappeared again just when I'd considered asking his opinion. He was nothing if not absolutely useless.

I gave up. Nothing that was going on made sense to me, so the only thing I could do was ask Finn.

The moon was full, but it hid behind some clouds the instant I stepped out of the car. The wind kicked up and blew hard in my face. I blinked against the sudden force, which seemed to stop as soon as it started. Running my hand through my hair, I glanced through the window into the Patricks' garage. All the other cars were gone—good. Less chance of running into Addie and Jack.

After two knocks, Finn opened the door. He looked bored.

Finn never looked bored. Something was definitely wrong, and it made my skin crawl. I could hear my own pulse in my ears and my lungs felt like they wanted to breathe much faster than usual.

"Feel that?" Darkness spoke quietly and crystal clear inside my head. "Those are *my* instincts that you're feeling. They're primal. They're sensitive … and they're *never* wrong. Be careful."

I walked into the kitchen and Finn sauntered in behind me.

"So what have you been up to?" I kept my voice low and casual.

"Nothing. Just been here all night." He gestured back toward the living room, where the TV was on.

I nodded, trying to look calm while my brain was freaking out. "So, I was thinking, about our conversation the other day … I really think you should go for it."

"You do?" All his attention was focused on me now and every trace of boredom was gone.

"Yeah. I think Stanford would be awesome. And so what if it's halfway across the country?" I leaned back against the counter, feeling around for the wooden owl statue that was always kept in that spot. I knew Finn hated the idea of going to a West Coast university, for reasons that I'd yet to figure out—so any response other than his customary "Uh, no way in hell" would be a dead giveaway.

Finn smiled and relaxed his stance, but there was something in his eyes that made every hair on my arm stand on end. "Yeah, so what? Stanford seems so cool."

My fingers finally brushed the wooden statue and I pulled it tight against my palm. Drawing in a deep, slow breath, I smiled back. Whoever this Taker was, they were using Finn's body and I would *not* hurt him … not seriously, anyway.

"It's really too bad, though." Fake-Finn turned his back on me and I took one silent step forward. Then his voice turned ice cold and he spun to face me with a knife in his hand and his lip curled back in an arrogant sneer. "I didn't want to kill you *yet*."

I took a step back. "Who are you? Cooper—right?"

"None of your business." Finn looked a little surprised when I said the name, then lunged forward, swinging the knife toward my stomach. He missed by mere inches, narrowly avoiding slicing me open. The front of my shirt had a long gash across the middle. Fear and adrenaline made every detail around me crystal clear.

I kicked the chair toward him and he stopped it with his foot. It hadn't been intended to hurt him, more to put something else between myself and Finn's very sharp knife.

Now, with the chair between us, I threw the wooden owl at him. It thudded against his shoulder when he ducked. It was solid and pretty heavy; Finn winced when he tried to raise the knife again. Using his momentary distraction, I reached for the only things that were handy. Ripping spices off Mrs. Patrick's spice shelf behind me, I popped off the tops and started throwing them as fast as I could at Finn. The first was some kind of Italian seasoning, and he just looked at me like I'd lost my mind, but the third was pepper and he was coughing and sneezing before I threw cinnamon and a dozen other spices into a cloud around him.

He'd covered his eyes with the sleeve of his shirt and sounded like he was hacking up a lung when I ran for him. I slammed my elbow down on his wrist and the knife clattered to the ground; then I jumped on him and pinned him face-down in the spices covering the floor. I grabbed the dishtowel and tied his wrists behind his back with it, then picked up the knife, jerked his head up by his hair, and put the blade against his neck.

"Who are you?" Power surged through my veins and I felt pure strength. I was totally in control. He had to answer me. I would make him.

Finn sputtered and coughed, but gave no response.

"Tell me your name." My voice was barely a growl. Finn looked scared for the first time. I pressed the knife closer and a single drop of blood crossed my blade. I could see my reflection in it. It was me, shining in silver and red blood—Finn's blood. He still hadn't answered me. I put a tiny bit more pressure on the blade and another drop fell.

The back door opened and Addie and Mia walked in.

"What the—?" Mia stopped and Addie ran into her back. Addie stepped around her and sneezed, then looked down at me. She froze and her eyes went from me to Finn. "Get off him! What's wrong with you?"

I looked up at her and back down at the blade and the few drops of my best friend's blood. The knife fell from my fingers with a sudden clatter and I kicked it aside. Closing my eyes tight, I knelt back on Finn's legs to keep him from moving and reached inside my head. Shutting out every word from Addie, Mia and Finn, I focused inside my mind and found Darkness.

I'd seen enough. We'd done enough. Darkness had to be stopped before he killed someone I loved. He wailed out in agony as I used every piece of my strength to push him into some dark corner, to wall him off, to cage him in. It took almost a full minute of pure pain. Every time he'd start to regain some ground, I would focus on the image of Finn's blood on the blade and he would retreat.

Then everything was silent.

"He's totally lost it. I don't even know—" Finn's words finally cut through. I was so relieved to hear his voice, even if it wasn't Finn using it. I'd almost killed him. Just an ounce more pressure and I would have murdered my best friend. If I'd . . . if he'd been . . . I shoved the horrifying thought aside.

"It wasn't on purpose! This isn't the way it looks." My voice was full of panic. I tried to ease it by focusing on the blissful silence in my head, by strengthening the wall I'd built around Darkness. I hadn't hurt Finn. That was the only thing that mattered right now.

But also important was the fact that while Finn's body was okay, this still wasn't Finn, and so far I was the only one who knew that.

Addie was still trying valiantly to push me off what she thought was her brother. I opened my eyes and turned to face her.

"Where's Jack?" I grabbed her hands and held her wrists in place.

"I don't know. Why, did you want to attack him, too?"

This was getting me nowhere, and Finn was starting to sputter below me. I only had one true ally in the room right now. She was my only hope.

"Mia—this isn't Finn. I can explain everything, but first, do you know where Jack is?"

She looked from me to Finn and back again. "We—we just dropped him off at your house."

"Call him." I kept my voice low and calm. I didn't need them to freak out more. "Ask him to come over here *now*."

"Okay." Mia dialed a number and I heard her speaking low into the receiver. "Jack—I don't know what's happening, but get over here right away." Then she lowered the phone and I could see that she hadn't hung it up. Good—that could work in my favor.

"Addie, I don't know what's wrong with him." Finn turned his head to the side and looked up at his sister. "Please help me. Get him off of me."

Addie pushed all her weight against my shoulder and tried to push me against the cabinets. I withstood her full weight by clamping my knees around Finn's sides. Then I grabbed another dishtowel and stuffed it in his mouth.

Addie growled and looked ready to fight me again, so I

stared straight into her eyes. "Listen to me and I'll explain. I'm not hurting him . . . I promise you, Addie."

"He's bleeding! You had a knife to his throat! To Finn!" Her voice choked off in a sob. "How could you do this, Parker?"

I'd never thought I was capable of something like this either. I nodded toward where the knife lay on the floor. "I don't have the knife anymore," I said, my voice ragged. "But I'll sit right here. I won't move until you let me explain."

Addie picked up the knife with shaking fingers, and when she saw at Finn's blood on it, her grasp on it tightened. She held it up. Her eyes were a sea of confusion and mistrust, but she was listening.

"This"—I looked down at Finn and then back up—"is not your brother. He attacked me."

Her brow furrowed and she shook her head.

"You remember what Jack told us about the Takers?"

Addie's eyes widened and she looked from me to Finn.

Mia, who stood behind her, spoke up first. "How do we know it's not you who isn't . . . yourself?"

"Watchers bodies can't be taken over." I kept speaking low and steady in spite of the turmoil inside me. The knife Addie was holding made me feel sick and kept my adrenaline pumping. Mia still held the phone in her hand, so I nodded toward it. "Ask Jack."

Mia looked a little sheepish as she lifted the phone to her ear. "Did you hea—"

I heard Jack talking rapidly in the background, then Mia said, "Okay, hurry." And hung up.

"He says we should move Finn to his room, gag him, and tie him up. He's on his way over."

"I don't—I don't know..." Addie's hands were shaking and it looked like she might drop the knife at any moment. Her eyes were still glued to Finn.

"Think of any question that no one but Finn could answer. And it needs to be something that happened before..." I calculated in my head. Tuesday was the last day Finn had been normal, but I'd go further back just to be safe. "Think of something that happened before your vacation and ask him about it. I promise he won't be able to answer you."

Addie reached down with her free hand and pulled the dishtowel from Finn's mouth. He immediately started talking.

"He's going crazy, Addie. I don't even know what he's talking about. Don't believe him!"

"Answer my question and I'll help you." She bent down until she could see his face, but she had to cover her mouth against the cloud of spices that kicked up every time Finn squirmed. "What did Grandpa Patrick call me before he died?"

Finn wiggled again and coughed for a while, but there was definitely a more forced sound to it this time.

"Answer her." I twisted his arm a little further and he stopped faking.

"Okay—I just don't remember. It feels like he's been gone a long time..."

Addie's face paled three shades before she stood up and dropped the knife into the sink. "I don't know who this is, but Finn would know our grandpa is alive and well in Florida. Let's take him in the other room."

Between the three of us, a rope from the garage for his hands and feet, and a new, more reliable, gag, we managed to get Finn into his room just before Jack showed up. Addie and Mia straightened up the kitchen while Jack and I pushed Finn into his closet and force-fed him one of Mrs. Patrick's sleeping pills. Harder than you might think when the prisoner is trying extremely hard to bite fingers off.

Finn was nodding off when we left him. We gathered around the kitchen table and tried to come up with a plan.

"We should take him to my house," I said. "My mom is working all weekend, and it will seem weird if your parents come home and don't see him."

"Or find him tied up in his own closet." Mia was biting her lip so hard I was afraid she'd start bleeding. I reached out and squeezed her hand.

"He's going to be okay." I glanced over at Jack, but was surprised to find Addie staring at my hand. Mia quickly pulled her hand away with an apologetic glance in my direction. I focused my attention on Jack again. "Finn wasn't asleep when I got here, and it's already dinnertime. If a Taker took him over last night, why didn't Finn wake up today back as himself again?"

Jack rubbed his thumb back and forth across the stubble on his chin. "The Taker must still be sleeping. Remember, it's about the Taker. When he wakes up, Finn will be free."

"So the sleeping pill we gave him will wear off, the Taker will wake up, and Finn will wake up back as himself again, right?"

Jack nodded, but it was slower than I liked and there was definitely some hesitation to it.

"What?"

"No, nothing." Jack frowned, but gave me a firm nod this time. "That's what should happen."

"Okay, so we need to get him back to my house. Since it was definitely one of us that Finn last made eye contact with, by morning everything will return to normal." The girls agreed and I stood up, but Jack frowned so I sat back down.

"Dude—just say it." I was trying very hard to be patient, but Jack was driving me mad lately just by existing. Even calling him for help felt superhuman. It was something I would only do when desperate—only to save Finn. I took a slow, deep breath before continuing with considerably less growl. "What are we missing?"

"I told you. It isn't about Finn's eye contact," Jack said. "It's just like with a Watcher. If you make eye contact with Mia at the end of a day, does it matter who she, the Dreamer, makes eye contact with after that? No. It isn't Finn that matters, it's the Night Walker. The Taker has to wake up and look into someone else's eyes to break his connection with Finn." Jack rubbed his hands across his face before finishing. "Someone has to go find the Taker, who I assume must be that Cooper guy. We need to wake him up and force him to make eye contact with someone."

Addie's hands were shaking, but she responded first. "Well, I thi—"

Jack and I interrupted her at the same time: "I'll do it."

"So Mia and I will be left alone in your house with an

unconscious Finn in your closet?" All emotion had left Addie's face. All I saw left was determination... and sarcasm. "Yeah, that won't be suspicious at all when your mom comes home." She stood up and pushed out her chair. "We'll stay here. Once we're sure he's out, we'll get him comfortable in his closet—still tied up, of course—and then I'll lie and tell my parents he's spending the night at your house. You guys keep your phones on. We'll call you if there are any problems, and then you come back here when you're done and we'll decide what to do from there."

Jack was the only one still seated. "I think Parker should stay here too."

"Why?" Addie got the words out before I did.

"Because we don't know where this search for Cooper is going to lead us. If we end up at the Takers' base or they get an easy chance to take Parker, they'll do it." Jack frowned and slowly got to his feet. "I don't want to give them an opportunity like that when I can do this alone."

"First—you don't even know what Cooper looks like. Second—Finn has been my best friend my entire life and I'm coming." I started backing toward the door. "Third—if you try to stop me, I'll go find Cooper on my own."

Addie turned to Jack. I thought I saw a tiny smile curving up one corner of her mouth before she tilted her head to one side and I couldn't see her whole face anymore. "Looks like he's coming—and it will be safer with two of you there, anyway."

Mia stepped over to me and lowered her chin as she met my eyes. "You two watch out for each other." She glanced over her shoulder at Addie and Jack. "No more fighting. Finn needs you—*both of you.*"

TWENTY-ONE

The only thing we discussed on the car ride was where to begin. Since Jack still didn't want to tell me where the Takers' base was, and we didn't know how connected Cooper was with the other Takers anyway, we decided that starting at Thor's place would be the best plan. I parked the car up the street from the run-down house.

For all we knew, Cooper might not even be here, but if he wasn't, Thor probably knew where he was. The fact that Finn had been here just a few hours ago, while under the control of someone else, made me pretty sure that Thor had a lot more to do with the Takers than I'd previously believed.

That thought made me want to put my fist through Thor's head more than I'd ever wanted to in the past, and considering he was the biggest asshat I'd ever met, that was really saying something.

Jack held his finger up to his lips as I turned off the car

and reached for my door handle. It was hard to resist the temptation to roll my eyes.

"Got it," I whispered. I was pretty proud of myself for showing some restraint.

Hiding in the shade of a tree, we waited. I wasn't sure what for, until I noticed that Jack's eyes weren't on the house but on the sky. The moon was out, almost full, and shining brightly down on this creepy little neighborhood. But there was a big cloud moving toward the moon and within a couple of minutes, it would be covered. The street would be darkened.

Time passed slowly, and I found myself thinking about the way Finn had looked coming at me with that knife. I knew it wasn't him, but it was still a memory that would be hard to shake. Just like the memory of his blood on the blade in my hand. I shivered and Jack glanced over at me.

"You sure you're up to this?" There was a slight smirk on his face, so I interrupted him before he could go on.

"Yes, I'm sure." I straightened the dark gray jacket I'd borrowed from Finn's closet and peered back up at the moon...almost time. "But if you want to wait in the car, I understand."

Jack didn't say a word, but the muscle flexing in his jaw was answer enough.

The moon finally slipped behind the cloud and the street sank into darkness. The nearest streetlamp was out— jagged shards of broken glass stuck out from the light socket that was supposed to provide safety from the shadows. The only illumination on the street came from a few windows and an occasional front porch lamp that still worked.

We stuck close to the trees as I led Jack down the street. When I got to Thor's yard, we crept around the back. Every crackle of gravel, every snap of a twig beneath my feet felt amplified, over and over. It felt like a megaphone announcing our presence to every person in the homes surrounding us. But there was no response. No one noticed. No one cared.

When I got around to the back I could see one of those screened-in sunrooms they have on older homes. Thor sat in a spindly old rocking chair that really didn't look reliable enough to bear his weight, and he was talking, but from my position I couldn't see the other person.

"…know if they can get more."

"They'll have to." The voice was soft and low. I couldn't even tell if it was male or female. My eyes scanned the shadows on the opposite end of the room. I could barely make out a figure there, but the only light came from inside the building and the figure was in a shade so deep they'd have to step forward for me to tell even how tall they were, let alone anything else.

"What if they can't?" Thor's voice sounded much younger and more vulnerable than I ever would've guessed. He also had a thick accent—Romanian? Or Russian maybe? I scratched my chin. The things you learn about someone when they finally stop growling and have a conversation.

"Then we'll make good on our promise. Besides, we're almost ready to start. We've gotten all the money we need for supplies and setup."

Money…all the weird sleep issues in Oakville, the people draining their savings accounts, even possibly the police commissioner quitting his job so abruptly. All the dozens of snippets of news articles or reports over the last few months that I'd wondered about. The Takers had been behind all of it, and now they were ready for whatever was coming next.

The other person stepped forward and I recognized Cooper immediately. Good, he was awake. I also noticed that he didn't have any sunglasses on and was looking straight at Thor. The only Taker I knew in town had just made eye contact with someone besides Finn. The connection should be broken now. This had been an easier job than I'd expected.

Jack grabbed my elbow and nodded back toward the car. I turned and started to follow him, but the next words I heard froze me mid-step and I barely kept myself from falling over.

"The chemist doesn't seem to be all that cooperative."

Chemist? Dad!

I'd always suspected that if there were Takers in town, it was related to Dad. But since Cooper hadn't made a move to come after me, even knowing I was a Watcher, I'd started to think maybe Cooper wasn't involved with Dad. After all, just because someone was a Taker didn't mean he knew all the other Takers. Hell, I hadn't even known there were other Watchers before Jack told me last week. But hearing them talk about "the chemist" made me certain that not only were Cooper and Thor heavily involved, they probably knew where Dad was that very moment.

Jack pulled hard on my sleeve but I ignored him, listening harder.

"He knows we can hurt them any time we want. He knows we aren't afraid to kill. We can become anyone at any time. The people close to you have the easiest time crushing you. We're on the inside. He can't fight that." Cooper was supremely confident.

Thor stood and walked closer to the screen. He could see me clearly if he just looked down. My heart pounded so hard my chest hurt. I'd waited too long, and now they were going to catch me. Jack froze, his fingers still gripped around my jacket. I could hear his breath coming in quiet puffs. The moon came out from behind the cloud just as Thor turned back toward Cooper.

"Parker shouldn't be underestimated. That's what got Jeff killed. You guys should've learned from that little experiment."

The words "little experiment" rang in my ears as we snuck along the side of the house, into the front yard, and back out to the car.

———

I drove on autopilot across town back to Finn's house. I thought I heard Jack call Addie to tell them we were on our way, but I didn't remember a word he said. All I could think about was what kind of "experiment" could have been done on Jeff. Had he been under the control of a Taker when he'd trapped Mia and me and started the fire? If so, he'd been as innocent as Finn was tonight.

Memories of Jeff from years ago flooded back. So many times, we'd hung out behind the junior high. Went to the movies or kicked the soccer ball around after school. Had I killed a complete innocent? Was I responsible for the death of my friend?

Mia and Addie met us out front and snuck us around the back of the Patricks' house, but I didn't go inside. Instead I sat on the garden wall by the basketball hoop, feeling sick and needing to think. I needed time to sort this out.

This wasn't like with Dr. Freeburg. I hadn't attacked Jeff, but if I'd known he wasn't himself... would I have tried harder to save him?

Could I have saved him?

After a few minutes, Addie came out and sat next to me. "So, they didn't say anything about Finn?"

"No. But they mentioned my dad." My voice sounded hollow, even to me. "I think they probably even know where he is and what's happening to him."

"Do you want to talk about it?" Her voice was quiet, hesitant. And the answer was no. I didn't want to talk to her right now. I knew I'd screwed up and made mistakes, but she wasn't the only one who'd been hurt. Right now, I needed someone I could trust not to hurt me again. More importantly, I needed someone who would be able to answer some of my questions.

"Thank you, Addie—but right now, I need to talk to Mia." My words were soft, but I could tell from the way she pulled back that they still stung. I tried to soften the blow. "She's the only one who was there... that night at school, with the fire."

The tension drained out of her shoulders and she looked less angry, if a little deflated. After a moment, she nodded. "Okay. I'll get her."

A few minutes later, Mia sat beside me. She was quiet, waiting for me to be ready.

"I heard something at the house about an experiment on Jeff."

Her body stiffened at Jeff's name, but she inclined her head for me to continue.

"Do you think he could've been under a Taker's control that day?" I didn't feel the need to clarify further, and she didn't ask me to. Even though we hadn't really talked about what had happened, we both knew too well what day I was referring to.

We could never forget.

Mia bit her lip and curled a strand of hair around her finger for a few seconds before finally answering. "I don't think so."

It surprised me that she felt so sure. "Why not?"

"Because of all the things he said." Her brow furrowed. "About his mom and the team, all the bitterness... that wasn't some Taker out for a joy ride. Jeff really felt those things."

"It wasn't a Taker." Jack's voice came from the door of the house. I hadn't realized he was listening, but it didn't surprise or bother me. He was the one who knew about this world, and apparently the one who could really answer my question.

"How do you know?" I shifted my position so I could see him over my shoulder, but his face was still hidden in shadow.

"Because it was a Watcher." Jack stared straight down at the ground between his feet. He seemed to shrink in place. "I know, because it was me."

TWENTY-TWO

I stood up and felt Darkness begin to push against the wall I'd locked him behind. He was surging to fight—to take action. But now that I knew exactly what we were capable of together, it was a little easier to find the strength to hold him back.

Mia was the first person to find words. She walked slowly toward Jack with both hands clenched by her sides. "What do you mean? Y-you made Jeff do that to us?"

"Not exactly."

"Well then what, exactly?" Addie stepped out around Jack and stood next to Mia.

"I was just trying to find out for sure. To figure out if Parker was a Night Walker." Jack still looked down but kept talking, his voice growing firmer. "It seemed like the best plan. Parker's dad agreed. I noticed how much attention Parker was paying to Mia, so I pushed Jeff in his dreams to grow more and more jealous of Parker. I didn't realize the Takers had already messed with him and left him a little unstable. Or that he was capable of taking it that far. I didn't realize he'd already been jealous of Parker to start with."

"How was messing with Jeff's dreams supposed to get you the answers you wanted? You almost got us killed." My voice came out cold and malevolent. I forced Darkness back again and he roared in anger. I sat down, trapping my hands under my legs, doing everything I could to keep him under control. Still I felt his rage, his frustration, boiling through my veins.

"I thought if I pushed him, he might make things difficult for you at school and then you'd go into his dreams and push him back. If you'd done that, I could have felt your resistance there when I went back into Jeff's dreams. It's like a fingerprint, kind of—a Watcher can tell if another Watcher has recently been in a dream. I would've been able to see and feel the difference in him. Then I'd know you were a Watcher."

After an uneasy pause, Jack continued. "I was so stuck on this idea that I even watched Mia's dreams once. You were paying so much attention to her, I thought maybe I could tell from her dreams what you were, but her nightmares were awful and clearly not influenced by a Watcher. Seeing them almost convinced me that you weren't one."

Then he looked up at me, staring straight in my eyes. "I messed up with Jeff. It didn't even occur to me that you might not know *how* to push him in his dreams—or that my influence would send him so far off the edge. It was an accident, and a massive mistake."

When no one responded, Jack stepped away from the wall, toward Mia. "I'm so sorry for everything that happened.

If I'd known he would—" He turned to face me. "If I'd known any of it, I would have stopped him."

I drew in a deep breath, and by the time I released it, even Darkness had calmed down a little. It was all becoming so complicated and confusing. Nothing was what I'd believed, and I needed some time to figure out how to respond to the changes.

Climbing slowly to my feet, I shuffled toward the house, making eye contact with Mia on my way. "Let's go get ready to deal with Finn's questions. He's going to freak out when he finds himself tied up in his own closet."

———————

Addie and Mia slept in their rooms, and Jack and I kept watch over Finn. Strangely, Finn was still asleep. Since we were in the same room as him and planned on taking shifts, we untied Finn's hands so he could sleep more comfortably. We didn't know what kind of shape he would be in when he woke up, or what he'd remember, if anything at all, so we didn't want to scare him more than necessary. We still kept him in the closet and left his feet bound in a very tight and complicated knot. If we'd been wrong about Cooper and it was some *other* Taker in control of Finn—which was a distinct possibility—Finn wouldn't be able to get anywhere very fast.

Jack agreed to take the first watch. As I was about to enter the Hollow, I heard him whisper my name.

"Huh?" I kept my eyes closed, not wanting to accidentally make eye contact with him.

He whispered across the room to me. "I really am sorry."

"I know." Stretching one arm up, I rested my forearm across my eyes. "But just so you know, that was a pretty sucky plan."

He laughed softly. "What was I supposed to do, walk up and ask if you were a Watcher? If you weren't, you would've thought I was crazy. I couldn't mention your dad, and you could've been a Taker or even a Builder. This was supposed to be the safest way, the least intrusive into your life."

I scoffed. "Well, it felt pretty damn intrusive to me."

Jack didn't respond, and I almost drifted off again before I heard another whisper. "You need to let Addie go."

I groaned and pulled my pillow over my head. "I really don't want to have this conversation with you."

"You're dangerous—to her and everyone else." His voice was pleading, worried. "She's already been hurt. What will it do to you if you hurt her worse next time? Can't you let her go?"

"In case you haven't noticed ... *I don't have her.*" I was exhausted and this conversation was just pissing me off. I didn't even try to hide it.

"Yeah, but she's still holding on ... still waiting for you to get better." Jack shifted his position against the wall. "You should tell her that you aren't going to."

"Why?" I pulled the pillow off my head. "To give you a better shot at her?"

"No." His voice dropped to a low mutter and I had to strain to hear him. "I don't have that anyway."

"What?"

"She...uh, hasn't spoken to me about anything but Builder training since I kissed her the other day. If you hadn't thrown me away from her, she probably would have. She wasn't exactly kissing me back."

I couldn't help but smile into my pillow and a bit of my tension seemed to ease. "Sounds rough."

He sounded a little angry when he responded. "Anyway, you just need to think about what's more important: Addie being with you...or Addie being safe."

That thought sobered me up and I rolled over with my back to him. "Fine, I get it. I'm going to sleep now. Good night."

And I lay there awake, thinking about his words for way longer than I wanted to admit.

———

The soft sound of whimpering woke me up and it took me a minute to realize I wasn't hearing it in someone's dream. There was a soft nudge against my foot, and when I peeked through my barely parted eyelids, my blood ran cold. Addie was standing over me wearing a lime green shirt with pajama bottoms, her back pressed against Finn's stomach, her long auburn curls draped over his elbow. His right arm was wrapped around her shoulders. His feet were untied, and he'd managed to get his hands on the scissors from the desk. He held the blade tight against Addie's throat as he backed her toward the door.

Jack was out cold on the bed; so much for taking turns keeping watch. I glanced at the clock. It was barely six a.m. Everyone else was probably still sleeping.

And Finn was obviously not back to normal.

My eyes scanned the room, but I couldn't see anything I could use quickly enough to save Addie without risking her neck—and life—at the same time. There was a heavy crystal paperweight on the dresser, but after Freeburg's dream...I shuddered. No, I couldn't.

I heard Addie's breathing quicken as they walked out into the hallway. A rush of anger and adrenaline pounded through my veins.

Okay, I could, but this time I'd do it differently. I got silently to my feet and gripped the paperweight in my right hand. Sneaking slowly into the hallway, I carefully side-stepped the creaky board on the right and caught up with them before they left the kitchen. Swinging hard, I brought the paperweight down on Finn's shoulder. The scissors fell to the floor as his arm dropped. He yelled out in pain just as I wrapped my left arm around his head and covered his mouth. He tried to bite my fingers, so I jerked my arm up under his chin until his jaw was wrenched shut. Finn fought against my arm and tried to elbow me in the stomach.

Now free, Addie jumped forward, grabbed the scissors off the floor, and spun around, holding them against his chest. Her voice came out as a soft snarl and it was clear she meant every word. "I'm studying anatomy, and I know exactly where I can cut you with these without killing my brother. Do *not* struggle."

Finn's eyes got huge and he complied as I led him back into the bedroom. I kicked Jack's foot on the bed and he jumped forward, crashing his knee into the dresser and swearing under his breath.

"I've never seen anyone that jumpy when they wake up." I wrestled Finn onto the bed face-down and pinned his wrists together with my knee. "Care to help out and grab some of the rope from last night?" Finn grunted loudly as I shifted my weight. "And the gag, please."

Jack stared with bloodshot eyes from me to Finn and back, then abruptly jumped up and rushed into the closet. I heard Addie talking in the kitchen and held up my hand for Jack to be quiet just as we got the gag in place. When Finn started to struggle, we threw the comforter over him and Jack sat on his legs.

"Sorry, Mom. I turned on the TV and it was much louder than I thought." Addie let out a very loud yawn and I smiled. She'd always been a great actress. "I'm still tired, though. I think I'll go back to my room and try to sleep a little more."

"Okay, honey. Whatever you do, try to keep it down." Mrs. Patrick sounded barely awake as I heard her slippered footsteps head back to their room.

"I will." Addie walked toward her room but then slipped through the door into Finn's instead. "We need to get him out of here and then figure out why Finn isn't back."

I nodded. "I'll pull the car up in front of the garage. Addie, wake up Mia and write your mom a note. We'll load him in and go to my house. It's a Saturday. Mom always works all day on Saturdays."

Jack and I finished tying Finn up, very securely this time. The deep frown on Jack's face concerned me. The fact that he kept shaking his head and muttering under his breath freaked me out further, but I could ask him questions later. For now, we had to get out of here before the Patricks caught us with their son tied up and gagged. I knew there would be no explaining that.

My car was parked down the street, so I started it, got a little momentum, and then cut the engine as I pulled up the driveway … just to be safe. Addie and Mia came out, and I followed them through the back door and grabbed Finn's feet. Jack had Finn's head wrapped up in the comforter, so what little noise he could make through the gag was muffled. We had him out and tossed into the backseat in under thirty seconds.

I threw my keys over to Mia, who was still a little bleary-eyed.

"You drive. Jack and I will make sure our passenger doesn't cause any problems."

We pinned Finn in the middle of the seat, using the blanket and the seat belt to further secure him and keep him upright. Addie sat up front and leaned over the backrest, keeping the scissors handy. After she and Jack gave me a nod, I loosened Finn's gag.

"So you're not Cooper, I take it?" I had to keep reminding myself that no matter how much it looked like him, this was not Finn.

Finn smiled, but didn't respond.

I looked over him at Jack. "How can any Taker be asleep for this long? Is it possible that the Taker woke up and didn't make eye contact with anyone else before going back to sleep?"

Jack shrugged and looked out the window, but Finn

leaned his head on the seat and chuckled. "You haven't told him?"

Jack whipped around and wrapped the fingers of one hand around Finn's throat, cutting off his laugh with a gurgling sputter.

"Stop! This is Finn's body." I pried Jack's fingers back and Finn coughed on the side of my face.

I rubbed my cheek against my shoulder and looked from Jack's furious expression to Finn's glare as they stared each other down. Jack daring him to speak … the Taker daring Jack to attack again.

"What haven't you told me, Jack?"

Everything was silent until Jack finally released his breath and turned to me. "I was afraid yesterday that this might be the case … when Finn was still being controlled so late in the day. But I didn't want to tell you until I was sure. But now, this morning, this pretty much confirms what I was afraid of."

I stared at him. Wanting him to go on, but afraid of what he might say.

"What?" Mia asked loudly from the front seat, and Addie jumped. "I'm trying to drive here and you're killing me. What does this mean?"

"It means that they've done it, Parker." Jack looked at me hard until I realized what he meant.

"No … he wouldn't." My words were soft and raw. I was so horrified that my throat felt constricted and closed off. Barely letting breath out, barely letting life in.

Jack turned and leaned his forehead against the window. Addie stared at me, her hands shaking, waiting. I cleared my throat and tried to find the right words to explain it. Something to make her feel better, but the truth wouldn't do that and I'd promised to stop lying.

"It means the Takers have found a drug that will let them take over people's bodies indefinitely. They call it Eclipse. It lets Takers keep the brain power and body of a Dreamer for a really long time... until they wear the Dreamer's body out."

Addie gasped and Mia swerved to the shoulder of the road and stopped the car. They both leaned over the front seat, staring at me, waiting for the "but" that would provide some speck of hope.

It was something I would not be able to give them. Instead I plowed on with more bad news. "It also means they've somehow convinced my dad to make this drug."

Finn's smile was cold and full of menace. "And it means Finn is never coming back."

TWENTY-THREE

I threw the blanket back over Finn's head and tried to figure out what to do. I wasn't done. This wasn't over, not by a long shot. Finn never gave up on me, and I wasn't about to give up on him.

"Parker?" It took me a minute, but when I finally heard Mia speaking my name, it was clear it wasn't the first time.

"Sorry, what did you say?"

"I asked you what we're supposed to do now." Mia didn't turn around, even though she still hadn't gotten the car back on the road. Instead, she met my gaze in the rearview mirror and I saw her eyes brimming with tears. Jack still stared firmly out the window, but his shoulders were hunched in like they bore the weight of the world. And truthfully, they did. Everything he'd been hiding from and fighting against his whole life was now happening. I saw a slight tremble in his neck and knew he felt the crushing fear that pounded through my veins.

Last, I turned my eyes on Addie. She was staring at me with empty desperation. She needed me … she was *counting on me* to help her.

This time, I wouldn't let any of them down.

"Head to my house." I set my jaw squarely and used Darkness's anger, bubbling just below the surface, to drive me forward. "Addie, you need to think up an excuse for all of us to be gone for a few days."

Jack turned away from the window and raised one eyebrow at me.

"We're going after my dad."

Mia nodded and put the car in gear before Jack even had a chance to shake his head, but I was done hearing his arguments and excuses. I cut him off before he got to speak.

"Anyone who wants to come is welcome. If you don't think it's a good idea"—I lowered my gaze and felt my jaw clench tight out of instinct—"just stay out of my way."

Jack didn't respond, but he closed his eyes and frowned.

"You said my dad was safe as long as he didn't give them the formula." I felt my fear building. "If this means they have it now … isn't he in real danger?"

Jack opened his eyes and stared at me hard. He didn't answer. He didn't have to.

"I'm going," I repeated.

"You don't even know where the Taker base is." Jack looked exasperated and a little scared.

"Thor and Cooper do." I nudged Finn sitting between us. "Even this Taker probably does. I'm sure I can find someone to point me there, if you won't."

Even if I wasn't stupid enough to ask a Taker to walk me into their headquarters, it still wasn't an empty threat. The way Jack had described it, the Takers would be happy to trap me to ensure my dad's continued cooperation. I knew what I was risking, and it only took one look at the blanket and ropes wound around my best friend's body to know it was worth it.

I ignored Jack's slack-jawed expression, pulled my phone out of my pocket, and dialed my mom's phone. It was after seven; she should be leaving any minute now.

"Hello?" I could hear keys jangling in the background from the second she picked up the phone.

"Hey, Mom." I made an effort to sound way more tired than I actually was.

"Good morning, early bird." Her smile came through her voice even over the phone. "I didn't know you could dial a phone this early on a Saturday morning. You're always full of surprises."

"I wanted to ask you..." The lie started to roll off my tongue before I even thought about it. Lying came so naturally to me now, without thought or really any effort. It was a habit, and I didn't even know why I did it. It often didn't work out well for me in the end. But I couldn't tell Mom the whole truth about this... it was too much right now, and I knew if she understood she'd never let me go. Yet maybe this could be a first step to a change with her, too. "Mom, is it all right if I spend a couple of days camping with Finn and Jack? There's something I need to do. I'll take my phone and I promise a full and complete explanation as soon as I get back."

She hesitated and the sound of her motions in the background stopped. "What's going on? Can I help?"

"You can't help. Not yet. Remember when I told you I wasn't on drugs, Mom?" I spoke fast, but as honestly as I could. "This is like that, and I need you to trust me. I promise to answer any question you have when I get back. Just please let me do this."

Then she asked the one question I couldn't answer truthfully. "Are you sure you'll be safe?"

I knew I couldn't hesitate, so I just did my best to put a smile in my voice as I responded. "Everything will be okay, Mom."

It was silent on the other end of the line for one–two–three, and then I heard the keys jangling again. "Okay, honey. Please call me often. Be smart, be careful, and you and Finn take care of each other."

I glanced at the lump of blankets next to me and felt my stomach drop. "I promise."

When I hung up the phone, I leaned over the front seat and touched Mia's shoulder. "Park up the street and I'll make sure she's gone before I wave you in to the garage."

"Okay."

When I sat back, Jack was staring at me, his lips in a grim line. "I don't understand. What do you think you're going to get out of going there?"

"If my dad is the one that did this to Finn … " I looked down at my hands and rubbed them hard along my knees before glancing up and straight into Addie's eyes. "Then he's the one who is going to help me undo it."

We pulled into the back of a grocery store on the way home to give Mom a few extra minutes to leave the house. Addie and Mia ran in to grab some breakfast and provisions for our trip.

Jack still hadn't told us where we were going, but he did give a noncommittal grunt when we asked him what we'd need, followed by, "We won't need much."

As planned, Mom was gone by the time we got to my house. We brought Finn in and Jack escorted him to the restroom with a wicked-looking knife held against his back. I'd jumped a big step away when Jack had pulled it out of his boot.

"I like to keep a few surprises to myself." Jack shrugged, held the knife directly in front of Finn's nose to make sure he got a good look, and then walked him into the bathroom.

Addie was on the phone with her mom, telling her about the camping trip we had planned and how excited we all were. Her mom sounded a little concerned about Jack coming and seemed to ask more than a few questions.

"No, it isn't like that, I promise. We are *all* just friends." She glanced over her shoulder and I pretended not to notice, staring straight down at the eggs I was cooking.

After gaining approval, she hung up and walked over, resting her hand on my arm. "How can I help?"

I ignored the way her simple touch made me feel like my skin was on fire. "Grab tortillas, cheese, and salsa from the fridge."

She and Mia helped me put together some breakfast burritos. Jack volunteered to keep Finn under control while he ate. He pulled a chair up directly behind Finn's and kept his knife in view as I tied Finn's feet together. Finn kicked me in the side of the head once, and pushed back his chair hard in an effort to knock Jack over, but the knife whizzed past his ear so fast it left a small gash there before burying itself in the side of one of my Mom's cupboards.

I whistled low and rubbed the side of my head as I went to pull the knife out. It had left a slice in the wood, but it wasn't that noticeable unless you were looking for it. "There's one more thing to explain to Mom when we get back."

Jack pulled another knife out of his other boot and put it against Finn's throat. "Don't do that again or next time I'll forget to miss. These guys are attached to Finn. He and I really didn't get along all that well ... get my point?"

Finn sighed, nodded, and took a giant bite of his burrito.

Addie sat down next to him and it seemed like she was trying to stare a hole through his forehead. "You won't tell us who you are? I'm getting tired of thinking of you as my fake brother."

Finn scowled. "What good does it do you to know my name?"

"Do you know us?" Mia asked, swallowing another bite. "Would we recognize your name?"

"Maybe ... some of you might." Finn stared down and I noticed this weird twitch he'd developed now that his hands were free. He kept trying to tuck his hair behind his right ear ... only it was too short.

"You're that girl!"

He looked up, startled, then immediately looked down and I knew I was right. "No."

"Yes, you're the girl from the car in the parking lot with Thor and Cooper. Are you Thor's…girlfriend or something?"

"Eww—no! And his name is Joey Thornton, not Thor!" Finn growled down into his plate and stopped his hand midway to tucking the nonexistent hair again.

"You're a girl?" Addie looked disgusted. "Why would you want to be in my brother's body?"

"I didn't. It was supposed to be a trial run." Finn looked ready to explode. "It was supposed to be you or Mia. Getting Finn was an accident."

I couldn't help but chuckle. Finn would've enjoyed the irony. "If I remember right, you were pretty." I gestured to Finn's long form before finishing. "This must've been quite the disappointment."

Finn shrugged, although I caught a hint of a blush rising in his cheeks, which just felt weird. "Gender doesn't really matter to us. I've taken men, women, kids; it doesn't matter. He's healthy. If things go well, I can get a few good years out of him."

"Before what? You trade up?" Mia folded her arms and if her eyes could shoot daggers, this Taker would be toast.

"Yes."

"So you do know how to get out of Finn's body?" I leaned closer.

Finn seemed to have realized his—her—mistake and focused down on his—her—food. Screw it; the gender was getting too confusing. This wasn't Finn, but for now that's how I'd think of him.

Jack was the one to answer. "If your dad's predictions are correct, the only way to get this Taker out would be if Fi—if the host body dies."

That obviously wasn't an option. I needed more information. "So, does it feel different when you take Eclipse?" I asked. "I mean, what your body does while you're in Finn's?"

Instead of answering, Finn pushed his plate away. "I'm done. Did you guys feel like tying me up again?"

"That's the one thing I don't understand about their plan ... " Jack frowned, handed me his knife, and picked up the rope. "Their bodies can't be just anywhere. I'm sure they've planned for this."

"What if this Taker's body dies?" I leaned back in my chair and stared hard into Finn's eyes. "I know what she looks like. What if we find her body and ... " I didn't need to finish. Everyone knew the choice we'd have to make.

Jack shrugged. "I don't know. There hasn't been a lot of experimenting with this, but it's possible that they'd both die, or Finn would be left brain-dead from the trauma. Your dad would have a better guess." He tied up Finn's hands then picked up the gag.

"Wait." Mia leaned in close, staring into Finn's eyes. "Chloe? Is that you?"

Finn didn't answer, but it would have been hard to miss the momentary flicker of panic.

"You know her?" I asked.

Mia sighed. "I thought I did, but she wasn't like this. She's Thor's half-sister."

"His name is *not* Thor!" Finn yelled, leaned forward and biting down on the gag, ripping it free from Jack's hands. Then Finn glared at Jack until he shrugged, walked around, and secured it firmly in place.

———

We packed everything, including the Taker, into the car. It seemed fine for me to drive since Finn had been pretty cooperative ever since Jack's knife-throwing demonstration. I turned around in the seat and looked at Jack.

"It's time to decide, Jack. You tell me. Are you going to help us get into the base safely, or should I drop you at the nearest bus stop and have another chat with our friend here?" I gestured toward Finn, and he glanced over at Jack with a little spark in his eyes.

"Fine. I didn't think it was possible, but you're even more stubborn than your dad." Jack sighed, rubbing his hands over his eyes. "We're heading to the old Benton Air Force base, five hours north of here. Your dad always thought the best place to hide was right under your enemy's nose...so that's exactly where he hid you."

TWENTY-FOUR

By the time we'd stopped for gas, it was nearly noon when we got on the road. Jack insisted on taking over the driving, and he put Addie in the front seat. When he'd whispered something to her outside the car, I'd done my best not to react. I needed better control, and I was learning... but that didn't stop me from thinking of a hundred ways I could bend him into a pretzel.

Once we were on our way, Addie leaned over the seat and looked straight at me. There was still some reservation in her eyes, still some fear, but the trust and faith seemed be returning.

"Jack wants us to sleep."

I blinked and glanced over at Jack's back. "Huh?"

"I've been in her dreams recently, you haven't." Jack kept his eyes on the road, but I could see from the way he gripped the steering wheel that he wasn't thrilled about this. "You've convinced me to take you into a hornets' nest ... but I want you to be as strong and prepared as she can make you before we get there."

Addie waited for me to look in her eyes again, then leaned back her seat and closed her eyes. Finn, sitting between Mia and me, was still very tied up and already had his eyes closed, although I doubted he was sleeping. Either way, he wasn't in a position to make much trouble. I leaned back and closed my eyes. Even with all the adrenaline in my system, I was pulled into Addie's dream within minutes.

———————

The dream was quiet ... so quiet I thought I might be in the Hollow until I turned and saw Addie. She smiled a little and looked straight at me. I wasn't touching her, but it was clear that it didn't matter anymore. She could see me anyway. I could tell already that she was a much quicker study of what Jack had taught her than I'd been.

We stood in a park with dark green grass and tall trees. Addie looked up and a slight breeze ruffled the leaves above us and cooled our faces. She walked over to a spot at the base of one particularly large tree and sat, crossing her legs and leaning against it.

"So I guess you finally get to see what a Builder can do." She patted the grass in front of her with her open palm.

"I guess so." I walked closer, but hesitated before sitting down. I believed she knew what she was doing, but for some reason it still didn't feel like it would work. The doors that had always kept me from my own sleep in everyone's dreams but Mia's were still there. I could feel them. And as long as they were there, I knew this wouldn't work.

"Building requires a lot of trust, and . . . " Addie looked down for a second.

"And you don't trust me anymore." My words came out as deflated as I felt. Addie, the only person who'd always believed I was inherently good, wasn't sure of me anymore.

"You've given me a lot of reasons not to." She sighed and then took my hand. "But I believe I still can. I was talking about the trust you have to have in me."

"Of course I trust you."

"I have to get inside your head to do this." Addie leaned back against the tree and watched me close. "You've never known what that's like before. You'll have no secrets from me, and I know how much you value those . . . "

My world felt oddly upside down, but I just nodded. "I told you before that I was done keeping secrets from you. I meant it."

She leaned forward and patted her lap. "Lay down, put your head here, and try to relax."

I froze for a minute and all I could picture was this same situation, but with Jack's head on Addie's lap. My mind replayed the images of them kissing on the front porch. Instead of anger, now, all I felt was pain. Addie was the first girl I'd ever loved, and my own lack of control had driven her away.

But I wouldn't lose Finn, too. No matter what. I couldn't.

Resting my head gently in her lap, I looked up as she leaned over me and smoothed my hair out of my face. Her lips kept twitching into a frown and I knew this was hard for her, too.

"You sure you're up for this?" I asked.

"Shut up." She gave me a slight smile, then placed her fingertips on the sides of my head and closed her eyes. "Close your eyes and try to sleep."

I obeyed, and at first I didn't feel anything. Then it was tiny motions, like small, gentle probes were moving around in my brain. Touching on memories, on my weak spots and my strong ones—every spot she touched released a memory, and we relived my past together. I was frustratingly, achingly, terrifyingly vulnerable. I was exposed in a way I'd never been before, and I forced myself not to fight it.

She saw Dr. Freeburg's dream for herself, and I could almost feel her shrinking back from me. She saw the way Darkness controlled me sometimes and how helpless and terrifying those moments had been. She brought out the guilt I felt about the people I'd hurt or even thought I'd hurt. We both felt raw emotion when she pulled out my memory of dragging Finn's bleeding, unconscious body out of the fire and into the snow. Then she saw the conversation where I'd told Finn everything—including how I felt about her, and the conversation I'd had with my mom about how she might be better off with Jack. Jack telling me to give her a reason to let go of me, and the ways I'd thought of doing it.

She saw my version of the time I'd saved her on the swing when we were kids. I relived the way I'd looked for her after Finn and I came inside, my heart stopping in my chest when I saw her tangled in the swing, trying to make myself bigger than I was to shield her shivering body as the storm stung my skin with hard rain and bits of hail, the way my fingers ached as I worked and worked to free her long hair while lightning and thunder rocked the sky above us. I'd felt absolute panic and I knew that even if I had to break the chain that held her trapped, I'd find a way to do it. Last, she felt my heart shred apart all over again when she brought out the memory of when I'd told her I loved her and she told me it didn't matter.

My face was wet with tears and I opened my eyes to see that some were hers. Her eyes were still closed and heartbreak was written across her face. As she bent over me, concentrating on my pain and past, she looked more beautiful than I'd ever seen her. Then I closed my eyes and she went through every memory, one by one, and closed the wounds and scars my life had left me with. She took her own certainties that I was strong, that I was smart, that I was brave, and wrapped them around my fears. Again and again, she touched the broken pieces until they were healed, the pain smothered and put out like a campfire being buried in the warm earth.

Her touch became hot like a branding iron, but it didn't hurt. And she moved quickly now; I could feel the strength draining from her, into me. She continued, forming new bridges in my brain. My thoughts came easier and clearer, my heart slowed its rapid pace, my guilt started to ease. She didn't erase the doubts I held about myself; instead, she paired each concern with pieces of her faith in me. I could see both sides now. Darkness and myself. The person I was afraid I was, deep down, next to the man she thought I could become.

The doors in my mind were flung wide, and Addie's fingers caressed the sides of my face as I drifted off to sleep.

———————

I woke to a soft nudge of my arm. Sunlight still fell on my face, so I knew I couldn't have been out that long, but it could've been centuries from the way I felt. Everything about me felt better, stronger, sharper than I could ever remember feeling. My muscles didn't ache, and my mind felt alert and aware on a level above any I'd ever experienced.

And this was only after one dream with Addie.

Suddenly I understood what Jack had said about Mia. I'd be forever grateful to her, and she had absolutely saved my life, but this was something entirely different. This was like starting over. Addie had undone all the damage, the havoc I'd wreaked upon myself both physically and emotionally. She'd made me stronger than I ever knew I could be.

Opening my eyes, I sat up straight and looked down at the hand that had nudged me. Mia jerked back and jumped, my sudden movement obviously catching her off guard.

"Sorry." I whispered because Addie hadn't moved yet. "How long were we out?"

"Almost two hours." Jack was watching me closely in the rearview mirror. "Looks like it did what I'd hoped."

I nodded. "Yeah, wow."

"I told you."

"I know."

Then he glanced at Addie's still form for a moment

before turning his eyes back to the road. I saw resignation in his face, and he kept his voice low when he spoke again. "She's going to be exhausted after that. Let her sleep."

"It—did it hurt her?" With Addie's seat leaned back, I could see her clearly when I sat forward a little. I brushed a stray curl from her cheek with one finger and saw dried tear tracks on her face.

"Not physically. It's like when we alter dreams, but about twice as exhausting." He met my eyes in the rear-view mirror. "And I'm guessing you needed a lot of work done ... so let her sleep."

I watched Addie's eyelids flutter for a moment and wasn't entirely sure she wasn't already awake, but I sat back in my seat and stared at the scenery passing outside the window. Every detail and nuance of the world around me felt more vivid than ever. It was like it had all slowed down, or I'd just finally caught up with it. I felt wide-awake, quick, and strong ... all thanks to the girl I'd shared all my secrets with.

————————

The sun was setting by the time we got within a few miles of the base. Addie had been leaning against the passenger window since she woke up. I'd thanked her a few times and she'd squeezed my hand in response, but she hadn't spoken.

Now that Jack was finally on board and everyone was awake, he'd spent the last couple of hours telling us the lay-out of the underground bunkers that the NWS had set up as their North American headquarters, back before the Takers had wiped out many of them and taken control of the organization. Jack had never been here either, but my dad had spent hours going over the schematics with him in case he was ever captured. Our biggest concern was that they'd spent all their time going over how to sneak out ... never how to sneak in.

The closer we got, the more nervous Jack seemed. He kept twitching and rubbing at the patch on his jacket.

"I have a question." When I spoke, he lurched forward a bit before meeting my eyes in the rearview mirror.

"You have a lot more than one."

"You obviously know my dad better than I do." I was happy the bitterness didn't come out in my voice the way it had in the past. Maybe Addie had helped heal that a little, too. "Why would he cave in to their demands, after all this time? Why give them what they want?"

Jack slowly shook his head. "That's—your guess is as good as mine."

"One more."

His hands clenched tighter on the wheel and he waited.

"If my dad taught you all this, he obviously knew every way he could escape." I waited while Jack turned onto an old highway that meandered its way over small hills and along suburban streets. "So why hasn't he escaped?"

Jack looked in the rearview mirror again and his eyes seemed filled with emotion for an instant before it all went behind a wall and he stared at the road in front of him. "Same answer."

———

We parked the car next to a low-lying building just up the hill from the main base. The squat, dilapidated stone structure sat in a wooded area and obviously hadn't been touched in at least a decade. Everything inside had been cleaned out, and the shelves that lined the back wall were covered in a thick layer of dust. We put Finn in a back room that locked from the outside, and then Jack hid behind a nearby bush with some binoculars, looking everything over before the daylight was completely gone to see if he could locate a back entry he'd noticed on some of the schematics. We set Addie and Mia up with some water and supplies, along with the keys to the car.

Addie still hadn't spoken a word since she awoke, and I was starting to worry that seeing all my secrets had been too much. Maybe she was too horrified and she couldn't see me the same anymore. Maybe somehow giving me all her faith had drained it from her. As amazing as I felt, I was starting to wonder if letting her inside my mind had been a bad idea.

I held out one of Jack's knives out to her. "I know we don't want to hurt Finn, but he'd haunt me to the end of my days if I let his body hurt you … okay?"

Mia stood up from a desk and brushed the dust off her jeans as she walked toward the door. "I'll—uh—go see how Jack is doing."

Addie took the knife and laid it on the desk beside her with a slight nod, then rubbed her hands together. She looked uncomfortable, like she didn't know what to say to me anymore. The last thing I wanted was to make her feel that way. My secrets were hard for me; they must be impossible for her. Even though it broke me in half, I knew Jack was right. Addie deserved so much better. Leaving her alone seemed like the kindest thing I could do.

I started backing toward the door. "And if we aren't back by morning..."

She looked up at me. Dark circles had appeared below her eyes and tears ran down her cheeks. She growled so low and threatening that I froze mid-step. "Don't you *dare* do that to me."

"Addie..."

She hopped off the desk, ran at me, and wrapped both arms around my neck. Her body pressed so tight against mine that I staggered a few steps backward. Her lips found mine and she kissed me like it was the only thing she had left in her. Wrapping both arms around her, I lifted her off the floor and squeezed her so tight I knew I had to stop or she might not be able to breathe. My hands ran slowly up her back and curled around her hair. Then I slowed down, kissing her, teasing her, because if this was the last thing I ever experienced before walking into the den of lions, I was going to enjoy it. I kissed her lips, throat, cheek, and ear, and breathed in the scent of citrus that was so much a part of Addie to me.

When I pulled back and kissed the tears off her cheeks, she grabbed my face with her hands and stared me straight in the eye. Every emotion she'd always kept so carefully hidden was exposed and raw for me to see. It stole my breath away.

"I love you, Parker. I've loved you since we were kids and you saved me from the storm." She gave a soft sob and held one of my hands to her face. "I've loved you when you were my friend and taught me to play Uno and Mario

Kart and how to throw a frisbee. I've even loved you when you acted crazier than any guy has a right to act."

Leaning in, I kissed her forehead, and she pulled me close and buried her face against my neck.

"More than anything, though, I love you right now, when you show me who you really are and risk everything to save your best friend." She kissed the skin of my neck below my ear and her voice dropped to a soft whisper. "Promise me that you'll come back to me. Promise me I won't miss finding all the other ways I can love you."

I tipped her head back and kissed her. I kissed her for all the times I should have been kissing her but hadn't because of my own stupid mistakes and a world of misunderstandings. I kissed her for all the times I hoped to kiss her from here on out.

Then I drew back, kissing her nose and her forehead before pulling her against my chest. "I love you, Addie."

She squeezed her arms around me and snuggled up into my neck. "And ... ?"

"And ... I promise." It was the first lie—okay, half-truth—in weeks that I didn't feel at all bad about.

———

Jack had timed the security patrol that checked the perimeter of the occupied part of the base. They passed by every fifteen minutes, and it took them seven minutes to get out of earshot from the entry point Jack had found for us. Much of the base was underground, and the forgotten hatch we'd be entering through looked half-buried in dirt and overgrown weeds.

Jack said that the later it got, the more relaxed security would be. We waited until the clock reached three a.m., and then watched the patrol make one full round to be certain the timing hadn't changed. They were still like clockwork. Since they went in a circle, we'd wait for them to pass and then we'd have six minutes to get down to the hatch, open it, get inside, and close it before they came into range around the back side of the base. Also, we had no idea if the hatch was sealed shut, locked, or possibly completely rotted.

No problem.

As soon as the guards passed, I checked my watch and we waited. The seconds ticked by slowly...then the minutes. By the time all seven had passed, my chest felt as though I'd been holding my breath the whole time. We scrambled down the hill toward the hatch as silently as we could. It was sheltered from the main path by a squat building that looked like it used to be some sort of supply depot. The metal on the building's doors was tinged with rust, but through the windows I could see shelves that were currently in use. One wall across from the door shimmered with bits of silver.

Freezing in place, I turned and waved Jack over. Rubbing the dust off one window pane, I cupped my hands over my eyes and peered closer. A small smile spread across my face as I recognized a pegboard—on each nail hung a ring with a small plastic tag and a single key. We'd spotted a parking lot full of vans and trucks not far from the hatch.

Jack gave a quick nod toward the keys, and I knew he'd seen them too. I tapped on my watch and we kept moving.

Only three minutes left, and we weren't even at the hatch yet. We both sprinted across the last few feet. Rust coated the edges of the metal platform and a thick layer of dust and dirt caked every square inch of the hatch. The lever was chipped and eroded. We brushed back some of the dirt and cobwebs around the old metal. Good news—the entrance obviously wasn't used much, so we probably wouldn't get caught immediately when we got inside. Bad news—we wouldn't get in at all if the lever broke off when we tried to open it.

Less than two minutes left.

Jack squatted down and pulled to the right with all his weight, trying to get the bolt to release so we could pull up the hatch. The lever didn't break, but it didn't budge either. I circled to the opposite side of Jack and, wrapping both hands firmly around the lever, I pushed. Sweat beaded up on my forehead and my heart pounded against my chest. It gave an inch... two, and then made an awful screeching sound and froze up again.

Sixty seconds left.

I pushed harder, grunting and straining at the effort as the rough edges dug into my palms. It still wasn't moving. Jack looked at me, eyes huge, afraid. Now was the time. We had to hide and try to find another entry point, or give it one more try and risk being caught. I sat down and pulled back, gave one massive kick against the lever with both feet. It came unstuck, and Jack fell backward when it swung free. We lifted the hatch and it released an awful squeak. Inky blackness was the only thing I could see down the hole.

Less than thirty seconds.

Jack jumped into the darkness without so much as a glance at where he'd land. I followed behind. My left hand caught on a rung near the top of the hole, which nearly jerked my arm out of my socket, but I didn't make a sound. I pulled the hatch shut and locked it.

Then I listened and waited.

According to my watch, we'd taken too long. The security patrol could have been close enough to hear us, but I didn't know if they had. And if they had, I didn't know if they'd recognize what it was they'd heard. I listened, but all I could hear was the echoing sound of my own breath, the pounding in my ears.

Then my vision filled with light. I let go of the rung on instinct and fell right on top of Jack. But the light wasn't coming from the top; it was coming from Jack's flashlight, and I'd just smashed it. We sat at the bottom of the hole and I heard Jack moving around and banging the flashlight a few more times, but nothing happened.

"Well, that's perfect." His voice echoed strangely, like he'd somehow managed to be on all sides of me at once.

"Tell me we brought two."

"I could, but it would be a lie."

I got to my feet, feeling along the walls. Everything around me felt like cold metal and I could hear the scurrying of rodents from somewhere off to the left. "Did you see anything while the light was on?"

"Enough to know that this tunnel goes both directions."

"Do you know which way to go?"

He breathed out in a big gush and I could actually hear him scratching his head. "I'm a little turned around from the fall...but I'm pretty sure it's that way."

"Uh...you know I can't see you, right?"

He grabbed my shoulder, found my chin, and pointed my face to the left. I jerked back from his grasp. "I've got it."

"Besides, that's where I can hear the rats." I heard him start walking. "And rats follow food."

We walked for two minutes, feeling along the walls until we came to a door. I cursed under my breath. What I wouldn't give for a window about right now. I listened intently, but couldn't hear anything on the other side. Jack turned the handle; it wasn't locked, but it wasn't quiet either. Apparently everything in old abandoned bases creaked. Who needed an alarm when every door had a loud screech to warn you about intruders? He pushed it open a crack and light spilled into our tunnel.

I listened for rushing footsteps or shouts, but there was nothing but the faint buzzing of fluorescent lights. Jack pushed it open further and peeked his head in. He waved for me to stay put while he stepped into the room. He was gone for one second—two—three—and then opened the door wide and smiled.

"Welcome to the old NWS headquarters, a.k.a. Taker Central. Don't expect a warm welcome."

Stepping out beside him, it took my eyes a minute to adjust to the light. The room we were in was mostly empty and about the size of our two-car garage. In the very center two power cords hung from the ceiling, and below them sat electronic equipment of every shape and size. I recognized a couple of machines from trips to the hospital. They measured heart rate and blood pressure, stuff like that. I didn't know what the rest did, but it seemed pretty clear that it was all medical equipment. Two walls were formed of metal, while the other two were partitions made from white sheets that hung from the ceiling. Given the partitions, it was impossible to tell the actual size of this room, but it was clearly massive.

Walking to the white sheet on the right, I peered around one edge without touching it. This next room was the same, except it only had one metal wall; the section we'd come in from was in a corner.

We walked through section after section like this. We'd passed through a dozen, maybe more, before I heard the first voice.

" ... does it seem to be going?"

A second, more nasal voice responded. "She's been in almost a full week."

"Any adverse reactions?"

"None. Her vitals all look strong."

"And the host?"

"She's checked in with Cooper a couple of times and seems to be adjusting well."

Pushing away Jack's hand, I peeked around the edge of the curtain and saw a single hospital bed in the next room. Two men stood beside it, one in a suit coat and the other in some kind of camouflage military vest. They continued to talk about pulse and brain wave activity. The one in the suit belonged with the nasal voice I'd heard and was clearly the person with medical training. The other seemed to be in charge—of the Takers, the experiment, the whole base? I couldn't tell, but he projected a clear sense of authority.

Even with all that, the most interesting person to me was the one in the bed. The one hooked up to over a dozen tubes, wires, and monitors... I couldn't see her face, but I didn't think I needed to. Chloe had told us she was the first Taker to do a trial of Eclipse. We'd just found where they were keeping her body.

And it looked like they were prepared to handle many, many more Takers just like her.

TWENTY-FIVE

As Jack found a path through more of the partitions, I mem-
orized each and every step. I'd already made up my mind.
When we left, we were taking Chloe with us. Red-hot anger
flowed through my every cell, and I fought with each breath
to keep Darkness locked up. Even without his influence, a
big part of me wanted to end this Taker if we couldn't save
Finn. Why should she live when she'd cost him his life?

I followed close behind Jack as he led the way out of the
medical center and into the main halls of the base. He seemed
to have figured out exactly where we were, because he was taking each turn with increasing speed and confidence. Except
for slowing to check each hall and room for people, we were
making great progress. The halls were mostly empty. Jack had
explained that most of the Night Walkers didn't actually live
here, so they were operating under a skeleton crew at night.

We came to a desk with a security guard sitting at it.

We waited, watching for the opportunity to get past him. He had a tablet out and was staring at some old TV rerun. Jack gave me a nod and I snuck into a room behind us and knocked over a stack of empty boxes. When the guard came in to investigate, Jack wrapped one arm around his neck. But the guard was stronger than he looked. He rammed himself backward, slamming Jack into the wall. My heart sped up in my chest when I saw him grab for the gun on his belt, and I moved much faster than I'd expected. The dream with Addie had really worked wonders. I hooked my arm through his, pushed it back, and kept the gun out of his reach. Then I pulled it from the holster and slid it across the floor. Jack still clung on, and the guard was turning purple...then faded to a pale blue before finally collapsing to the floor.

Just as he stopped struggling, Jack held one finger to his lips and we caught our breath, listening. It took only a second before I heard it too. Footsteps crept through the hall outside our room. They were deliberately soft, and then there was a whispered voice. I couldn't make out the words, but the voice still made my spine stiffen. It meant two things. There was more than one person—

And they knew we were here.

I stood closest to the door and held my breath as I heard someone get close. As soon as he reached around the doorway to flip on the light switch, I grabbed his wrist and jerked him into the room. I barely processed the shocked look on his young face—he wasn't much older than me—before I swung hard and fast. My arm vibrated as my fist connected with his cheekbone. My knuckles were throbbing. When he fell back, he hit his head against a shelf and collapsed to the floor.

I spun in time to see Jack knocking a walkie-talkie from an older guard's hand. He reached for a gun at his waist, but Jack kicked the front of his right kneecap and the man screamed and crumpled like wadded-up paper. In two movements, so fast my eyes could barely keep up, Jack grabbed the gun from the guard's belt and slammed the butt down against the top of his head. Then he moved over to the guard I'd decked, who was moaning, and knocked him out as well.

And then there was silence. Jack picked up the walkie-talkie, turned it down almost all the way, and clipped it to his belt. He stood at the door, listening intently for noise in the hallway as I pulled the guards into the back of the storage room and tied them up with some rope we'd brought in my backpack. I shoved them back behind a row of shelves.

The entire process had taken about two minutes. Jack was more than well trained; he was more than efficient. Seeing him in here…the way he never freaked out or seemed scared…he was like a machine.

Probably a good thing I'd never let Darkness convince me to get in a full-on fist-fight with Jack. He was very good and could probably kill me with his pinky or something…if he wanted to.

Finally, we came to a maze of hallways where every door was barred. My heart skipped a beat and I stopped, my feet glued to the floor. We'd been in such a hurry, and I'd been so worried about Finn and getting inside and everything else we were doing that I'd never stopped to think about what would actually happen when I found Dad.

I was about to see him for the first time in nearly five years. I'd recognize him, I knew, because I'd seen him when Jack had made him appear in Mom's dream. But would Dad know me? Would he recognize me? I'd changed a lot since I was eleven.

I didn't even want to think about the other question hovering in the back of my mind:

Did he even want to see me?

Jack continued moving down the hallway, peeking through the small square windows into each cell. He'd made it around the corner before he noticed he'd lost me and came back. His jaw was tight, and I was suddenly nervous about what we might find waiting in these cells.

"Come on." His words were barely a whisper across the air. He grabbed my wrist, pulling me along beside him until I started moving of my own volition.

We worked together. He went left, I went right, checking every cell. The conditions I saw inside made my stomach turn. Most of the cells had no light or only a single bulb hanging overhead. They were dank and cold, with shivering prisoners in horrifying conditions. Each cell was about half as big as my bedroom, with only the barest necessities inside: a sink and a hole in the corner that served as a toilet. Very little else. Most prisoners didn't even have cots, although I saw a thin blanket occasionally. One after another … there were people in all of them.

As I checked the next one on my side, my feet halted

their forward motion. My gut clenched tight with fury and sadness.

The little blond girl was curled in a tiny ball in the corner of her cot. She held one corner of her ragged blanket between her fingers and tugged on the loose threads with small trembling fingers. I recognized her immediately. It was the seven-year-old who'd gone missing; we'd talked to her parents. It was Audrey Martin.

I grabbed Jack's elbow and pointed into the cell. When he peeked in, his shoulders hunched forward. I whispered, "Why would they take her? She's so young…"

"Some of these people are probably other Watchers or suspected Builders, but most are probably just regular people who got in a Taker's way or served a purpose. At her age, any Night Walker ability wouldn't have developed yet… I'd bet she's leverage. The parents must have something the Takers want." Jack shook his head and shrugged.

The Takers had caused even more trouble than we knew. I wondered how many of their prisoners were people we'd seen reported missing on the news. From the stories Jack had told me about Takers killing suspected Builders, I wondered if any of the kidnapping victims hadn't survived even long enough to be thrown into this hellhole.

Jack moved on and gestured for me to follow him, but I didn't move.

He walked back and looked into Audrey's room again before closing his eyes tight and frowning. "Your dad first… then we'll figure out the rest."

My jaw tightened and I gave him a reluctant nod before moving on to the next room on my side.

We kept checking left and right, again and again. I tried not to look at the people once I realized they weren't Dad. Not looking too close made it hurt less every time I walked away. I'd never seen, never even imagined, anything like this. No one deserved this.

When Jack got to the last room on his side of the hall, he stopped and looked back at me. I could tell from the look in his eye, from the way he hesitated, that he'd found what we were looking for.

And now he looked scared.

Stepping around him, I took a long deep breath, braced myself for anything I might see, and peeked through the window. The room was dark; there wasn't even a light bulb hanging overhead, just a barren socket. I could barely make out a form in the back corner on the cot and I didn't know how Jack could be sure it was Dad, but when I glanced at him, he just gave me a grim nod and waited.

My hands were shaking as I wrapped my fingers around the door release and pried it up. The noise it made wasn't overly loud, but it wasn't exactly quiet either. I checked the hall around us and listened, but I didn't hear anyone coming. So I counted to three, then pulled the door open and stepped inside.

If possible, inside the room was even quieter than the hallway. I crept closer, not wanting to scare him even more than our presence already would. I heard Jack slip into the room behind me and lodge something at the bottom of the door so that it closed most of the way, but not completely.

Seconds felt like minutes, or possibly even hours, passing as I crept closer to the form on the bed. Time didn't exist, because my heart was pounding too fast and hard for it to keep up. I kept waiting for movement, but the light was too dim. I couldn't make out anything. Flashbacks of Dr. Freeburg lying dead in his bed didn't help, and I swallowed back the bile that rose in my throat. This was not the same thing. He was not going to be dead when I finally found him. My dad was alive ... he had to be.

Jack's breath was heavy right behind me and when I looked over my shoulder, I saw sweat on his forehead as he stared at the form on the bed. It wasn't hot here; if anything, it was very cool down in this bunker. Was he as nervous as I was?

Then a shadow broke away from the far wall and slammed into Jack so hard I actually heard the breath leave his body. He was tall, taller than Jack, taller than me. He had Jack on the floor squirming under the weight across his throat in seconds ... no, pieces of seconds.

It was so fast my eyes couldn't follow the movement, but other than the gush of air from Jack and the thud when they hit the ground, it was nearly silent. Then the figure raised his face and the sliver of light caught on the light blue of my dad's eyes—my eyes—but the stark desperation in them reminded me more of Darkness's eyes. The thought chilled me to my core.

He stared up at me as he spoke two words that stole the air from my lungs. "Hello, son."

I blinked and he smiled, showing smile lines around his eyes that felt out of place on a face so similar to my own. When Dad looked back down at Jack, everything about him stiffened and he pressed harder on his neck. Jack's face faded from red to violet. Nothing that was happening made sense, but until it did, I wasn't going to let anyone die.

Grabbing my dad's shoulder, I jerked on it, but my movements were hesitant and he was too strong. It was barely enough to make him notice me.

"What are you doing?" His expression was incredulous as he turned his face up toward mine again.

"Me? What about you?" I finally snapped into action as Jack's eyes started to bulge out. Searching around me, I pulled the lump off the bed that we'd thought was a person ... it was strategically wadded-up clothes beneath a blanket. I grabbed a shirt and wrapped it across the front of my dad's shoulders, then took hold of the ends and leaned back with all my weight. Leveraging my body to pull Dad back just enough, I felt a little give, then an inch more ... and then I heard Jack gasp in a short breath of much-needed air.

This was not at all how I'd pictured our reunion, but I had to do something before Jack wasn't alive anymore to tell me his half of whatever the hell was going on here.

"Get off of him." I pulled harder and Dad glanced back at me, his expression beyond surprised. He looked flat-out shocked.

"Parker ..."

"Get off, *now*." I jerked him back hard again and inclined his head.

"Okay, fine." He eased off enough that Jack took a huge breath and started coughing, his face color returning to normal. But when I dropped the shirt, Dad didn't move any further. He looked very much like the version of himself that Jack had shown me in the dream—his dark hair long and wavy, his beard a little thicker—but there was a raggedness that hadn't been there before. It wasn't in his appearance, it was in his eyes. It was a crazed desperation I'd only seen one other place: in myself.

"I don't know what you think, Parker..."

I pointed down at Jack with my free hand and kept my voice low. "I don't know what *you* think. In fact, I don't know you at all, *Dad*..."

He flinched and I saw the pain I'd caused in his face. Darkness flared deep inside me, enjoying the punishment I was delivering, reveling in the fact that Dad deserved it. I swallowed hard, pushing Darkness down firmly behind his wall. Ignoring his angry bellowing, I went on, softening my tone.

"Look down at him." We both turned our eyes on Jack. His arms were by his side and tears rolled down his cheeks. He wasn't even trying to defend himself. "Does he look like someone you need to fight? Does he look like your enemy? What are you doing?"

Jack shook his head. "No, he's right, Parker. It's my fault he got caught. I ignored his warnings. I thought I knew better. I wanted to prove I *was* better." He took a deep, shuddering breath. "They used me to get him."

Dad leaned forward, his face and expression furious, but he didn't try to choke Jack again. His voice was a feral growl.

"That's all, huh? Don't you have more to confess to your brother?"

"M-my wha—" I knelt back from them in complete shock, but no one seemed to notice.

"No, that's all. What are you talking about?" Jack was physically trembling beneath him.

"No more lies."

This time Jack actually looked a little offended. "I'm not lying!"

"You practically gift-wrapped me for them!" Dad slammed the side of his fist against the ground next to Jack's head. "You called and told me they had you!"

"They were holding a gun to my head!" Jack spit out, pushing him off.

"But when I came, you weren't here." I could hear in Dad's voice, as he leaned back, that he was starting to doubt. "Instead, they had a whole army waiting to greet me."

"I only agreed to call you because *I knew you wouldn't come*!" Jack pushed Dad again and slid up the wall into a sitting position. It was silent for ten—twenty—thirty seconds before Jack uttered four words that were absolutely drenched in pain and regret. "*Why* did you come?"

"Why wouldn't I come?"

"You've been teaching me my entire life how to escape from here. You've gone over plan after plan after plan, and never once—not in one single scenario—did you ever come back to get me. It isn't like I'm…" His eyes darted to me, but he didn't finish his sentence.

Dad's back stiffened. "I didn't know if I could—if I'd be alive to come in after you. I wanted you to be prepared."

"Well done, *Danny*. You were very convincing," Jack scoffed. I saw Dad flinch, and for the first time ever the guy who was apparently my brother sounded just like me. "Because I didn't believe for even one second that you'd come after me. No matter what you heard on the phone."

"But they …" Dad's voice was soft now and full of pain. "Once I was caught, they said you'd joined their side. They showed me pictures of you with Parker. You were fighting. They told me you would kill him if I didn't make Eclipse. I thought you had, I thought you were—oh my God."

"The better question is …" Jack wiped tears off his cheeks angrily. "How could you have believed them?"

Dad lowered his face into both hands and shook it slowly back and forth. "He came back again, fiercer this time. I guess I haven't been thinking straight."

When Jack didn't respond, Dad scooted closer. "Jack, I'm so sorry. You know—you've seen how hard it can be for me to see the truth. Without you here to help … he's too strong." His voice dropped to a low whisper, packed with emotion. "I can't even say … I'm just … I'm so sorry. I should never have believed them. I know you would never …"

Jack closed his eyes tight before taking a deep breath that seemed to drain the fight out of him. "I know. I've seen. I understand."

"Super, because I don't." I was stunned, confused, and furious. I'd just found out the guy who'd been living in my house for weeks was secretly my brother. Obviously not full-blooded, because Mom didn't know it either. So Dad had cheated on her...or with her?

"You're my brother?" I glared from Jack to Dad and back again. Then a sudden realization dawned. "The Builder you mentioned? The one who died when you were twelve?"

Dad flinched and turned away. Jack gave a slight nod, but he looked braced for a fight.

"You said she was your sister."

"I lied." Jack didn't look away or even blink.

Every thought made me more and more furious, and Darkness was threatening to burst free. I took a deep breath and decided I didn't care. It didn't matter what ran in our blood. How could I call them family when they'd both left me alone with this maddening ability my entire life?

"It doesn't matter. I'm getting out of here as quickly as I can. I just need you to tell me how to undo what you did. All I care about right now is saving my best friend." I got to my feet and fought Darkness back, drawing in measured breaths and blowing them out between my teeth. Calm...I needed to stay calm.

Dad looked at Jack with wide eyes and Jack gave a soft nod. Climbing to his feet, Dad grabbed my arm and waited for me to face him. "I'm sorry, Parker. I had no idea you were...that you'd become Divided, like me. If I'd known you were so far in, I would've sent Jack sooner. I promise."

"You're like me? You could've saved me from this!" I jerked my arm out of his grasp. "How come the answer isn't ever 'I would've come myself'?"

Dad's face was wracked with pain. "It's complicated. Staying away kept you safe."

"Save it," I muttered. "You left me and stayed with your other son. Obviously it wasn't about keeping your kid safe."

Dad shook his head desperately, frantically. "His mom was dead and no one knew he was mine. That's why I made him call me Danny. If I'd had the option to give Jack another life than the one we had, I would've chosen it. If anything had happened to you or your mom because I was selfish and stuck around, I wouldn't ever have forgiven myself. You're a man now, Parker. Tell me there isn't anyone you would stay away from if it meant saving their lives."

Flinching, I looked at my feet and Jack answered for me, his voice exhausted. "He understands. He's mad and he doesn't want to, but he still understands."

"Gee, thanks, bro." I glared at him and spit out the last word like it disgusted me. My head was pounding, my heart ripping through my chest. I was losing control. This was all too much. Closing my eyes, I pictured Addie and Finn in my mind and tried to calm down.

"It's fighting him." Dad's voice was close, although his first words weren't directed at me. "Breathe, Parker. Don't give in."

It took me a couple of minutes, but the soothing voice of my dad along with thinking about my friends smoothed everything over. I opened my eyes.

"Thanks."

Dad squeezed my shoulder. The circles under his eyes were deep and scary dark, worse than mine had ever gotten. He reached out suddenly and wrapped one long arm around me and grabbed Jack with the other, crushing us both against his shoulders.

"I love you both." He rubbed his hand through my hair and I didn't try to pull away. "I've missed you more than I can explain, both of you."

I'd spent many long nights thinking of all the words I would use to hurt my dad if he ever walked back into my life. Each syllable I'd imagined uttering came back to me. The possibility was right here, within reach. And he still loved me. I could see it in his eyes, feel it in the way he hugged me. That love would make it so easy to hurt him the way he'd hurt me. The ultimate revenge, right here within my grasp, and I did the one thing I hadn't imagined doing. Without a second thought, I waved them all away and wrapped my arm around his back.

"I missed you too, Dad."

When he pulled back, there were tears in his eyes and he was smiling. The same smile I remembered from long before he left, from when I was much younger.

"Now, tell me what's going on with Finn?"

TWENTY-SIX

"You remember Finn?" I frowned and rubbed my thumb across my chin.

Dad's brow furrowed. "Of course. You've been friends forever. And I've kept an eye on you over the past five years, you know."

Jack shook his head like I was a lost cause. "I tried to explain that, but it's clear who got the brains in the family."

"Oh, right." I glared at Jack. "He was your spy."

Jack flinched at the word "spy" and I almost felt bad... almost. Then he turned to Dad. "Finn was the trial-run subject for Eclipse." His face was sober, but Dad's face drained of color completely.

"No ... no, it wasn't supposed to happen." He rubbed one hand through his hair, tugging on the ends like I'd always done. It was like watching a vision of me in the future. "I swore I'd never make that drug again, but when they told me you'd betrayed me, showed me pictures of you and Parker... told me you'd threatened to use everything I'd taught you against Parker... it was confusing. He made me believe them."

I knew now that Dad was talking about his own version of Darkness. I couldn't claim not to understand how terrifyingly real hallucinations could seem.

"Tell me you know how to reverse it," I said.

"I don't..." Dad turned toward me, his face stricken. "I don't think it's possible. Any options are untested, unsafe."

"We'll start there. Tell me what you know."

"It's not that simple. You'd need to do something that cannot be done." He was muttering under his breath as he turned away, arguing so low the only person it could've been with was himself. I made a mental note to be even more careful not to argue with Darkness in front of other people. It didn't—well, it didn't look good.

"Dad?" My voice was low but firm. "I'm not a kid anymore. You tell me what I have to do. I'll decide whether or not I can do it."

He stared at my face and raised one rough palm to my cheek. "Right... right. You're no child, but don't overestimate yourself. Even you can't do this."

"Tell me."

"It's like they always said, though..." Dad muttered to himself before walking back to his hiding spot by the back wall as though he'd completely forgotten we were here. "Sometimes it takes one who is broken to heal one who is not."

I turned to Jack, but I could see it in his eyes. Dad hadn't been watching out for me in this frame of mind. He wasn't really capable of it anymore—but Jack was. He'd been doing what Dad would've wanted, and he'd been handling this entire mess almost entirely on his own. Jack's eyes brimmed with tears that never quite fell as we watched our dad display how far a Watcher could fall.

My heart shattered for them both and for the first time, I didn't think about how they should have been around for me. I thought about how I should have been around for them. Was this the future for all Watchers, if we survived this long without a Builder? Or was it just for those like Dad and me? The Divided? For the first time, I wondered if it could be a blessing to die young.

Jack stepped silently to my side, both of us watching Dad's back.

"How long has he been like this?" My voice cracked a little.

"It's been a slow decline. He's had a harder and harder time fighting back."

"I'm not deaf." Dad whirled to face us, his eyes sharp. "And I don't know how much your brother has told you, but you've already been here too long and we must act quickly." He was speaking fast, but each word was quiet and clear. I was thrown again when he said the word "brother," but I moved past it, knowing that if what he was about to tell me was how to save Finn, it was much more important right now.

He stood beside his cot and patted his hands across the front of his dirty jeans and shirt like he was looking for something to write with ... never mind the fact that we had nothing to write *on*. "Finn's personality has gone quiet. It's being slowly overwritten by the Taker in his body. Like code in a computer, he's being replaced. The longer this continues, the more of him will be gone. Understand?"

I gave him a shaky nod. Finn was being erased from the inside out. How could I fight that? "Tell me how to stop it."

"This is a bad idea, Parker." He frowned and turned in a small circle beside his bed before staring at me again. "There is a good chance that you—that neither you nor Finn will survive it."

"I understand. Just tell me what you know." I placed one hand on his wrist to keep him focused.

"It's the Taker. You must find the Taker's body and bring it with you, but make sure you take the IV also. Once you unhook the drug, you'll have one hour to find a way to release Finn before the Taker's body will begin to shut down. Once that happens, they'll both be lost for good."

I frowned. "This sounds like more than an untested theory."

His brow furrowed. "This part we know for sure. They've done a couple of low-dose temporary tests to make sure Eclipse was safe before the official trial involving your friend."

"Okay..." I said, resisting the sinking feeling in my gut. Everything he said was only making it sound less like there was an answer.

"The dangerous part is this: only a mind stronger than the bond between the Taker and Finn will be able to break him loose. The only mind strong enough to do that..." He stopped fidgeting, grabbed one of my shoulders, and stared hard into my eyes. "Is one that's been Divided—and permanently rejoined again."

"That's possible?" My mind and mouth gaped at the ramifications. Would Darkness be gone? Could I be like before? For the first time in days, Darkness was utterly silent behind his wall.

Dad's frown deepened at the hopeful tone in my voice. "When a person like us becomes Divided, that new portion of personality stretches out into new space. It actually utilizes a different portion of the brain, which makes the mind stronger and the personality weaker."

"That makes sense." I spoke slowly, my mouth struggling to form words from my rampaging thoughts. "But has anyone ever actually been rejoined?"

"It's happened a couple of times." Dad looked down and closed his eyes like he was in sudden, intense pain. "The risk, though, has outweighed any possible reward."

My brain stopped whirring and every limb went suddenly cold. "What is the risk?"

"We have no proof whether it can be different, but every time thus far, every time one of the Divided has tried…" Dad opened his eyes, but he looked everywhere except for at me. "It has been the Id—the adapted personality—that's taken full control."

My body went rigid and for a moment it seemed as though everything had gone still both within me and without. I heard my voice speak words that I didn't remember deciding to say. "I understand."

"I know how important Finn is to you, Parker." Dad

squeezed my shoulder with his long, thin fingers until I looked up into his face. "But this is too dangerous. You shouldn't try it. The danger is too great."

My stomach roiled inside of me at the choice I'd have to make. And all I could manage was to speak the same words again. "I understand, Dad."

"Good." He nodded, checked his pockets for a pen again, and then turned back to Jack. "Now then, we need to go to my lab."

"Why?" Jack was already shaking his head.

"To make sure no one can ever make Eclipse again."

We snuck back into the hallway and Jack crept down to the corner, checking to be sure the nearest section was still empty. He gestured for me to follow, but instead, I walked to the nearest occupied cell, pulled up the door release as quietly as possible, and then moved on to the next one. The prisoner from the first, a ragged older man, staggered out behind me. I glanced ahead at Jack and my—*our*—dad. "You guys want to help me out here?"

"Now?" Jack looked torn. It was a lot harder to sneak around with a massive group of people.

I paused and looked at them both. "Do you really think we'll get the chance to come back later?"

Without a word, they looked at each other and then began opening the cells, one at a time. Dad skipped one and I asked why.

"I know him." His mouth pressed in a hard line. "He's a Taker."

I peeked in. The man looked only a little older than Jack, and his face was pressed against the glass. He mouthed the word, "Please."

"Then why did they lock him up?"

He shrugged and moved on to the next cell.

Looking back in, I met the man's eyes and then muttered under my breath as I lifted the latch, "The enemy of my enemy... I hope."

The Taker came out, thanked me, and turned toward the huddled group in the middle of the hallway.

I stopped him halfway there. "Why were you locked up?"

He sighed but turned, his face sincere as he responded. "Not all of us think Eclipse is the answer. I think I just disagreed a little louder than most."

Dad raised his eyebrows from down the hall and I heard him mutter, "Maybe there is hope yet."

By the time we got down the first hallway, we had a team of ten people opening doors and spreading our message: "We're all getting out of here. Move quick. Stay quiet."

I opened Audrey's door myself. When I walked in, she cowered farther into the corner.

"I've talked to your mom and dad. They miss you."

Her brown eyes got huge and she stopped shaking, but she didn't move.

"I'd like to take you home to them."

I counted one second—two—three. Long enough that

Jack poked his head in the door looking for me, but I didn't want to rush her... or scare her.

"Parker..." Jack said my name, but hesitated when I glanced at him over my shoulder.

Then I felt a tiny cold hand in mine and looked down to see Audrey's bare feet next to my own.

"Please take me home." Her voice trembled, but before I could respond, she followed Jack out into the hallway and pulled me along in her wake.

Jack led everyone down the next hall. We found Delilah Jones, the grandmother I'd seen on the Missing Persons poster in the Newton City Jail. She took Audrey's hand so I could continue opening cells. Perfect strangers moved together with one purpose. Some assisted older people and children to move quickly, to stay quiet. Jack took command like he was born to it and they followed him easily. This was what the NWS should have been about. Helping others to survive, to live full lives in spite of what our genes and reckless scientists had done to us. This was what Dad had always wanted.

By the time we got out of the prison wing, there were more of us than I couldn't quickly count... more than fifty. Dad lead us down a side hallway to his lab.

We found a large, dark, empty workshop halfway there and had all the prisoners hide inside.

"Stay here. Stay quiet, and we'll be right back," Jack whispered to a room full of wide eyes. Then he pointed to a workbench along one wall with tools and pieces of metal pipe. "And if they come here before we do... feel free to defend yourselves."

Dad's lab was more than ten times the size of the cells. There were tables set up with chemistry equipment and several different instruments I didn't recognize. The shelves on one wall were lined with row upon row of small jars, each with a neatly printed label. A large whiteboard stood on a stand in the back. It was covered with incomprehensible scribbles that I could only assume were formulas and advanced equations that were way over my head.

The moment we entered, Jack slid a metal lock quietly across one door and sent me to guard another entry. There were several more, though, and we couldn't cover them all.

"We need to hurry." Jack's voice was calm, but we could both hear more activity in the surrounding halls than had been there before. He held the walkie-talkie to his ear, but it was turned down so low I couldn't make out any noise from where I stood. If no one had noticed the empty cells yet, they would soon.

Dad moved from shelf to shelf picking up different chemicals, turning on burners, mixing concoctions. Every few seconds I heard him whisper, "No … no, this won't work," under his breath and then move on to the next shelf.

Boots ran directly past my door and I glanced out to see three guards running by with guns raised. They definitely knew about the prisoners now. When I turned back, I saw Dad speaking low and fast to Jack, whose skin looked ashen.

They both jumped when I spoke. "Um … Dad? You almost ready?"

He stopped in place and stared at me, slowly shaking his

head. His eyes looked sad but sure as Jack left him to stand by a third doorway. "Yes. Give me a couple more minutes."

"That may be all we have," Jack said.

Now Dad moved with purpose, mixing this and that in a small pot over a burner. He brought over a few other ingredients, nodded twice, and then pulled a paper and pen out of a desk drawer.

Boots ran past again and I held my breath as I waited. This base was so big, it would take them a couple minutes to organize an effective search.

At least, that's what I kept telling myself.

"I'm done. Come over here, quickly." Crumpling up the paper, Dad waited as we both came back to the table.

"You're ready?" Jack's voice sounded uncertain and his eyes were locked on Dad's vials and ingredient labels.

"Yes." Dad pushed the paper into Jack's hand and then drummed the fingers of his right hand against his thigh. "This is for after."

"After what?" Jack opened the paper. His eyes squinted at the scribbles while Dad turned to me.

"Is this what I think it is?" The mixture of awe and anguish in Jack's voice snapped me out of it.

"Yes." Dad lead us toward the door we'd come in through and peeked out into the hallway. "You must get out of here as fast as you can. Take care of each other." He put one hand on each of our shoulders and pulled us in for another hug.

"You—you're coming with us. You have to come with us." My voice shook, my body shook, my whole world was shaken at the idea of losing him again.

"I'd hoped I could…but this lab *must* be destroyed to ensure the end of Eclipse. There's too much information they could use to build on here. And I don't have the right ingredients for a time-delay." He gave me a sad smile. "I'm afraid I have to stay here to make sure you both can escape."

"No…you can't." My heart ripped a new tear with each beat and I was flooded with memories of losing him the first time.

"From the moment I realized what Eclipse could do, my life was over." Dad's eyes were haunted, tortured. "But I've never told anyone how to make it or even what goes into it." He gestured to the wall with a proud half-smile. "I've requested hundreds more ingredients than I actually needed. Even if they had a list, it could still be a century before they figured it out."

Then the smile turned fierce. "And I'm going to do everything in my power to make sure they don't have any list…or me to chase down anymore."

"No—no—" The repeated word was empty hope, but I clung to it anyway.

"This hasn't been a life, Parker." Dad's eyes were sad and so tired. "Not for me, and not for Jack. This is my gift to you, your mother, your friends, and everyone you will ever love. They know the prisoners are out of their cells by now, but they don't know you're here. I can distract them, and then destroy this lab while you two get yourselves and the prisoners out safely. This is the only thing I can give my boys that's worth anything. Please don't take that from me."

He turned toward Jack. "Remember me as Dad. You'll never have to call me anything else ever again."

Jack's shoulders were trembling, but when Dad looked at him, he gave him a firm nod and a hug. Dad whispered. "You'll be the answer. You'll know what to do."

"I love you...Dad."

Jack's eyes were wet, but I was numb. How was I supposed to know how to finally find, and then lose, my father in under an hour? How could I do this? But knowing what he was about to do, about to sacrifice, so that our lives wouldn't have to be spent on the run like his had...how could I not give him whatever he needed from me?

Dad pulled me against his chest and rubbed his hand across my hair as tears broke free and fell down my face. "I'm so sorry you couldn't see me, but know that I was always watching over you. I've always been more proud of you than you've ever known. I couldn't be there for you myself, but I gave you the greatest treasure I've ever had—your mom."

He lifted my face and smiled. "Now it's your turn to take care of her. And when you finally decide to tell her all of this, please tell her that I have never, *will* never, stop loving her."

I drew in a shaky breath. "I will. I love you."

Dad turned his gaze on Jack, then released me as he reached out and pulled Jack into his arms. "I know you can do everything you'll need to. I'd never trust anyone else with that paper. *No one else.*" Jack hugged Dad back, but he kept a firm hold on his emotions as Dad continued. "I've always had more faith in you than you've had in yourself. Now is no different. I love you and I know you can fix everything I've broken."

"Are—are you sure—" But before Jack could finish, Dad patted him on the shoulder and turned him back toward the door.

"Now go. Be careful. Make sure you get *everyone* out safe." Dad met my eyes and I understood his message. Then he grabbed the walkie-talkie from Jack's belt and waved us out.

We listened, waiting for boots in the hall. I looked back one last time before following Jack around the corner. Dad gave us a brave smile, then ducked back into his lab.

"Wait…"

Jack looked at me, his voice still choked up with emotion. "What? We can't… he won't…"

"I know. Is he… how is he going to do it?"

Jack blinked at me. "He's a phenomenal chemist with a lab full of chemicals. You have any wild guesses?"

"That's what I thought." My words shook as I swallowed back the massive lump of loss in my throat. Then I walked quietly toward the room we'd left the prisoners in. "Let's make sure we hold up our end of the deal."

———

"How many are there?" I whispered, my voice so small I could just barely hear it.

"Eight in the hall, more inside."

I could hear whimpering and crying from the prisoners on the other side of the wall we were leaning against. The walkie-talkie of one of the guards sparked to life and I heard Dad's voice loud and clear. "This is Daniel Chipp. You've done just about all you can do to make my life a living hell. You've stolen my family and my freedom. Eclipse isn't what I started out trying to make, and I'll be damned if I give you a way to extend your lives when you've cost me so much of mine."

I peeked around the corner just in time to see the guards exchange panicked looks. One spoke sharply to the others. "We've got this situation under control. You five go check his lab and cell. Find him!"

Five gone—at least three to go.

As soon as the group of guards was dispatched, I decided to move. Even though I knew this might be the stupidest thing I'd ever done, I didn't let myself think about it too much, just untucked and rumpled my shirt and messed up my hair, letting it hang down across my face. "Don't let them kill me, okay?"

Before Jack could even question me, I turned the corner into plain view of the remaining guards. Stumbling noisily as I walked down the hall, I yelled, "Jennifer! Are you here?" I sniveled and argued with myself. "No, she isn't. She wouldn't leave us."

"You, stop there!" The guards turned their attention on me.

"I'm not, you are. No—no, I can't." I kept muttering, careful to keep my hands open so they could see I had no weapons. I slid one foot like I had a limp and breathed as loudly as I could.

The front guard drew his gun. "I said, stop!"

But I was almost there...just a few more feet and I'd make it. I'd seen Jack at work; for this to have even a chance, the positioning had to be right.

"Jen-ni-fer?" I sung out the name and slowed down, leaning against the far wall like it was the only thing keeping me upright. Then I grew even more agitated with my muttering. "You promised she wouldn't leave me. Shut up! Yes, you did."

"STOP!" The front guard pointed the gun at my right temple and I froze, breathing hard, knowing I wasn't quite in the right position yet. I still needed another couple of feet.

I stared straight at the gun and squinted as my palms sweated like mad. "Jennifer?"

Then I fell straight forward, letting my body go limp and pushing off my toes so my face crashed into the floor first. My head exploded in pain, but I knew I'd made it. The guards bent over me, their backs exposed to Jack as they muttered about "another prisoner going crazy."

And my brother didn't waste the opportunity.

He sprinted silently up and kicked the legs out from under one guard, sending him crashing headfirst into the stone wall. Then Jack grabbed the now-lowered gun out of the hand of the other guard before he could react and brought it down hard on his head. More guards came out into the hallway, just as Jack pressed the gun to the third guard's temple.

"Everyone drop your guns and move back inside the workshop." Jack voice was low and almost sinister.

The first guard to follow orders lowered his gun directly in front of my face. When I grabbed it from him and climbed to my feet, the guards' eyes went wide.

"Jennifer?" Jack grinned over at me. "Nice ... but maybe clue me in next time?"

"Just the first thing I came up with. I'm hoping there won't be a next time."

Jack kicked the foot of one the guards who was moving too slow. "Then you're more optimistic than I am."

As soon as we were back inside, a couple of prisoners stepped forward and tied the guards up while Jack and I kept our guns trained on them. As soon as they were secure, I took one of the walkie-talkies and we lead the group down the halls toward the medical center where we'd come in.

We hadn't made it far when we heard an emergency beacon come over the walkie-talkie. "Red Alert: All security to the lab. Red Alert: All security to the lab."

By listening to the team's coordinates, we were able to avoid the guards remaining in our section. Dad had security fully distracted, as he'd promised ... now we had to get out of here before he finished his plan. I reminded myself not to think about Dad and pushed back another devastating wave of loss. Focusing on getting Audrey and the other prisoners out alive, I forced myself to keep everyone moving.

I stood beside Chloe's bed, trying to decide on the best way to move her. The curtain shifted aside, and the nasal man with the medical training stared at me before suddenly laughing.

"I should've known you might be here. Your father is

so—" He made a soft whining noise as Jack swung twice and knocked him out cold. Jack stepped on the man's fingers.

"Do *not* talk about our dad" were the only words he spoke as he turned and lead the way through the labyrinth of curtains.

Most of the people behind us stepped carefully around and over the man, but I saw a couple of light kicks as well. I figured he might be a little sore . . . if he survived the coming explosion.

And after what they'd done to my family and these prisoners, I didn't feel even a little bit bad about that.

Picking up Chloe, I swung her IV bag over one shoulder and her body over the other. Then I felt a slight tug on my arm. Audrey reached up and took the IV bag for me.

"Thank you."

She gave me a shy smile, and when she said "You're welcome" it made a little whistling sound between her teeth.

Jack found a couple of flashlights in a nearby supply room. We'd reached the end of our secret tunnel when he turned to face the rest of us. "Okay, looks like the easy part is over. Everyone ready?"

The prisoners stared back, determined and terrified. And they waited for directions.

"We'll be leaving through this hatch directly above me. To the left is a building where they have keys for the cars in the parking lot on the right. We'll be going out in groups of about eight, so everyone find a group. Make sure you have someone who can drive. The driver is responsible for getting everyone in the group back to their homes. I'll go out first and break into the building to hand out keys. I'll signal my brother when it's time to send a new group. When you climb out, come to me to get the key, then go to your vehicle and duck down inside it and wait. If you start the car and leave early, they'll catch you and you'll die. Only start your car when you hear my whistle, or if you hear nearby gunshots. If we all leave at the same time, I can dump the rest of the keys and they won't be able to catch us. Everyone understand?"

Murmurs of assent spread through the group. I was impressed.

"Dad teach you that?" I asked as Jack reached one hand up onto the ladder.

He gave me a sad smile and nodded. "Dad taught me everything I know."

Instead of my normal jealousy, I felt curiosity... and a little pity. I'd had a pretty normal childhood. Jack had been raised to fight and to lead. "Maybe when all this is over, you can tell me more about that."

"Deal." He climbed up to the top and listened. I silenced the prisoners and we waited. After a few minutes, Jack gave me a thumbs-up and opened the hatch. I handed Chloe off to one of the stronger prisoners and climbed to the top, then watched the path for the security patrol as Jack took off his black jacket, wrapped it around his fist, and punched through the glass pane next to the door of the key shed. The glass was so old that it broke like spun candy. Jack unlocked the door and crept inside.

Then I saw the patrol coming in the distance. It seemed that due to the breakout, they'd doubled the frequency of their perimeter sweep. It was obvious from the lack of a bigger search out here, though, that they believed the prisoners were still inside the base.

I lowered the hatch, hoping Jack had seen them ... but the door to the key shed was still open. It would be obvious. Turning off my flashlight, I waited, hoping and praying in the hushed shadows of night. Just before the patrol rounded the closest corner, I saw the door close softly and silently. I finally relaxed.

Listening close, we stood motionless in the pitch-black tunnel. Every tight breath and muted gasp of the prisoners felt like it was lending its tension to me. We were their only chance, and I wasn't sure how long Dad would give us to get out of here. He probably thought we were already gone. How would he know? I heard a soft sob from a couple of the prisoners, but nothing loud enough to be heard outside. Finally the patrol was out of the area, and I lifted the hatch an inch. Jack already had the door open again and was using something metallic to bounce the moonlight back at me—car keys.

"First group, time to go."

TWENTY-SEVEN

It took about twenty minutes to get almost everyone into the vehicles, but Jack's plan worked smoothly. At the end the only stragglers were Audrey, Delilah, and a grumpy middle-aged man named Mason. He kept watching Audrey like she was an animal he didn't trust.

"You sure we shouldn't ... tie her up? Or gag her or something?" he grumbled to me when Audrey wasn't looking. Delilah's eyes went wide.

"Um, why?" I stared at him and could almost swear he flushed behind his full beard.

"She's a kid," he said as she looked up and he took a small step away from her. "Kids are loud."

Delilah smothered a laugh behind her hand and turned away.

"Yeah ... I'm pretty sure she's been quieter than half the other people in the group."

Mason turned away and I barely made out his response. "So far…"

He was definitely not a kid person, but at this point it didn't matter. This last group would go with Chloe's body and me in one of the vans.

Jack put one key in his pocket and brought all the rest back to me as we climbed out. I handed him Chloe—my shoulder was aching. Taking the final key we'd need, I tossed the rest of the keys down the hatch.

"They might have some trouble finding them down there." Jack grinned as I closed the hatch and locked it as securely and tightly as I could. Then I took Chloe and her IV bag back and motioned for my group to follow me. Jack picked up a few handfuls of dirt and threw them over the hatch. The sky was still pitch black as Jack led us to the parking lot and helped me load Chloe into the backseat of our van.

"I'll go help Mia and Addie get Finn into the car and then give the signal. You be ready to go." Jack glanced over his shoulder; the patrol unit's flashlight was far enough away that we knew they couldn't see us, but they'd be here soon enough. Mason sat in the passenger seat, silent as a stone. Audrey was shivering next to Delilah in the second row of seats.

"Have Addie call me when you get on the road and let me know everyone is safe," I said.

"I will."

Jack snuck across the road and up the hill so quickly that after a moment, I couldn't even make him out in the brush across from me.

"Everyone stay low and still," I whispered to the others

as I ducked down in the driver's seat and waited, counting down the minutes until we could leave. Counting down until Jack would tell me that my friends were all still okay.

The patrol came by, and there was an urgency to the swing of their flashlights that turned me cold. They'd figured out now that we'd left the base. They were looking for us—hunting the prisoners they'd spent so much time collecting ... and the people who'd freed them.

Our van was parked in the first row. The guards walked to the empty car next to us before I realized that we hadn't locked our doors ... I could see Mason remember this at the same time, and when he lifted his hand up to push down the button, I heard a guard outside yell, "There! That one!"

The van's side door was yanked open and before I could blink, there was a gun to Audrey's head. She whimpered and tried to pull back, but the guard wrapped his fingers around her frail arm.

"You better not even breathe, sweetheart. I'm not in a good mood." The man leaned back and I saw his face in the moonlight. His eyes were so dark they bordered on black, and the dark circles under his eyes were like giant pits in his face. Wrinkles hung across his loose skin in unnatural directions that made him look sick. He was far more ragged than Cooper had been, and ten times worse than me on my roughest day. This was a Taker nearing his end ... there was no doubt about it. That kind of future bred desperation, and you could see it in his eyes. It was the kind of hunger that deprived you of your humanity. Deprived you of your soul.

The shockwave from the explosion shattered the front

window of the small sedan next to us, sending the guard reeling backward. His gun went off, shooting into the sky, and then he dropped it. Mason and I both shoved him back and locked all the doors. It didn't matter. The guards weren't paying attention to us anymore. One was running toward the nearest entrance to the base while the other was searching the ground for his gun.

My eyes were glued to the inferno that lit up the night.

On the opposite end of the parking lot, some of the ground caved in and a few motorcycles and four-wheelers went down with it. All my eyes could see was the giant ball of flame that shot up into the sky before snuffing out into nothing. My ears rang, and above the din my heart raced in my chest. If there was a whistle from Jack, I didn't hear it, but then all around me vans were starting and racing toward the exit. I knew I needed to move, to fall in line. Just as Jack had planned, no Takers who survived the blast would have a clue which vehicles to follow.

But all I could do was stare at the flames and think about what it meant. People were dying in there. Knowing this was the plan and seeing the carnage were two different things. I saw figures in flames. I felt the heat from the fire warming the air even inside the van. This was the war. This was what Jack had grown up knowing. It didn't mean victory or a real chance at escape and a future, like it was supposed to. All it meant was that my dad was dead.

I rested my face on the wheel and breathed ... through smaller explosions in the distance, I breathed. The voices of Mason, Audrey, and Delilah started soft, but soon they were yelling my name. They wanted me to move, to drive, to go—but everything in my body had slowed to a screeching halt. Even with the sound of vehicle after vehicle driving past, I just kept breathing through the finality of the pain that was expanding in my chest and threatening to take over my world.

And then I remembered Finn and Addie.

And I remembered that if I just sat here breathing, the people in my van would be hurt. And everything my dad had just done would be for nothing.

I sat up straight, started the car, and got in line behind the other vans driving toward the exit.

———————

One time—five times—a dozen. I had no idea how many times I called Addie's phone. It was all a blur. Everything that had happened over the past few weeks had created some kind of protective barrier around me against the pain, and losing Dad had been the final straw. My mind, my fragile sanity, my emotions were all wrapped in a giant bubble—I wasn't even capable of responding normally anymore.

It became a pattern: I drove toward home hitting redial. I got voicemail, drove a little farther, and called again. Over and over until it seemed like the only logical option was to keep doing it. One by one, the other vans we'd taken disappeared, the prisoners heading back to the lives they'd been ripped from. Some had taken back roads or split off onto other highways. Several had waved as they departed, and one older woman blew me a kiss. Now we were the only van left on this road.

There had been no sign of any pursuit. Dad took care of that.

"Is it your mama?" Delilah's whispered words floated up from the backseat. "Or your dad you want to hug first?"

Dad—the word sent a fresh storm of anguish through my mind and I did my best to force it away. I couldn't deal with that pain ... not yet ... not right now.

"Both of them," Audrey replied, excitement evident in her every word. "And my dog. He's a Chihuahua. His name is Bubba."

Delilah laughed softly. "Of course it is."

Mason and I stared straight ahead. Neither of us spoke, but I thought I saw him wipe a stray tear off his cheek once. My wall of anxiety and fear wouldn't even let that kind of emotion through.

I pressed *call* on my phone again, glancing down at the smiling picture of Addie on my screen. I'd taken it the day they found out about their trip. Mr. Patrick had given them all Mickey Mouse ears. Addie was wearing them in the photo and even though she was grinning, the look in her eyes and the cock of her eyebrow was saying something more like *"Uh oh. Now what?"*

I'd teased her, saying that this was her permanent expression around me.

"This is Addie's phone. I'm obviously doing something extremely important or I would have answered your call. Leave a message. Bye!"

I pressed the *end call* button and threw my phone as hard as I could. It bounced off the dashboard and fell down on the floor. The van around me went silent. Then Mason reached down, picked it up, and handed it to me.

"Jack doesn't seem like the type to give up." Mason's voice was a low and quiet, but the southern twang came through loud and clear. "It don't seem right that you give up on him neither."

"Right...thanks." I put the phone back on my lap and glanced over my shoulder at Audrey and Delilah. "Sorry."

Audrey's eyes looked heavy and she lay down on Delilah's lap. Delilah smiled. "Now stop that. It'd be hard for you to do anything worth apologizing for after getting us out of there."

I inclined my head and turned back toward the road. About a mile farther on, I pushed *call* again. Even if Addie didn't answer, hearing her voice on her message kept me from totally losing it.

———————

By the time the sun rose, I had to stop for gas. Handing twenty dollars to Mason, I sent the others inside to get food and drinks. I put the gas nozzle in and pulled the handle. Every motion was done without thought. I couldn't think anymore. The ticking of the gas meter was oddly soothing. I rested my forehead against the van as other vehicles came and went around me.

"Hey, buddy, you okay?"

I looked up. At the pump across from me stood a thirty-something man with a receding hairline and a toddler in his backseat.

I tried to give him a quick smile, but nothing happened so I just nodded and fell back on my old go-to response. "I'm fine, just tired. Thank you."

"Okay." He gave me another worried look as he got in his car and drove away.

A new vehicle pulled up behind me as I finished up and put back the handle. I didn't even glance back. I didn't want to risk any more questions.

"You look terrible." Addie's warm voice made me spin in a circle—then she was wrapped around me before I could really get a look at her. Mia ran up behind her and hugged us both. The bubble around me popped, and every emotion I'd been holding back exploded. We laughed until we cried, and then laughed again. Jack stepped out of the car and grinned from behind the rear passenger door. He had a few cuts on his face, but it was all superficial.

"Glad we found you." He inclined his head my direction. "My phone is dead and in the rush after the…" He cleared his throat and looked down. "We left Addie's behind."

I kissed the top of Addie's head and gave Mia a tight squeeze before disentangling myself from them. Peeking into the car, I could see a lumpy form wiggling around a bit in the back. Finn—or his body, anyway—was fine too.

Walking up to Jack, I grabbed him and gave him a tight hug. "Thank you. Thank you for getting them all out safe."

Jack seemed absolutely stunned at first, then hugged

me back. "No problem. I—I'm glad they're all okay. Where's your group?" He glanced into the van.

"Chloe is in the backseat and the others went in to get some food." It was amazing how much better I felt just knowing my friends were okay. I walked back to Addie and pulled her against my side. "Let's drive over to that storage unit complex and switch our passengers around. I'd like to spend the last hour of our drive having a little chat with Finn's parasite."

————————

"I think you need to understand that things have changed." I held the knife in plain view as I spoke.

Mia was driving the van, and even though Finn's body was still tied up, we'd removed the gag and hood and placed him securely in the backseat. Audrey and Delilah had moved to my car, which Jack was driving, but Mason sat next to Finn, a disapproving glare firmly in place.

No response. Finn's mouth was set in a hard line and he stared straight ahead.

"My dad just blew up the NWS compound."

Finn laughed. "That's not possible."

"Why not? Because you'd be dead?"

Finn rolled his eyes and shook his head in such a distinctly feminine way and I almost laughed. "For starters..."

"We stole your body just before the explosion. It's lying across the seat behind you. If you weren't tied up you could see it yourself."

Finn's skin paled and his mouth opened and closed a few times. "You're bluffing."

"Not even a little bit." I stared him down, showed I was telling the truth.

"On top of that, your body is down to the last little bit of the drug. No more Eclipse will be made again, *ever*. My dad took that secret w-with him."

Mia's face whipped around toward me, but I kept my eyes on Finn.

"You know what that means, right?"

Finn shrugged, but he was pale—scared. "If that's true... then your friend and I will both be gone."

"That's one option." I blew a puff of air out and looked down at the knife.

"You think you have another?" Finn seemed incredulous and highly suspicious. The Taker had no idea if any of what I was saying was true.

"I hope so. And right now, I have no reason to lie to you, so you should consider believing me." I leaned a little closer. "Whether you help me or not, I'm going into that brain you share with Finn and I'll do everything in my power to separate you two."

"Th—that's not possible."

"How do you know?"

"I—I ... " he stuttered, eyes wide.

"You don't know." I shrugged. "And to be honest, I don't know if it's really going to work, but I'm going to try. The question is: will you help me?"

Finn blinked once ... twice ... no response. Then Mason

elbowed Finn in the side, hard. I turned toward him in surprise, and he shrugged and looked out the window at the sunrise while Finn caught his breath.

"The only question you need to answer is, which path do you want to choose?" I continued. "Do you want to die for sure? Or do you want to at least try to help me, for the chance to live in your own body again? Think about it. Let me know what you decide."

I turned back and faced the road. It took about thirty seconds longer than I'd hoped, but finally I heard the words I'd been waiting for.

"What do you want me to do?"

———

As we neared home, I had Mason call my mom's office to make sure she'd gone into work like I hoped. Her office line didn't have caller ID, and when she answered, Mason said he'd gotten the wrong number and hung up. It was all I needed to know. We had to have the house to ourselves today.

We drove to Audrey's house first. I knew Delilah and Mason could make it home on their own from my place, but I needed to know that the little girl was safe with her parents before I tried something that could end up killing me, or else let Darkness take over.

When we arrived at the address Audrey had carefully recited, Delilah and I walked Audrey to the front door. She hugged us each tight, then rang the doorbell.

Her dad was in mid-sentence when he pulled the door open and saw her.

"Audrey!" He reached down and crushed her against him, picking her off the floor as tears ran down his cheeks. I heard a clanging sound from the kitchen and her mom stepped into the hallway. Neither of them looked like they'd slept since I'd seen them last. Her mom's short blond hair was ratted in bunches on one side and every one of her long red nails had been broken or bitten off.

She ran forward and grabbed Audrey's face in her hands and stared at her, then kissed her cheeks. In between sobs, she repeated four words over and over: "You're here. You're safe." Meanwhile Bubba, the crazy Chihuahua, ran in circles around their feet and barked.

Delilah grabbed my elbow and with a smile pulled me back toward the van. Tears streamed down her cheeks. "Now it's my turn."

Before we got to the driveway, I heard Audrey's dad yell out "Wait!"

He released Audrey to his wife and jogged toward us. I expected him to grill me for answers that I couldn't give him, but instead he just wrapped one arm around me and one around Delilah.

"I have no idea how you brought her home, but you—I just—" Drawing back, he closed his eyes and tried to contain his emotion. "Thank you. That's all ... just thank you."

"You're welcome." I smiled. Somehow bringing this

girl back home had healed a small piece of the scar left by my dad's sacrifice. What we did for her ... it mattered.

And that mattered to me.

When we got home, it was nearly eleven in the morning, but we were all too anxious about saving Finn to even think about how tired we were. Jack and Mia parked the vehicles in front of my house and we got our stuff—and Chloe's body—out of the van.

"You sure you have everything under control here, kid?" Mason watched Jack lead Finn into the house. He and Delilah wrote down their contact information, and I gave them mine in case they had any more trouble.

"Yeah, we'll be fine," I said. At least, I hoped so ...

Delilah hugged everyone, and then hugged me again. "Thank you again."

"You're welcome."

Mason stuck out his hand and I shook it. "You have somewhere you can get rid of that van when you get home?" I asked.

His mouth split into the widest grin I'd seen on him yet, and it caught me by surprise. "My buddy has a wrecking yard. We'll take care of it."

I laughed, and Jack came back outside to shake Mason's hand with a wry grin. "Could be good to have a friend like you."

"Anything you need. Any time. I mean it." Mason lowered his chin and stared hard at Jack, waiting. He didn't let go of his hand until Jack nodded and said, "I will definitely keep that in mind."

———————

We put Finn in my room and Chloe's body on the couch. It only took us a few minutes to set things up. I knew exactly what I had to do. The only thing I didn't know was if I *could* do it.

I pulled Jack aside while Mia and Addie made some food. "I need you to promise me something."

He looked over at the kitchen, then back at me and waited for me to continue.

"If when I come out of this you think I'm a threat to my mom or any of them ... if you think I'm not in control or I'm gone—"

"You sure you want to do this?" Jack looked like he was trying to decide whether to talk me out of it.

"Yes." I didn't hesitate. "I'm stronger now, with Addie's help ... and Finn is family to me."

"I know. I've seen it." He put his hand on my shoulder. "Look, you're the only one I've ever seen control your other half like you do now. You're stronger than any other Divided ... including Dad. Plus, your other half—he seems more rational lately, or something."

"Thanks?" I didn't feel like Jack had answered me, and it made me nervous. "But if I'm a threat ... "

"What I'm trying to say is...what I said before, about you being dangerous for Addie? I think I was wrong. You're different. If anyone can do this, I think it's you, Parker." Jack smiled. "I may be the smart one, I may have gotten the looks and the charm...but I think you're the strong one."

I laughed. "A few guards back there might have disagreed with you."

"You know what I mean." The smile faded from his face and he nodded. "But, yes, if it doesn't turn out the way we hope...I'll make sure you can't hurt anyone."

Addie brought me a bowl of eggs, but her hand was shaking so hard I was afraid she might drop it.

I took the bowl and swallowed two bites. "Thank you." I was talking to Addie, but I glanced back at Jack, and he inclined his head in my direction.

Food was the last thing on my mind, but anything that might give me a little extra strength would be good right now. I scarfed down the bowl and then went to set up in the bedroom. My brain still felt much improved since Addie had helped heal the breaks...but the last six hours had been draining, both emotionally and physically, and I could imagine fresh new cracks already forming. I could only hope the new damage wouldn't be the difference between success and failure.

I broke one of Mrs. Patrick's stolen sleeping pills in half. After Finn swallowed one half, I took the other. I didn't want to take the chance of one of us not falling asleep no matter how exhausted we both were. We'd put a sleeping bag on an air mattress on the floor, and Finn was already tied up inside it.

"Are the ropes still necessary?"

"Do you really think there's anything that can make us trust you after taking over Finn's body?" I raised one eyebrow.

Finn's shoulders hunched forward in defeat. "Fine."

I walked back out to the table. Everyone was sitting silently, staring at their half-empty plates.

"We both took our pills, so I'm going to go lie down. In a few minutes, come see if we're both asleep. If we are, take out Chloe's IV."

There was no response. I looked down at Jack and he answered without raising his gaze, but I saw the muscle in his jaw flex. "Got it. Be careful, Parker."

"I promise."

Mia stood up, hugged me, and whispered in my ear, "I'm sorry about your dad."

"Thank you." I smiled and patted her back. "Maybe someday you could paint me a picture of him?"

Her eyes welled up with tears and she took a deep breath before answering. "I'd like to be able to do that."

Addie walked me down the hall, both her hands wrapped tight around mine. "Is this as dangerous as I'm afraid it is?"

I didn't answer right away.

"The truth, please."

"Yes." I kissed her cheek before looking in her eyes. "But it's Finn."

It was all I could say and really all I had to say. There was nothing that Addie and I wouldn't do to save him, and we both knew it.

She wrapped both arms around my waist and buried her

face against my chest. I pulled her in tight, kissed the top of her head, and smelled her hair. When she looked up, I kissed her softly and whispered, "I'll do everything I can to come back to you, and to bring Finn with me."

"You better. And by the way, I was happy to find out about Jack being your brother. Having a brother is … it's the best." Addie smiled, gave me one more light kiss, and walked backward toward the table.

"He probably doesn't like you dating his sister, you know," Finn said when I went back into the room. "That's got to be weird. My brothers are very protective of me."

"Shut up." Once I'd gotten a good look in Finn's eyes, I flipped the light switch. Other than for the sunlight peeking around the very edges of my curtains, my room was dark.

Then something dawned on me. "Both Cooper and Thor are your brothers?"

"Yes."

"You have a messed-up family."

It was at least thirty seconds before I got a response, and Finn's voice sounded heavy with medicated exhaustion. "So do you."

Sitting on the edge of my bed, I picked up the camcorder on the desk out of instinct. It had been one of my better ideas. I wrapped it up in its power cord and put it in my bottom desk drawer. Whoever I was when I woke up, I wouldn't need it anymore.

I lay down on my bed, closed my eyes, and got ready to deal with Darkness.

TWENTY-EIGHT

In spite of how drugged Finn had sounded, I must have fallen asleep quicker than he did because I was in the Hollow and waiting. I'd actually been hoping to have a few minutes alone there before I got sucked into whatever madness awaited me in Finn's brain. Everything inside my own head was quiet and still. I didn't know what that meant, but with Darkness, it probably wasn't good. I mentally tore down the wall I'd trapped him behind and even though I could feel him watching, he didn't immediately come out.

"Are you seriously giving yourself the silent treatment?" My voice echoed through the white vastness around me. "Because that's just messed up."

He appeared, sitting cross-legged on the ground in front of me. "You haven't even begun to see messed up."

"You know everything that's going on, right?"

The look he gave me was full of so much disdain it was like he'd smacked me.

"Okay, you do."

"Why should I care if you save your little friend?" Darkness held more fury and challenge in his eyes than I'd seen in a long time. Locking him away had seriously pissed him off, even more than I'd expected.

"Because you feel my emotions too."

"I don't care as much about emotions as you do."

"Sure you do. It's just all the negative ones you pay attention to."

Instead of responding, Darkness seemed to be trying to bore holes in my forehead with his stare.

"I think I owe you an apology," I said.

He blinked.

"You've been telling me for a long time that we'd be stronger together, and all I've ever done is fight you and lock you up behind walls. If our positions were reversed—as you've made so abundantly clear to me—I'd be furious, too."

Darkness looked confused. "You can't trick me, you know ... I can hear your thoughts."

I sat down in front of him. "Then look close, because I'm not trying to trick you. I know better than that."

He sat perfectly still for a few seconds before saying, "Go on."

"Okay, it's like this. If we come out of here and you're in control, then Jack is going to kill us."

"Because you told him to."

"True." I held my hands out in front of me, palms up.

"But still, it's what will happen. Here's the other part that you may not have thought of. If *I* come out of here in control, then we live … but it probably means we didn't save Finn, which is not what I want."

"Wait … you don't want to be in control?" Darkness frowned.

"I want to take your suggestion and do what you've been trying to do all along. I want to try to become one again. Both of us together, good … bad … whatever. Permanently."

"Why are you changing your mind?" He looked more than suspicious.

"Because I realized that fighting with you doesn't make me normal. It makes me abnormal." I rested my elbows on my knees. "The things you want are instincts and needs. You have no morality and I don't always agree with you, but sometimes you *are* right, and you're always strong. The trick is to know that sometimes your instincts will win, and sometimes my moral code will win, and a lot of the time we'll make mistakes. And all of that just makes us human—or Watcher, or whatever the hell we are."

"How eloquent," Darkness said, but his expression was blank and unfortunately, I'd never been able to read his mind. It was like my part of the brain didn't have access to his part. I really wasn't very happy about the whole set-up.

"So … what do you think?"

Before he could answer, we both got sucked into the suffocating, solid black nothing that happens when a Taker and Watcher get stuck together.

The weight of it was oppressive, and my lungs didn't

feel like they could expand like normal. It was a very good thing that I wasn't claustrophobic, because this situation would be the worst nightmare for someone like that. I took a breath, then two, and then opened my eyes and tried to find the people I knew were stuck in here with me. There should be two, but I could only feel one.

I focused, trying to pull Chloe out of the nothing. Pull her out to where I could see her and feel her. My brain ached and I could feel Darkness withdrawing from me. He hadn't decided yet. I needed him to be all in, or I'd never be able to do this.

My brain stuttered. I was asking too much. It couldn't keep up. I shifted my focus to myself instead. Maybe if Chloe could see me, she'd come forward. I wished I'd spent years training on how to control this, like most Watchers had. It was still so new and difficult for me. I put all my energy into making myself visible; my nonexistent hands shook with concentration, and then there they were. I lay down on my back on … nothing really, but it felt solid, and I took a moment to catch my breath. I ran my hands over my face and when they came away, there was blood on my fingers.

My nose was bleeding … not good. There'd been a shift in my brain, but Darkness was still keeping himself apart.

"Come on. I may kill us if I keep doing this on my own."

No response.

Rolling onto my stomach, I reached out for Chloe again. Now that I was visible I could breathe a little easier. I pictured her body in my head, her eyes staring at me from over the steering wheel of their family's car. I pictured her here with me, but it was so hard and my head was pounding. The pain crashed in waves over me, tumbling me and carrying me down until I was drowning in it. Every cell in my body was being ripped in half from my effort, but I would not give up. I couldn't even though I was reeling. Still, I reached out for her again and again. It was like the world's worst game of tug-of-war, except the rope was attached to the inside of my brain.

Curling into a ball, I yelled as loud as I could and gave one final yank on the thread—and there she was. Chloe, her mind and body as one in our inky surroundings. It was definitely progress. She looked down at her body and then at me.

"Good lord, what did you do to yourself?" She scooted closer and her expression seemed torn between triumph and dismay. Reaching out one hand, she gently touched the side of my face. My ears were bleeding now too.

I could finally feel Finn, but like a whisper in the background, he was barely there. I couldn't even get ahold of him to pull. How was I supposed to win this battle by myself?

Lying back on the ground, I wrapped my arms around my head as if the pretend pressure from my arms could push my brain back together. No matter how hard it was. No matter how bad it hurt. I could never look Addie in the eye, could never live with myself, if I didn't do everything—*every single thing*—that I could. Even if it killed me, I had to try.

It was Finn. There were no other options.

Reaching out with my mind, I tried to grab him, but he was like smoke. A wisp here and there and then gone. I tried again, again, again. I tried until even my hair seemed to vibrate with the effort, and then I tried again. I would *not* give up on him. There were instants where I almost had him and then I heard screaming. Chloe was screaming. I tried again. My heart threatened to break through the wall of my chest. But I tried again. I would not give up on Finn. I couldn't.

I rolled onto my side and reached again. Chloe was shaking me and shouting my name. I opened my eyes, but everything was foggy. I couldn't lift my head. I couldn't speak. I had nothing left.

"He's here." Chloe leaned over me. "You brought him here, but you can't . . . you're bleeding so much, Parker, and he's not responding. I don't know what will happen to us if you die in here—with us like this."

Next to her I could see the top of Finn's head. He was lying on the ground. I'd done it. I had them both. Now all I had to do was separate their minds . . . and I couldn't do it. I had the will, but no part of my body was reacting to my commands anymore. I screamed at my body inside my head. Finn was right there. All I had to do was pull them apart somehow. I was capable of it. I knew I was.

But I had nothing left.

I was nothing anymore.

Still . . . it was Finn.

Screaming in agony, I reached out with my brain one last time, knowing it might be the last thing I ever did, and mentally tried to pull them apart. My brain transformed into one massive stick of dynamite. The more I pulled, the more fuses appeared; it was just a matter of time before I made the wrong move, lit a match, and it was over. Still, I held on to Finn with my mind and pulled with everything

I had left. My body was convulsing and Chloe was screaming and all I could do was pull.

Then something changed. My body stopped shaking as
Darkness began moving through my brain, snapping off the
fuses and removing anything that might spark. He fixed that
damage I'd been doing to us. When he was done, I heard him
speak.

"I'm trusting you not to let me down. I hope that moral
code you're always talking about makes you keep your promise." He sounded tired, resigned. My efforts had drained him
as well.

And then my body surged with life and strength. I sat up
and my ears and nose stopped bleeding. Using our combined
focus, we pulled with our mind ... my mind. We were one.
We were whole.

And we were crazy strong—but maybe still not quite
strong enough.

I found a crack in Finn's and Chloe's merged minds and
burrowed in until I filled the tiniest of crevices between them.
Then I pushed. Finn's body thrashed about on the ground
and Chloe curled up in a ball and screamed, over and over.

I prodded, shoved, and pushed harder and harder until
I didn't know if I could do any more. I couldn't catch my
breath. It was too much—even with Darkness. Like I'd been
warned, this was impossible. As I began to withdraw, my
chest felt like a vacuum of agony. My brain filled with shattering echoes of pain.

Then, in one instant, I saw Finn plastered across the
walls around us. A million images and memories from him

rose to the surface … and then one by one began fading away. His wide grin the first time he'd blocked my goal at practice. The time he'd worn a pumpkin over his head on Halloween night and insisted we call him "The Great Orange One." His expression when I finally told him I was a Watcher—and he believed me. Every image slammed me with new pain.

He was my best friend. I couldn't—I *wouldn't* lose this fight. I gathered all my focus and held tight to the memories, the images, gripping them all in my mind and letting them play out.

And then I felt it—the tiniest budge between Finn and Chloe. A tiny slip, like his mind was recognizing me, fighting beside me to retain the memories. A glimmer of hope filled me with determination and I visualized forcing every memory of Finn into the crevice between him and Chloe, pelting the miniscule crack again and again. It widened bit by bit under the assault until, finally, I could force all my focus into one massive ball of energy, squeeze it between them, and shove their minds apart with every ounce of strength I had left.

The last things I heard were horrific screams from both Finn and Chloe. Then everything disappeared in one blinking moment of the brightest light.

———

I sat bolt upright in bed. Jack was beside me, and he was on me in an instant, shoving me down and pinning me to the bed. I tried to struggle, and the urge to fight him off was intense, but my brain was pudding and I had no will left. I relaxed back and he leaned over me.

"Who are you?"

"We're one. I'm myself. I'm … whole."

"How can you prove it?" His eyes were piercing, his expression stuck midway between ecstatic and terrified.

"I guess the fact that even though I want to throw you against the wall right now, I'm not, is going to have to work for the moment." How could I prove that the other half of me hadn't taken over my body? I couldn't. He'd always been me—I just hadn't realized how much of me. Jack's weight on my chest was getting to be too much. "Could you please get off? I can't breathe."

Jack's mouth curved up, but I could see he was still hesitant. He leaned back and rubbed the top of my head. "Welcome back, little brother."

I groaned and stretched. Every piece of my body and brain throbbed with pain … but I'd survived when I really shouldn't have, thanks to Darkness. "Call me that again and I'll deck you."

He chuckled. "I'd like to see you try."

TWENTY-NINE

The bleeding hadn't only been in the dream. It took me a few minutes in the bathroom to wash all the blood out of my hair, my ears, and the stubble on my chin. I looked in the mirror, trying to see the difference inside me. I could still feel Darkness, but he was like a whisper... one of my many voices, one of many opinions and thoughts. He was still a part of me and he always would be... and I was surprisingly happy about that.

Finn and Chloe hadn't woken yet, and Jack thought it was a bad idea to wake them.

So we waited.

We'd all been asleep for nearly an hour before I woke up. Now it was more than two hours, going on three. I'd done everything I could. It had nearly killed me; I knew that without question. I had to believe that my efforts had made a difference. I had to believe it until someone proved otherwise.

Addie put her hand in mine and led me outside to get some fresh air. We sat with Mia on the bench in the backyard. The afternoon sunlight filtered through the leaves above. The trees had weathered the long winter and come through to the summer changed. They stood taller, reached farther, their branches stronger. Everything about them was better for having withstood their struggles. I couldn't help but hope my winter had done the same for me.

"You never know..." Mia whispered through her fingers.

"What?" Addie held my hand in one of hers and took Mia's with the other.

"You never know how important people are until it's too... until they're... "

"He's not." Addie said firmly, but her lower lip trembled. Then she repeated again to herself, "He's not."

"It's a good thing to feel needed." Finn's voice behind us was weak, but hearing it was like a giant burst of warmth in my chest. He leaned against the doorway of the house, one leg crossed over in front of him and his arms folded across his chest. I didn't know if Addie had brought him a change of clothes or what, but he had on a shirt that said *Sorry About What Happens Later.*

Mia was the first off the bench. She ran to him and wrapped both arms hard around his neck. Jack came out of the door with a grin and barely stabilized Finn before they both toppled over. Mia kissed Finn's cheek and kept hugging him. His face turned bright red and his eyes were wide. Then he caught my eye, wagged his eyebrows, and winked over Mia's shoulder.

Addie and I ran over and hugged Finn too. Having him back... it was all worth it. I'd made so very many bad choices in recent months, but I'd always had excellent taste in friends.

When Finn finally withdrew from the numerous hugs, it was clear he wasn't all that steady. We peeked in at Chloe on the couch; she was waking up and rubbing her forehead. Jack walked over and spoke quietly to her. She got to her feet, but she was wobbly and looked deflated and pale as she gathered her things. At least she was alive.

"You can take a shower if you'd like," I said as I joined them. Jack looked at me in surprise. "Then I'll give you a ride home when you're ready."

Chloe mumbled a quick "thank you," and her cheeks flushed slightly as she walked carefully down the hall to the bathroom.

"What did you say to her?" I asked Jack as the rest of us moved to sit at the table.

"I told her I would try to help her." Jack stared me in the eye like he was half ready for me to say he shouldn't.

"Good." I leaned forward and stretched my shoulders and neck. After the last twenty-four hours, I felt stiff everywhere. "I think she needs it."

Jack slowly inclined his chin but didn't comment.

Finn turned toward me, changing the subject. "You're really making it hard for me to keep up my end of this, you know?"

"Huh?"

"Less than seven months and you save my life twice?"

Finn tugged on his ear and winced. "They're going to take my man card and give me one that says 'damsel in distress.'"

I laughed. "It's the least I could do, considering both times were my fault. Besides, it turns out that life is considerably less fun without you around. I had no other option, really."

"I see. Well, in that case, I'd like to file a formal complaint. I feel kind of ripped off. If there's going to be body switching next time, I'd rather take over a girl's body than vice versa. Just for future reference." I could see pain and fear behind his eyes, but Finn was playing it off like always, dismissing living through the worst nightmare with a few jokes and a wave of his hand.

"Noted." I smiled and shook my head. "Glad to have you back, man."

"Glad to be here." Finn smiled and shot a quick look at Mia. She was beaming. I didn't remember ever seeing her look this happy.

Mia turned to Finn. "Would you go shopping with me later this week? I wa—" She glanced at me and smiled before finishing. "I want to buy a few paint supplies."

Finn grinned, then pretended to consider the request carefully. "Sure, as long as you occasionally paint something I want to see. I have very sophisticated tastes that really can't be met by the current market. I still haven't found a painting that can capture both the essence of Bruce Lee and the aroma of a good pizza—just for an example."

"I can probably manage that." Mia laughed softly before leaning her head against his shoulder. Finn tentatively put his arm around her, then grinned even wider when she moved closer.

"Well, I guess I need to pack up." Jack walked over and lifted his jacket off the back of one of the chairs.

I stood without thinking and my chair tipped over with a clatter. "What? Why?"

Jack pulled the paper Dad had given him out of his pocket with a sad smile. "Dad figured it out. He finally found the real solution for the Takers. It's a formula that will save them without hurting anyone else. It will enable them to get real sleep."

I stared at the tiny paper in awe of what it held. "Why didn't he give it to them before?"

"He told me he tried to, a few weeks ago, but as long as there was a chance for them to have Eclipse, they would never choose to be normal. Not when they could be what they considered gods. They wouldn't give up that kind of power."

"What are you going to do with it?" I didn't even know where he would start with something like that.

"I have to find phone numbers for a few of his contacts." Jack's hand trembled, so he folded the paper up and put it back in his pocket. "Dad wants me to work toward building a new NWS, one that sticks to the principles of the original: to help the Night Walkers. His contacts will help me make it happen, and this formula is my insurance that the Takers don't try to mess it all up again."

"But you have to leave? You can't do it from here?" It felt weird, knowing how angry I'd been at Jack before, but I really didn't want him to go. There were so many questions

I wanted to ask him about my—our—dad, but more than that, I wanted the chance to get to know my brother better.

"I'll stay for a couple of days, but then I have to go." Jack smiled, looking relieved that I wanted him around. "But this life is part of what Dad gave us. We don't have to hide. You have my number and I have yours. Call me. I'm going to try to set up a lab and a new NWS on the other side of the base once things settle down, *if* there's still enough structure left intact to support people living there again. I'll only be a few hours away and I can go back and forth."

"Okay." I picked my chair up from the floor and shrugged. "I guess that'll work."

Finn laughed out loud, looked at Addie, and rolled his eyes. "Men."

Man, it was so good to have him back.

I kissed Addie on the cheek and whacked Finn softly on the back of the head as I passed. Then I grabbed my phone and went into my room. I dialed Mom's number and she answered on the first ring.

"Parker?"

"Yep."

She released a breath. "I know you said not to worry, but I've been so nervous."

"I know, Mom. I'm back home and I'm sorry for scaring you." I looked at my desk and rolled one of the pencils back and forth to control my nerves. "When will you be home?"

"I have a couple more appointments ... unless you need me right now?" I heard her flipping through papers in the background and knew she was already trying to figure out how to make that happen.

"No, it can wait an hour or two. But tonight." I released one long breath. In spite of the wriggling feeling in my stomach, I was relieved to have finally opened this door. She needed to know about me. She deserved to know, and I wanted to talk to her about Dad. To give her the answers she'd waited so long for. "We have a lot to talk about."

After I hung up the phone, Addie walked up, her brow furrowed. "Everything okay?"

Lifting my right thumb, I ran it across her forehead until the lines there went away. Then I reached for her wrists, lifting them up and draping them around my neck. "Never better."

She smiled and kissed me long and sweet.

And there was more kissing.

And more kissing.

And still more kissing ...

The End

Acknowledgments

There are so many people who make a book happen. Often with my books, *Paranoia* included, it all starts during a brainstorming session with my incredible agent, Kathleen Rushall. Thank you for all of your amazingness. I truly could not navigate this crazy publishing world without you.

After the initial idea phase comes the writing, which includes hours of bouncing ideas off of my incredibly patient husband, Ande, while the most amazing kids in the world, Parker and Cameron, throw in the occasional suggestion that's so full of brilliance I wonder why they aren't the ones writing books instead of me. You three are my world; thank you for helping me build it.

Then comes the editing, which starts with my amazing critique partners: Kasie West, Renee Collins, Michelle Argyle, L.T. Elliot, Candice Kennington, Natalie Whipple, Bree Despain, and Sara Raasch. Thank you for helping me sort through my mess to find the gem buried beneath. Parker owes his story to you.

Then, of course, comes more editing with Flux. To Brian Farrey-Latz, for helping Parker put his best foot forward, and to the rest of the Flux team (especially Sandy and Mallory), thank you so much for having as much love for this book as I do. You've brought it to life in ways I never could've imagined. And another huge thank you to Lisa Novak for creating the incredibly chilling cover that captures the tone of Parker's story to perfection; any ideas I had paled in comparison to what you created.

Thank you to Taryn Fagerness, for working tirelessly to help the world find the Night Walkers. It blows me away to think of my story being translated into German, Italian, Czech, Spanish, Portuguese, Turkish, Hungarian, Chinese, and more. Thank you for all you do!

Thank you to Krista, Eric, Matt, Amanda, Mom, and Bill, plus Nick Whipple, Dave Cutler, and all the rest of my family and friends, for always wanting to read and pushing me to write more!

Thank you to the writing community, specifically here in Utah, plus The Lucky 13s and the Friday the Thirteeners, for providing me with strength and sanity during my debut year. You are the best!

Last, but most certainly not least, thank you so very much to all of my readers. You are the reason I get to write books. Thank you for finding meaning in Parker's madness and keeping my dreams alive.

© Michelle Davidson Argyle

About the Author

J. R. Johansson has two amazing sons and a wonderful husband who keep her busy and happy. In fact, but for the company of her kitten, she's pretty much drowning in testosterone. They live in a valley between huge mountains and a beautiful lake where the sun shines more than three hundred days per year. She loves writing, playing board games, and sitting in her hot tub. Her dream is that someday she can do all three at the same time.

Visit the author online at www.jrjohansson.com.